JUSTINE is [...]
by Lawrence Durrell [known as "The Alexandria]
Quartet." Few writers in our time have received
such extravagant praise from critics and reviewers.
Here are some of the things that have been
said about JUSTINE and its author—

✔ "It is safe to say that no artist in England
or America has produced in recent times so startling and intricate a drama as this kaleidoscopic
story...."   —*Saturday Review*

✔ "A beautiful and unique work, sensuous and
wise in its scrutiny of love..."   —GORE VIDAL

✔ "He makes Alexandria seem a glitteringly
sophisticated, dazzlingly beautiful and suffocat-
ingly evil place...."   —*Newsweek*

✔ "Here is a remarkable novel ... altogether
worth our delighted and admiring attention...."
                              —*New York Herald Tribune*

JUSTINE was originally published by E. P. Dutton &
Co., Inc., at $3.75.

Not for sale in the British Empire market.

Lawrence Durrell

JUSTINE

POCKET BOOKS, INC. • NEW YORK

This GIANT CARDINAL edition includes every word contained in
the original, higher-priced edition. It is printed from brand-new
plates made from completely reset, clear, easy-to-read type.

JUSTINE

E. P. Dutton edition published August, 1957

GIANT CARDINAL edition published April, 1961
1st printing .... February, 1961

Not for sale in the British Empire Market

C

GIANT CARDINAL editions are distributed in the U.S. by Affil-
iated Publishers, Inc., 630 Fifth Avenue, New York 20, N.Y.

To Eve
these memorials of her native city

NOTE

I am accustoming myself to the idea of regarding every sexual act as a process in which four persons are involved. We shall have a lot to discuss about that.

S. FREUD: *Letters*

There are two positions available to us—either crime, which renders us happy, or the noose, which prevents us from being unhappy. I ask whether there can be any hesitation, lovely Thérèse, and where will your little mind find an argument able to combat that one?

D. A. F. DE SADE: *Justine*

PART

one

THE SEA is high again today, with a thrilling flush of wind. In the midst of winter you can feel the inventions of Spring. A sky of hot nude pearl until midday, crickets in sheltered places, and now the wind unpacking the great planes, ransacking the great planes. . . .

I have escaped to this island with a few books and the child—Melissa's child. I do not know why I use the word "escape." The villagers say jokingly that only a sick man would choose such a remote place to rebuild. Well, then, I have come here to heal myself, if you like to put it that way. . . .

At night when the wind roars and the child sleeps quietly in its wooden cot by the echoing chimney-piece I light a lamp and limp about, thinking of my friends—of Justine and Nessim, of Melissa and Balthazar. I return link by link along the iron chains of memory to the city which we inhabited so briefly together: the city which used us as its flora—precipitated in us conflicts which were hers and which we mistook for our own: beloved Alexandria!

I have had to come so far away from it in order to understand it all! Living on this bare promontory, snatched every night from darkness by Arcturus, far from the lime-laden dust of those summer afternoons, I see at last that none of us is properly to be judged for what happened in the past. It is the city which should be judged though we, its children, must pay the price.

* * * * *

Capitally, what is this city of ours? What is resumed in the word Alexandria? In a flash my mind's eye shows

me a thousand dust-tormented streets. Flies and beggars
own it today—and those who enjoy an intermediate existence between either.

Five races, five languages, a dozen creeds: five fleets
turning through their greasy reflections behind the harbour bar. But there are more than five sexes and only
demotic Greek seems to distinguish among them. The
sexual provender which lies to hand is staggering in its
variety and profusion. You would never mistake it for a
happy place. The symbolic lovers of the free Hellenic
world are replaced here by something different, something subtly androgynous, inverted upon itself. The Orient cannot rejoice in the sweet anarchy of the body—
for it has outstripped the body. I remember Nessim once
saying—I think he was quoting—that Alexandria was the
great wine-press of love; those who emerged from it were
the sick men, the solitaries, the prophets—I mean all
who have been deeply wounded in their sex.

* * * * *

Notes for landscape-tones. . . . Long sequences of
tempera. Light filtered through the essence of lemons.
An air full of brick-dust—sweet-smelling brick-dust and
the odour of hot pavements slaked with water. Light
damp clouds, earth-bound, yet seldom bringing rain.
Upon this squirt dust-red, dust-green, chalk-mauve and
watered crimson-lake. In summer the sea-damp lightly
varnished the air. Everything lay under a coat of gum.

And then in autumn the dry, palpitant air, harsh with
static electricity, inflaming the body through its light
clothing. The flesh coming alive, trying the bars of its
prison. A drunken whore walks in a dark street at night,
shedding snatches of song like petals. Was it in this that
Anthony heard the heart-numbing strains of the great
music which persuaded him to surrender forever to the
city he loved?

The sulking bodies of the young begin to hunt for a
fellow nakedness, and in those little cafés where Balthazar went so often with the old poet of the city,* the boys
stir uneasily at their backgammon under the petrol-
lamps: disturbed by this dry desert wind—so unroman-
tic, so unconfiding—stir, and turn to watch every
stranger. They struggle for breath and in every summer
kiss they can detect the taste of quicklime. . . .

* * * * *

I had to come here in order completely to rebuild this
city in my brain—melancholy provinces which the old
man* saw as full of the "black ruins" of his life. Clang of
the trams shuddering in their metal veins as they pierce
the iodine-coloured *meidan* of Mazarita. Gold, phosphorus, magnesium paper. Here we so often met. There
was a little coloured stall in summer with slices of water-
melon and the vivid water-ices she liked to eat. She
would come a few minutes late of course—fresh perhaps
from some assignation in a darkened room, from which
I avert my mind; but so fresh, so young, the open petal
of the mouth that fell upon mine like an unslaked summer. The man she had left might still be going over
and over the memory of her; she might be as if still
dusted by the pollen of his kisses. It mattered so little
somehow, feeling the lithe weight of the creature
as she leaned on one's arm smiling with the selfless candour of those who had given over with secrets. It was
good to stand there, awkward and a little shy, breathing
quickly because we knew what we wanted of each other.
The messages passing beyond conscience, directly
through the flesh-lips, eyes, water-ices, the coloured stall.
To stand lightly there, our little fingers linked, drinking
in the deep camphor-scented afternoon, a part of
city. . . .

* * * * *

I have been looking through my papers tonight. Some
have been converted to kitchen uses, some the child has
destroyed. This form of censorship pleases me for it has
the indifference of the natural world to the constructions
of art—an indifference I am beginning to share. After
all what is the good of a fine metaphor for Melissa when
she lies buried deep as any mummy in the shallow tepid
sand of the black estuary?

But those papers I guard with care are the three vol-
umes in which Justine kept her diary, as well as the folio
which records Nessim's madness. Nessim gave them all
to me on parting saying:

"Take these and read them. There is much about us
all in them. They should help you to support the idea
of Justine without flinching, as I have had to do." This
was at the Summer Palace after Melissa's death, when
he still believed Justine would return to him. I think
often, and never without a certain fear, of Nessim's love
for Justine. What could be more comprehensive, more
surely founded in itself? It coloured his unhappiness
with a kind of ecstasy, the joyful wounds which you'd
think to meet in saints and not in mere lovers. Yet one
touch of humour would have saved him from such dreadful comprehensive suffering. It is easy to criticise, I know.
I know.

*   *   *   *   *

In the great quietness of these winter evenings there
is one clock: the sea. Its dim momentum in the mind is
the fugue upon which this writing is made. Empty ca-
dences of sea-water, licking its own wounds, sulking along
the mouths of the delta, boiling upon those deserted
beaches—empty, forever empty under the gulls: white
scribble on the grey, munched by clouds. If there are
ever sails here they die before the land shadows them.
Wreckage washed up on the pediments of islands, the

last crust, eroded by the weather, stuck in the blue maw
of water . . . gone!

* * * * *

Apart from the wrinkled old peasant who comes from
the village on her mule each day to clean the house, the
child and I are quite alone. It is happy and active amid
unfamiliar surroundings. I have not named it yet. Of
course it will be Justine—who else?

As for me I am neither happy nor unhappy; I lie suspended like a hair or a feather in the cloudy mixtures of
memory. I spoke of the uselessness of art but added nothing truthful about its consolations. The solace of such
work as I do with brain and heart lies in this—that only
there, in the silences of the painter or the writer can reality be reordered, reworked and made to show its significant side. Our common actions in reality are simply
the sackcloth covering which hides the cloth-of-gold—
the meaning of the pattern. For us artists there
waits the joyous compromise through art with all that
wounded or defeated us in daily life; in this way, not to
evade destiny, as the ordinary people try to do, but to
fulfil it in its true potential—the imagination. Otherwise why should we hurt one another? No, the remission
I am seeking, and will be granted perhaps, is not one I
shall ever see in the bright friendly eyes of Melissa or
the sombre brow-dark gaze of Justine. We have all of us
taken different paths now; but in this, the first great
fragmentation of my maturity I feel the confines of my
art and my living deepened immeasurably by the
memory of them. In thought I achieve them anew; as if
only here—this wooden table over the sea under an olive
tree, only here can I enrich them as they deserve. So that
the taste of this writing should have taken something
from its living subjects—their breath, skin, voices—
weaving them into the supple tissues of human mem-

ory. I want them to live again to the point where pain becomes art. . . . Perhaps this is a useless attempt, I cannot say. But I must try.

Today the child and I finished the hearth-stone of the house together, quietly talking as we worked. I talk to her as I would to myself if I were alone; she answers in an heroic language of her own invention. We buried the rings Cohen bought for Melissa in the ground under the hearth-stone, according to the custom of this island. This will ensure good luck to the inmates of the house.

* * * * *

At the time when I met Justine I was almost a happy man. A door had suddenly opened upon an intimacy with Melissa—an intimacy not the less marvellous for being unexpected and totally undeserved. Like all egoists I cannot bear to live alone; and truly the last year of bachelorhood had sickened me—my domestic inadequacy, my hopelessness over clothes and food and money, had all reduced me to despair. I had sickened too of the cockroach-haunted rooms where I then lived, looked after by one-eyed Hamid, the Berber servant.

Melissa had penetrated my shabby defences not by any of the qualities one might enumerate in a lover— charm, exceptional beauty, intelligence—no, but by the force of what I can only call her charity, in the Greek sense of the word. I used to see her, I remember, pale, rather on the slender side, dressed in a shabby sealskin coat, leading her small dog about the winter streets. Her blue-veined phthisic hands, etc. Her eyebrows artificially pointed upwards to enhance those fine dauntlessly candid eyes. I saw her daily for many months on end, but her sullen aniline beauty awoke no response in me. Day after day I passed her on my way to the Café Al Aktar where Balthazar waited for me in his black hat to give me "instruction." I did not dream that I should ever become her lover.

I knew that she had once been a model at the Atelier —an unenviable job—and was now a dancer; more, that she was the mistress of an elderly furrier, a gross and vulgar commercial of the city. I simply make these few notes to record a block of my life which has fallen into the sea. Melissa! Melissa!

* * * * *

I am thinking back to the time when for the four of us the known world hardly existed; days became simply the spaces between dreams, spaces between the shifting floors of time, of acting, of living out the topical. . . . A tide of meaningless affairs nosing along the dead level of things, entering no climate, leading us nowhere, demanding of us nothing save the impossible—that we should be. Justine would say that we had been trapped in the projection of a will too powerful and too deliberate to be human—the gravitational field which Alexandria threw down about those it had chosen as its exemplars. . . .

* * * * *

Six o'clock. The shuffling of white-robed figures from the station yards. The shops filling and emptying like lungs in the Rue des Soeurs. The pale lengthening rays of the afternoon sun smear the long curves of the Esplanade, and the dazzled pigeons, like rings of scattered paper, climb above the minarets to take the last rays of the waning light on their wings. Ringing of silver on the money-changers' counters. The iron grille outside the bank still too hot to touch. Clip-clop of horse-drawn carriages carrying civil servants in red flowerpots towards the cafés on the sea-front. This is the hour least easy to bear, when from my balcony I catch an unexpected

glimpse of her walking idly towards the town in her
white sandals, still half asleep. The city unwrinkles like
an old tortoise and peers about it. For a moment it re-
linquishes the torn rags of the flesh, while from some
hidden alley by the slaughter-house, above the moans
and screams of the cattle, comes the nasal chipping of a
Damascus love-song; shrill quartertones, like a sinus
being ground to powder.

Now tired men throw back the shutters of their balconies and step blinking into the pale hot light—
etiolated flowers of afternoons spent in anguish, tossing
upon ugly beds, bandaged by dreams. I have become one
of these poor clerks of the conscience, a citizen of Alexandria. She passes below my window, smiling as if at some
private satisfaction, softly fanning her cheeks with the
little reed fan. It is a smile which I shall probably never
see again for in company she only laughs, showing
those magnificent white teeth. But this sad yet quick
smile is full of a quality which one does not think she
owns—the power of mischief. You would have said that
she was of a more tragic cast of character and lacked common humour. Only the obstinate memory of this smile
is to make me doubt it in the days to come.

*   *   *   *   *

I have had many such glimpses of her at different times, and of course I knew her well by sight long
before we met: our city does not permit anonymity to
any with incomes of over two hundred pounds a year. I
see her sitting alone by the sea, reading a newspaper and
eating an apple; or in the vestibule of the Cecil Hotel,
among the dusty palms, dressed in a sheath of silver
drops, holding her magnificent fur at her back as a peasant holds his coat—her long forefinger hooked through
the tag. Nessim has stopped at the door of the ballroom
which is flooded with light and music. He has missed her.

Under the palms, in a deep alcove, sit a couple of old
men playing chess. Justine has stopped to watch them.
She knows nothing of the game, but the aura of stillness
and concentration which brims the alcove fascinates her.
She stands there between the deaf players and the
world of music for a long time, as if uncertain into
which to plunge. Finally Nessim comes softly to take her
arm and they stand together for a while, she watching
the players, he watching her. At last she goes softly, reluctantly, circumspectly into the lighted world with a
little sigh.

Then in other circumstances, less creditable no doubt
to herself, or to the rest of us: yet how touching, how
pliantly feminine this most masculine and resource-
ful of women could be. She could not help but remind
me of that race of terrific queens which left behind them
the ammoniac smell of their incestuous loves to hover
like a cloud over the Alexandrian subconscious. The
giant man-eating cats like Arsinoe were her true sib-
lings. Yet behind the acts of Justine lay something else,
born of a later tragic philosophy in which morals must
be weighed in the balance against rogue personality. She
was the victim of truly heroic doubts. Nevertheless I can
still see a direct connection between the picture of Justine bending over the dirty sink with the fœtus in it, and
poor Sophia of Valentinus who died for a love as perfect
as it was wrong headed.

* * * * *

Georges Pombal, a minor consular official, shares a
small flat with me in the Rue Nebi Daniel. He is a rare
figure among the diplomats in that he appears to possess
a vertebral column. For him the tiresome treadmill of
protocol and entertainment—so like a surrealist night-
mare—is full of exotic charm. He sees diplomacy
through the eyes of a Douanier Rousseau. He indulges

himself with it but never allows it to engulf what remains of his intellect. I suppose the secret of his success
is his tremendous idleness, which almost approaches the
supernatural.

He sits at his desk in the Consulate-General covered
by a perpetual confetti of pasteboard cards bearing the
names of his colleagues. He is a pegamoid sloth of a man,
a vast slow fellow given to prolonged afternoon siestas
and Crebillon *fils*. His handkerchiefs smell wondrously
of *Eau de Portugal*. His most favoured topic of conversation is women, and he must speak from experience
for the succession of visitors to the little flat is endless,
and rarely does one see the same face twice. "To a
Frenchman the love here is interesting. They act before
they reflect. When the time comes to doubt, to suffer remorse, it is too hot, nobody has the energy. It lacks
finesse, this animalism, but it suits me. I've worn out
my heart and head with love, and want to be left alone
—above all, *mon cher*, from this Judeo-Coptic mania
for *dissection*, for analysing the subject. I want to return
to my farmhouse in Normandy heart-whole."

For long periods of the winter he is away on leave and
I have the little dank flat to myself and sit up late, cor-
recting exercise books, with only the snoring Hamid for
company. In this last year I have reached a dead end in
myself. I lack the will-power to do anything with my life,
to better my position by hard work, to write: even to
make love. I do not know what has come over me. This
is the first time I have experienced a real failure of the
will to survive. Occasionally I turn over a bundle of
manuscript or an old proof-copy of a novel or book of
poems with disgusted inattention; with sadness, like
someone studying an old passport.

From time to time one of Georges' numerous girls
strays into my net by calling at the flat when he is not
there, and the incident serves for a while to sharpen my

taedium vitae. Georges is thoughtful and generous in these matters for, before going away (knowing how poor I am) he often pays one of the Syrians from Golfo's tavern in advance, and orders her to spend an occasional night in the flat *en disponibilité,* as he puts it. Her duty is to cheer me up, by no means an enviable task especially as on the surface there is nothing to indicate lack of cheerfulness on my part. Small talk has become a useful form of automatism which goes on long after one has lost the need to talk; if necessary I can even make love with relief, as one does not sleep very well here: but without passion, without attention.

Some of these encounters with poor exhausted creatures driven to extremity by physical want are interesting, even touching, but I have lost any interest in sorting my emotions so that they exist for me like dimensionless figures flashed on a screen. "There are only three things to be done with a woman," said Clea once. "You can love her, suffer for her, or turn her into literature." I was experiencing a failure in all these domains of feeling.

I record this only to show the unpromising human material upon which Melissa elected to work, to blow some breath of life into my nostrils. It could not have been easy for her to bear the double burden to her own poor circumstances and illness. To add my burdens to hers demanded real courage. Perhaps it was born of desperation, for she too had reached the dead level of things, as I myself had. We were fellow-bankrupts.

For weeks the old furrier followed me about the streets with a pistol sagging in the pocket of his overcoat. It was consoling to learn from one of Melissa's friends that it was unloaded, but it was nevertheless alarming to be haunted by this old man. Mentally we must have shot each other down at every street corner of the city. I for my part could not bear to look at that heavy pock-marked face with its bestial saturnine cluster of tormented features smeared on it—could not bear to think of his gross intimacies with her: those sweaty little hands covered as thickly as a porcupine with black hair. For a long time this went on and then after some months an extraordinary feeling of intimacy seemed to grow up between us. We nodded and smiled at each other when we met. Once, encountering him at a bar, I stood for nearly half an hour beside him; we were on the point of talking to each other, yet somehow neither of us had the courage to begin it. There was no common subject of conversation save Melissa. As I was leaving I caught a glimpse of him in one of the long mirrors, his head bowed as he stared into his wineglass. Something about his attitude —the clumsy air of a trained seal grappling with human emotions—struck me, and I realized for the first time that he probably loved Melissa as much as I did. I pitied his ugliness, and the blank pained incomprehension with which he faced emotions so new to him as jealousy, the deprivation of a cherished mistress.

Afterwards when they were turning out his pockets I saw among the litter of odds and ends a small empty scent-bottle of the cheap kind that Melissa used; and I took it back to the flat where it stayed on the mantelpiece for some months before it was thrown away by Hamid in the course of a spring-clean. I never told Melissa of this; but often when I was alone at night while she was dancing, perhaps of necessity sleeping with her admirers, I studied this small bottle, sadly and passionately reflecting on this horrible old man's love and measuring it against my own; and tasting too, vicariously, the desperation which makes one clutch at some small discarded object which is still impregnated with the betrayer's memory.

I found Melissa, washed up like a half-drowned bird,

on the dreary littorals of Alexandria, with her sex
broken. . . .

* * * * *

Streets that run back from the docks with their tattered rotten supercargo of houses, breathing into each
others' mouths, keeling over. Shuttered balconies swarm-
ing with rats, and old women whose hair is full of the
blood of ticks. Peeling walls leaning drunkenly to east
and west of their true centre of gravity. The black rib-
bon of flies attaching itself to the lips and eyes of the
children—the moist beads of summer flies everywhere;
the very weight of their bodies snapping off ancient flypapers hanging in the violet doors of booths and
cafés. The smell of the sweat-lathered Berberinis, like
that of some decomposing staircarpet. And then the
street noises: shriek and clang of the water-bearing Saidi,
dashing his metal cups together as an advertisement, the
unheeded shrieks which pierce the hubbub from time
to time, as of some small delicately-organized animal being disembowelled. The sores like ponds—the incuba-
tion of a human misery of such proportions that one was
aghast, and all one's human feelings overflowed into disgust and terror.

I wished I could imitate the self-confident directness
with which Justine threaded her way through these
streets towards the café where I waited for her: *El Bab*.
The doorway by the shattered arch where in all innocence we sat and talked; but already our conversation
had become impregnated by understandings which we
took for the lucky omens of friendship merely. On that
dun mud floor, feeling the quickly cooling cylinder of
the earth dip towards the darkness, we were possessed
only by a desire to communicate ideas and experiences
which overstepped the range of thought normal to conversation among ordinary people. She talked like a man

and I talked to her like a man. I can only remember the
pattern and weight of these conversations, not their substance. And leaning there on a forgotten elbow, drinking
the cheap *arak* and smiling at her, I inhaled the warm
summer perfume of her dress and skin—a perfume
which was called, I don't know why, *Jamais de la vie*.

* * * * *

These are the moments which possess the writer, not
the lover, and which live on perpetually. One can return
to them time and time again in memory, or use them
as a fund upon which to build the part of one's life
which is writing. One can debauch them with words, but
one cannot spoil them. In this context too, I recover another such moment, lying beside a sleeping woman in a
cheap room near the mosque. In that early spring dawn,
with its dense dew, sketched upon the silence which en-
gulfs a whole city before the birds awaken it, I caught
the sweet voice of the blind *muezzin* from the mosque
reciting the *Ebed*—a voice hanging like a hair in the
palm-cooled upper airs of Alexandria. "I praise the perfection of God, the Forever existing" (this repeated
thrice, ever more slowly, in a high sweet register). "The
perfection of God, the Desired, the Existing, the Single,
the Supreme: the perfection of God, the One, the Sole:
the perfection of Him who taketh unto himself no male
or female partner, nor any like Him, nor any that is dis-
obedient, nor any deputy, equal or offspring. His perfection be extolled."

The great prayer wound its way into my sleepy consciousness like a serpent, coil after shining coil of words
—the voice of the *muezzin* sinking from register to register of gravity—until the whole morning seemed dense
with its marvellous healing powers, the intimations of a
grace undeserved and unexpected, impregnating that
shabby room where Melissa lay, breathing as lightly as a

gull, rocked upon the oceanic splendours of a language she would never know.

*   *   *   *   *

Of Justine who can pretend that she did not have her stupid side? The cult of pleasure, small vanities, concern for the good opinion of her inferiors, arrogance. She could be tiresomely exigent when she chose. Yes. Yes. But all these weeds are watered by money. I will say only that in many things she thought as a man, while in her actions she enjoyed some of the free vertical independence of the masculine outlook. Our intimacy was of a strange mental order. Quite early on I discovered that she could mind-read in an unerring fashion. Ideas came to us simultaneously. I remember once being made aware that she was sharing in her mind a thought which had just presented itself to mine, namely: "This intimacy *should go no further,* for we have already exhausted all its possibilities in our respective imaginations: and what we shall end by discovering, behind the darkly woven colours of sensuality, will be a friendship so profound that we shall become bondsmen forever." It was, if you like, the flirtation of minds prematurely exhausted by experience which seemed so much more dangerous than a love founded in sexual attraction.

Knowing how much she loved Nessim and loving him so much myself, I could not contemplate this thought without terror. She lay beside me, breathing lightly, and staring at the cherub-haunted ceiling with her great eyes. I said: "It can come to nothing, this love-affair between a poor schoolteacher and an Alexandrian society woman. How bitter it would be to have it all end in a conventional scandal which would leave us alone together and give you the task of deciding how to dispose of me." Justine hated to hear the truth spoken. She turned upon one elbow and lowering those magnificent troubled eyes

to mine she stared at me for a long moment. "There is
no choice in this matter," she said in that hoarse voice I
had come to love so much. "You talk as if there was a
choice. We are not strong or evil enough to exercise
choice. All this is part of an experiment arranged by
something else, the city perhaps, or another part of ourselves. How do I know?"

I remember her sitting before the multiple mirrors
at the dressmaker's, being fitted for a shark-skin costume,
and saying: "Look! five different pictures of the same
subject. Now if I wrote I would try for a multi-dimen-
sional effect in character, a sort of prism-sightedness.
Why should not people show more than one profile at a
time?"

Now she yawned and lit a cigarette; and sitting up in
bed clasped her slim ankles with her hands; reciting
slowly, wryly, those marvellous lines of the old Greek
poet about a love-affair long since past—they are lost
in English. And hearing her speak his lines, touching
every syllable of the thoughtful ironic Greek with tenderness, I felt once more the strange equivocal power of
the city—its flat alluvial landscape and exhausted airs—
and knew her for a true child of Alexandria; which is
neither Greek, Syrian nor Egyptian, but a hybrid: a
joint.

And with what feeling she reached the passage where
the old man throws aside the ancient love-letter which
had so moved him and exclaims: "I go sadly out on to the
balcony; anything to change this train of thought, even
if only to see some little movement in the city I love, in
its streets and shops!" Herself pushing open the shutters to stand on the dark balcony above a city of coloured
lights: feeling the evening wind stir from the confines of
Asia: her body for an instant forgotten.

*   *   *   *   *

"Prince" Nessim is of course a joke; at any rate to the shopkeepers and black-coated *commerçants* who saw him drawn soundlessly down the Canopic way in the great silver Rolls with the daffodil hub-caps. To begin with he was a Copt, not a Moslem. Yet somehow the nickname was truly chosen for Nessim was princely in his detachment from the common greed in which the decent instincts of the Alexandrians—even the very rich ones —foundered. Yet the factors which gave him a reputation for eccentricity were neither of them remarkable to those who had lived outside the Levant. He did not care for money, except to spend it—that was the first: the second was that he did not own a *garçonniére,* and appeared to be quite faithful to Justine—an unheard of state of affairs. As for money, being so inordinately rich he was possessed by a positive distaste for it, and would never carry it on his person. He spent in Arabian fashion and gave notes of hand to shopkeepers; night-clubs and restaurants accepted his signed checks. Nevertheless his debts were punctually honoured, and every morning Selim his secretary was sent out with the car to trace the route of the previous day and to pay any debts accumulated in the course of it.

This attitude was considered eccentric and high-handed in the extreme by the inhabitants of the city whose coarse and derived distinctions, menial preoccupations and faulty education gave them no clue to what style in the European sense was. But Nessim was born to this manner, not merely educated to it; in this little world of studied carnal moneymaking he could find no true province of operation for a spirit essentially gentle and contemplative. The least assertive of men he caused comment by acts which bore the true stamp of his own personality. People were inclined to attribute his manners to a foreign education, but in fact Germany and England had done little but confuse him and unfit him

for the life of the city. The one had implanted a taste for
metaphysical speculation in what was a natural Mediterranean mind, while Oxford had tried to make him don-
nish and had only succeeded in developing his philosophic bent to the point where he was incapable of prac-
tising the art he most loved, painting. He thought and
suffered a good deal but he lacked the resolution to
dare—the first requisite of a practitioner.

Nessim was at odds with the city, but since his enormous fortune brought him daily into touch with the
business men of the place they eased their constraint
by treating him with a humorous indulgence, a condes-
cension such as one would bestow upon someone who
was a little soft in the head. It was perhaps not surprising
if you should walk in upon him at the office—that sar-
cophagus of tubular steel and lighted glass—and find
him seated like an orphan at the great desk (covered in
bells and pulleys and patent lights)—eating brown bread
and butter and reading Vasari as he absently signed letters or vouchers. He looked up at you with that pale al-
mond face, the expression shuttered, withdrawn, almost
pleading. And yet somewhere through all this gentleness
ran a steel cord, for his staff was perpetually surprised
to find out that, inattentive as he appeared to be, there
was no detail of the business which he did not know;
while hardly a transaction he made did not turn out to
be based on a stroke of judgment. He was something of
an oracle to his own employees—and yet (they sighed
and shrugged their shoulders) he seemed not to care! Not
to care about gain, that is what Alexandria recognizes
as madness.

I knew them by sight for many months before we actually met—as I knew everyone in the city. By sight and no
less by repute: for their emphatic, authoritative and
quite conventionless way of living had given them a certain notoriety among our provincial city-dwellers. She

was reputed to have had many lovers, and Nessim was
regarded as a *mari complaisant*. I had watched them
dancing together several times, he slender and with a
deep waist like a woman, and long arched beautiful
hands; Justine's lovely head—the deep bevel of that
Arabian nose and those translucent eyes, enlarged by
belladonna. She gazed about her like a half-trained panther.

   Then: once I had been persuaded to lecture upon the
native poet of the city at the *Atelier des Beaux Arts*—a
sort of club where gifted amateurs of the arts could meet,
rent studios and so on. I had accepted because it meant a
little money for Melissa's new coat, and autumn was on
the way. But it was painful to me, feeling the old man all
round me, so to speak, impregnating the gloomy streets
around the lecture-room with the odour of those verses
distilled from the shabby but rewarding loves he had experienced—loves perhaps bought with money, and lasting a few moments, yet living on now in his verse—so
deliberately and tenderly had he captured the adventive
minute and made all its colours fast. What an impertinence to lecture upon an ironist who so naturally,
and with such fineness of instinct took his subject-matter
from the streets and brothels of Alexandria! And to be
talking, moreover, not to an audience of haberdashers'
assistants and small clerks—his immortals—but to a dig-
nified semicircle of society ladies for whom the culture
he represented was a sort of blood-bank: they had come
along for a transfusion. Many had actually foregone a
bridge-party to do so, though they knew that instead of
being uplifted they would be stupefied.

   I remember saying only that I was haunted by his face
—the horrifyingly sad gentle face of the last photograph;
and when the solid burghers' wives had dribbled down
the stone staircase into the wet streets where their lighted
cars awaited them, leaving the gaunt room echoing with

their perfumes, I noticed that they had left behind them
one solitary student of the passions and the arts. She sat
in a thoughtful way at the back of the hall, her legs
crossed in a mannish attitude, puffing a cigarette. She
did not look at me but crudely at the ground under her
feet. I was flattered to think that perhaps one person had
appreciated my difficulties. I gathered up my damp brief
case and ancient mackintosh and made my way down
to where a thin penetrating drizzle swept the streets from
the direction of the sea. I made for my lodgings where
by now Melissa would be awake, and would have set
out our evening meal on the newspaper-covered table,
having first sent Hamid out to the baker's to fetch the
roast—we had no oven of our own.

It was cold in the street and I crossed to the lighted
blaze of shops in Rue Fuad. In a grocer's window I
saw a small tin of olives with the name *Orvieto* on it, and
overcome by a sudden longing to be on the right side of
the Mediterranean, entered the shop: bought it: had it
opened there and then: and sitting down at a marble
table in that gruesome light I began to eat Italy, its dark
scorched flesh, hand-modelled spring soil, dedicated
vines. I felt that Melissa would never understand this.
I should have to pretend I had lost the money.

I did not see at first the great car which she had
abandoned in the street with its engine running. She
came into the shop with swift and resolute suddenness
and said, with the air of authority that Lesbians, or
women with money, assume with the obviously in-
digent: "What did you mean by your remark about the
antinomian nature of irony?"—or some such sally which
I have forgotten.

Unable to disentangle myself from Italy I looked up
boorishly and saw her leaning down at me from the mirrors on three sides of the room, her dark thrilling face
full of a troubled, arrogant reserve. I had of course for-

gotten what I had said about irony or anything else for that matter, and I told her so with an indifference that was not assumed. She heaved a short sigh, as if of natural relief, and sitting down opposite me lit a French *caporal* and with short decisive inspirations blew thin streamers of blue smoke up into the harsh light. She looked to me a trifle unbalanced, as she watched me with a candour I found embarrassing—it was as if she were trying to decide to what use I could be put. "I liked," she said, "the way you quoted his lines about the city. Your Greek is good. Doubtless you are a writer." I said: "Doubtless." Not to be known always wounds. There seemed no point in pursuing all this. I have always hated literary conversation. I offered her an olive which she ate swiftly, spitting the pit into her gloved hand like a cat where she held it absently, saying: "I want to take you to Nessim, my husband. Will you come?"

A policeman had appeared in the doorway, obviously troubled about the abandoned car. That was the first time I saw the great house of Nessim with its statues and palm loggias, its Courbets and Bonnards—and so on. It was both beautiful and horrible. Justine hurried up the great staircase, pausing only to transfer her olive-pit from the pocket of her coat to a Chinese vase, calling all the time to Nessim. We went from room to room, fracturing the silences. He answered at last from the great studio on the roof and racing to him like a gun-dog she metaphorically dropped me at his feet and stood back, wagging her tail. She had achieved me.

Nessim was sitting on the top of a ladder reading, and he came slowly down to us, looking first at one and then at the other. His shyness could not get any purchase of my shabbiness, damp hair, tin of olives, and for my part I could offer no explanation of my presence, since I did not know for what purpose I had been brought here.

I took pity on him and offered him an olive; and sit-

ting down together we finished the tin, while Justine
foraged for drinks, talking, if I remember, of Orvieto
where neither of us had been. It is such a solace to
think back to that first meeting. Never have I been closer
to them both—closer, I mean to their marriage; they
seemed to me then to be the magnificent two-headed
animal a marriage could be. Watching the benign
warmth of the light in his eye I realized, as I recalled
all the scandalous rumours about Justine, that whatever
she had done had been done in a sense *for him*—even
what was evil or harmful in the eyes of the world. Her
love was like a skin in which he lay sewn like the infant
Heracles; and her efforts to achieve herself had led her
always towards, and not away from him. The world has
no use for this sort of paradox I know; but it seemed to
me then that Nessim knew and accepted her in a way impossible to explain to someone for whom love is still entangled with the qualities of possessiveness. Once, much
later, he told me: "What was I to do? Justine was too
strong for me in too many ways. I could only out-love
her—that was my long suit. I went ahead of her—I an-
ticipated every lapse; she found me already there, at
every point where she fell down, ready to help her to
her feet and show that it did not matter. After all she
compromised the least part of me—my reputation."

This was much later: before the unlucky complex of
misfortunes had engulfed us we did not know each other
well enough to talk as freely as this. I also remember him
saying, once—this was at the summer villa near Bourg
El Arab: "It will puzzle you when I tell you that I
thought Justine great, in a sort of way. There are forms
of greatness, you know, which when not applied in art
or religion make havoc of ordinary life. Her gift was mis-
applied in being directed towards love. Certainly she
was bad in many ways, but they were all small ways. Nor
can I say that she harmed nobody. But those she harmed

most she made fruitful. She expelled people from their old selves. It was bound to hurt, and many mistook the nature of the pain she inflicted. Not I." And smiling his well-known smile, in which sweetness was mixed with an inexpressible bitterness, he repeated softly under his breath the words: "Not I."

*　*　*　*　*

Capodistria . . . how does he fit in? He is more of a goblin than a man, you would think. The flat triangular head of the snake with the huge frontal lobes; the hair grows forward in a widow's peak. A whitish flickering tongue is forever busy keeping his thin lips moist. He is ineffably rich and does not have to lift a finger for himself. He sits all day on the terrace of the Brokers' Club watching the women pass, with the restless eye of someone endlessly shuffling through an old soiled pack of cards. From time to time there is a flick, like a chameleon's tongue striking—a signal almost invisible to the inattentive. Then a figure slips from the terrace to trail the woman he has indicated. Sometimes his agents will quite openly stop and importune women on the street in his name, mentioning a sum of money. No one is offended by the mention of money in our city. Some girls simply laugh. Some consent at once. You never see vexation on their features. Virtue with us is never feigned. Nor vice. Both are natural.

Capodistria sits remote from it all, in his immaculate shark-skin coat with the coloured silk handkerchief lolling at his breast. His narrow shoes gleam. His friends call him *Da Capo* because of a sexual prowess reputed to be as great as his fortune—or his ugliness. He is obscurely related to Justine who says of him: "I pity him. His heart has withered in him and he has been left with the five senses, like pieces of a broken wineglass." However a life of such striking monotony does not seem to depress him.

His family is noted for the number of suicides in it, and
his psychological inheritance is an unlucky one with its
history of mental disturbance and illness. He is unper-
turbed however and says, touching his temples with a
long forefinger: "All my ancestors went wrong here in
the head. My father also. He was a great womanizer.
When he was very old he had a model of the perfect
woman built in rubber—life-size. She could be filled with
hot water in the winter. She was strikingly beautiful. He
called her Sabina after his mother, and took her everywhere. He had a passion for travelling on ocean liners
and actually lived on one for the last two years of his
life, travelling backwards and forwards to New York.
Sabina had a wonderful wardrobe. It was a sight to see
them come into the dining-saloon, dressed for dinner. He
travelled with his keeper, a manservant called Kelly. Between them, held on either side like a beautiful
drunkard, walked Sabina in her marvellous evening
clothes. The night he died he said to Kelly: 'Send Deme-
trius a telegram and tell him that Sabina died in my arms
tonight without any pain.' She was buried with him off
Naples." His laughter is the most natural and unfeigned
of any I have ever heard.

Later when I was half mad with worry and heavily in
Capodistria's debt, I found him less accommodating a
companion; and one night, there was Melissa sitting half
drunk on the footstool by the fire holding in those long
reflective fingers the I.O.U. which I had made out to
him with the curt word "*discharged*" written across it in
green ink. . . . These memories wound. Melissa said:
"Justine would have paid your debt from her immense
fortune. I did not want to see her increase her hold
over you. Besides, even though you no longer care for me
I still wanted to do something for you—and this was the
least of sacrifices. I did not think that it would hurt you
so much for me to sleep with him. Have you not done

the same for me—I mean did you not borrow the money from Justine to send me away for the X-ray business? Though you lied about it I knew. I won't lie, I never do. Here, take it and destroy it: but don't gamble with him any more. He is not of your kind." And turning her head she made the Arab motion of spitting.

* * * * *

Of Nessim's outer life—those immense and boring receptions, at first devoted to business colleagues but later to become devoted to obscure political ends—I do not wish to write. As I slunk through the great hall and up the stairs to the studio I would pause to study the great leather shield on the mantelpiece with its plan of the table—to see who had been placed on Justine's right and left. For a short while they made a kindly attempt to include me in these gatherings but I rapidly tired of them and pleaded illness, though I was glad to have the run of the studio and the immense library. And afterwards we would meet like conspirators and Justine would throw off the gay, bored, petulant affectations which she wore in her social life. They would kick off their shoes and play piquet by candlelight. Later, going to bed, she would catch sight of herself in the mirror on the first landing and say to her reflection: "Tiresome pretentious hysterical Jewess that you are!"

* * * * *

Mnemjian's Babylonian barber's shop was on the corner of Fuad I and Nebi Daniel and here every morning Pombal lay down beside me in the mirrors. We were lifted simultaneously and swung smoothly down into the ground wrapped like dead Pharaohs, only to reappear at the same instant on the ceiling, spread out like specimens. White cloths had been spread over us by a small black boy while in a great Victorian moustache-cup the

barber thwacked up his dense and sweet-smelling lather
before applying it in direct considered brush-strokes to
our cheeks. The first covering complete, he surrendered
his task to an assistant while he went to the great strop
hanging among the flypapers on the end wall of the shop
and began to sweeten the edge of an English razor.

Little Mnemjian is a dwarf with a violet eye that has
never lost its childhood. He is the Memory man, the
archives of the city. If you should wish to know the an-
cestry or income of the most casual passer-by you have
only to ask him; he will recite the details in a sing-song
voice as he strops his razor and tries it upon the coarse
black hair of his forearm. What he does not know he can
find out in a matter of moments. Moreover he is as well
briefed in the living as in the dead; I mean this in the
literal sense, for the Greek Hospital employs him to
shave and lay out its victims before they are committed
to the undertakers—a task which he performs with relish
tinged by racial unction. His ancient trade embraces the
two worlds, and some of his best observations begin with
the phrase: "As so-and-so said to me with *his last breath.*"
He is rumoured to be fantastically attractive to women
and he is said to have put away a small fortune earned
for him by his admirers. But he also has several elderly
Egyptian ladies, the wives and widows of pashas, as permanent clients upon whom he calls at regular intervals
to set their hair. They have, as he says slyly, "got beyond
everything"—and reaching up over his back to touch
the unsightly hump which crowns it he adds with pride:
"*This* excites them." Among other things, he has a gold
cigarette case given to him by one of these admirers in
which he keeps a stock of loose cigarette-paper. His
Greek is defective but adventurous and vivid and Pombal
refuses to permit him to talk French, which he does much
better.

He does a little mild procuring for my friend, and I

am always astonished by the sudden flights of poetry
of which he is capable in describing his *protégées*. Leaning over Pombal's moonlike face he will say, for example, in a discreet undertone, as the razor begins to whisper: "I have something for you—*something special.*"
Pombal catches my eye in the mirror and looks hastily
away lest we infect one another by a smile. He gives a
cautious grunt. Mnemjian leans lightly on the balls of
his feet, his eyes squinting slightly. The small wheedling
voice puts a husk of double meaning round everything
he says, and his speech is not the less remarkable for being punctuated by small world-weary sighs. For a while
nothing more is said. I can see the top of Mnemjian's
head in the mirror—that obscene outcrop of black hair
which he had trained into a spitcurl at each temple, hoping no doubt to draw attention away from that crooked
papier mâché back of his. While he works with a razor his
eyes dim out and his features become as expressionless as
a bottle. His fingers travel as coolly upon our live faces
as they do upon those of the fastidious and (yes, lucky)
dead. "This time," says Mnemjian, "you will be delighted from every point of view. She is young, cheap
and clean. You will say to yourself, a young partridge, a
honey-comb with all its honey sealed in it, a dove. She is
in difficulties over money. She has recently come from the
lunatic asylum in Helwan where her husband tried to
get her locked up as mad. I have arranged for her to sit
at the Rose Marie at the end table on the pavement. Go
and see her at one o'clock; if you wish her to accompany
you give her the card I will prepare for you. But remember, you will pay only me. As one gentleman to another
it is the only condition I lay down."

He says nothing more for the time. Pombal continues
to stare at himself in the mirror, his natural curiosity
doing battle with the forlorn apathy of the summer air.
Later no doubt he will bustle into the flat with some ex-

hausted, disoriented creature whose distorted smile can
rouse no feeling in him save those of pity. I cannot say
that my friend lacks kindness, for he is always trying to
find work of some sort for these girls; indeed most of the
consulates are staffed by ex-casuals desperately trying to
look correct: whose jobs they owe to Georges' importunities among his colleagues of the career. Nevertheless there
is no woman too humble, too battered, too old, to receive those outward attentions—those little gallantries
and *sorties* of wit which I have come to associate with the
Gallic temperament; the heady meretricious French
charm which evaporates so easily into pride and mental
indolence—like French thought which flows so quickly
into sand-moulds, the original *esprit* hardening immediately into deadening concepts. The light play of sex
which hovers over his thought and actions has, however, an air of disinterestedness which makes it qualita-
tively different from, say, the actions and thoughts of
Capodistria, who often joins us for a morning shave.
Capodistria has the purely involuntary knack of turning
everything into a woman; under his eyes chairs become
painfully conscious of their bare legs. He impregnates
things. At table I have seen a water-melon become conscious under his gaze so that it felt the seeds inside it stirring with life! Women feel like birds confronted by a
viper when they gaze into that narrow flat face with its
tongue always moving across the thin lips. I think of
Melissa once more: *hortus conclusus, soror mea spon-
sor. . . .*

* * * * *

"*Regard dérisoire*," says Justine. "How is it you are so
much one of us and yet . . . you are not?" She is comb-
ing that dark head in the mirror, her mouth and eyes
drawn up about a cigarette. "You are a mental refugee
of course, being Irish, but you miss our *angoisse*." What

she is groping after is really the distinctive quality which
emanates not from us but from the landscape—the me-
tallic flavours of exhaustion which impregnate the airs
of Mareotis.

As she speaks I am thinking of the founders of the
city, the soldier-God in his glass coffin, the youthful body
lapped in silver, riding down the river towards his tomb.
Or that great square Negro head reverberating with a
concept of God conceived in the spirit of pure intellectual play—Plotinus. It is as if the preoccupations of this
landscape were centred somewhere out of reach of the
average inhabitant—in a region where the flesh, stripped
by over-indulgence of its final reticences, must yield to a
preoccupation vastly more comprehensive: or perish in
the kind of exhaustion represented by the works of the
Mouseion, the guileless playing of hermaphrodites in
the green courtyards of art and science. Poetry as a
clumsy attempt at the artificial insemination of the
Muses; the burning stupid metaphor of Berenice's hair
glittering in the night sky above Melissa's sleeping face.
"Ah!" said Justine once, "that there should be something free, something Polynesian about the licence in
which we live." Or even Mediterranean, she might have
added, for the connotation of every kiss would be different in Italy or Spain; here our bodies were chafed by the
harsh desiccated winds blowing up out of the deserts of
Africa and for love we were forced to substitute a wiser
but crueller mental tenderness which emphasized loneliness rather than expurgated it.

Now even the city had two centres of gravity—the true
and magnetic north of its personality: and between them
the temperament of its inhabitants sparked harshly like
a leaky electric discharge. Its spiritual centre was the
forgotten site of the Soma where once the confused
young soldier's body lay in its borrowed Godhead;
its temporal site the Brokers' Club where like

Caballi* the cotton brokers sat to sip their coffee, puff
rank cheroots and watch Capodistria—as people upon a
river-bank will watch the progress of a fisherman or an
artist. The one symbolized for me the great conquests of
man in the realms of matter, space and time—which
must inevitably yield their harsh knowledge of defeat
to the conqueror in his coffin; the other was no symbol
but the living limbo of free-will in which my beloved
Justine wandered, searching with such frightening single-
ness of mind for the integrating spark which might lift
her into a new perspective of herself. In her, as an Alexandrian, licence was in a curious way a form of self-abne-
gation, a travesty of freedom; and if I saw her as an exemplar of the city it was not of Alexandria or Plotinus
that I was forced to think, but of the sad thirteenth child
of Valentinos who fell, "not like Lucifer by rebelling
against God, but by desiring too ardently to be united
to him."* Anything pressed too far becomes a sin.

Broken from the divine harmony of herself he fell, says
the tragic philosopher, and became the manifestation of
matter; and the whole universe of her city, of the world,
was formed out of her agony and remorse. The tragic
seed from which her thoughts and actions grew was the
seed of a pessimistic gnosticism.

That this identification was a true one I know—for
much later when, with so many misgivings, she allowed
me to join the little circle which gathered every month
about Balthazar, it was always what he had to say about
gnosticism which most interested her. I remember her
asking one night, so anxiously, so pleadingly if she had
interpreted his thinking rightly: "I mean, that God
neither created us nor wished us to be created, but that
we are the work of an inferior deity, a Demiurge, who
wrongly believed himself to be God? Heavens, how prob-
able it seems; and this overweening *hubris* has been
handed on down to our children." And stopping me as we

walked by the expedient of standing in front of me and
catching hold of the lapels of my coat she gazed earnestly
into my eyes and said: "What do you believe? You never
say anything. At the most you sometimes laugh." I did
not know how to reply for all ideas seem equally good
to me; the fact of their existence proves that someone is
creating. Does it matter whether they are objectively
right or wrong? They could never remain so for long.
"But it matters," she cried with a touching emphasis. "It
matters deeply my darling, deeply."

We are the children of our landscape; it dictates behaviour and even thought in the measure to which we
are responsive to it. I can think of no better identification. "Your doubt, for example, which contains so much
anxiety and such a thirst for an absolute truth, is so different from the scepticism of the Greek, from the mental
play of the Mediterranean mind with its deliberate re-
sort to sophistry as part of the *game* of thought; for your
thought is a weapon, a theology."

"But how else can action be judged?" "It cannot be
judged comprehensively until thought itself can be
judged, for our thoughts themselves are acts. It is an attempt to make partial judgements upon either that leads
to misgivings."

I liked so much the way she would suddenly sit down
on a wall, or a broken pillar in that shattered backyard
to Pompey's Pillar, and be plunged in an inextinguish-
able sorrow at some idea whose impact had only just
made itself felt in her mind. "You really believe so?" she
would say with such sorrow that one was touched and
amused at the same time. "And why do you smile? You
always smile at the most serious things. Ah! surely you
should be sad?" If she ever knew me at all she must later
have discovered that for those of us who feel deeply and
who are at all conscious of the inextricable tangle of hu-

man thought there is only one response to be made—
ironic tenderness and silence.

In a night so brilliant with stars where the glow-worms
in the shrill dry grass gave back their ghostly mauve
lambence to the sky there was nothing else to do but
sit by her side, stroking that dark head of beautiful hair
and saying nothing. Underneath, like a dark river, the
noble quotation which Balthazar had taken as a text and
which he read in a voice that trembled partly with emotion and partly with the fatigue of so much abstract
thought: "The day of the *corpora* is the night for the
spiritus. When the bodies cease their labour the spirits in
man begin their work. The waking of the body is the
sleep of the spirit and the spirit's sleep a waking for the
body." And later, like a thunderclap: "*Evil is good perverted.*"*

* * * * *

That Nessim had her watched I for a long time
doubted; after all, she seemed as free as a bat to flit about
the town at night, and never did I hear her called upon
to give an account of her movements. It could not have
been easy to spy upon someone so protean, in touch with
the life of the town at so many points. Nevertheless it is
possible that she was watched lest she should come to
harm. One night an incident brought this home to me,
for I had been asked to dine at the old house. When they
were alone we dined in a little pavilion at the end of the
garden where the summer coolness could mingle with
the whisper of water from the four lions' heads border-
ing the fountain. Justine was late on this particular occasion and Nessim sat alone, with the curtains drawn
back towards the west reflectively polishing a yellow jade
from his collection in those long gentle fingers.

It was already forty minutes past the hour and he had
already given the signal for dinner to begin when the

little black telephone extension gave a small needle-like
sound. He crossed to the table and picked it up with a
sigh, and I heard him say, "yes" impatiently; then he
spoke for a while in a low voice, the language changing
abruptly to Arabic, and for a moment I had the sudden
intuitive feeling that it was Mnemjian talking to him
over the wire. I do not know why I should feel this. He
scribbled something rapidly on an envelope and putting
down the receiver stood for a second memorizing what
he had written. Then he turned to me, and it was all of a
sudden a different Nessim who said: "Justine may need
our help. Will you come with me?" And without waiting
for an answer he ran down the steps, past the lily-pond in
the direction of the garage. I followed as well as I could
and it could only have been a matter of minutes before
he swung the little sports car through the heavy gates
into Rue Fuad and began to weave his way down to the
sea through the network of streets which slide down towards Ras El Tin. Though it was not late there were
few people about and we raced away along the curving
flanks of the Esplanade towards the Yacht Club grimly
overtaking the few horse-drawn cabs ("carriages of love")
which dawdled up and down by the sea.

At the fort we doubled back and entered the huddled
slums which lie behind Tatwig Street, our blond headlights picking out the ant-hill cafés and crowded squares
with an unaccustomed radiance; from somewhere behind the immediate skyline of smashed and unlimbered
houses came the piercing shrieks and ululations of a
burial procession, whose professional mourners made
the night hideous with their plaints for the dead. We
abandoned the car in a narrow street by the mosque
and Nessim entered the shadowy doorway of some great
tenement house, half of which consisted of shuttered
and barred offices with blurred nameplates. A solitary
boab (the *concierge* of Egypt) sat on his perch wrapped

in clouts, for all the world like some discarded material object (an old motor tyre, say)—smoking a
short-stemmed hubble-bubble. Nessim spoke to him
sharply, and almost before the man could reply passed
through the back of the building into a sort of dark backyard flanked by a series of dilapidated houses built of
earth-brick and scaly plaster. He stopped only to light his
cigarette-lighter, and by its feeble light we began to quest
along the doors. At the fourth door he clicked the machine shut and knocked with his fist. Receiving no answer
he pushed it open.

A dark corridor led to a small shadowy room lit by the
feeble light of rush-lamps. This was apparently our destination.

The scene upon which we intruded was ferociously
original, if for no other reason than that the light, pushing up from the mud floor, touched out the eyebrows
and lips and cheek-bones of the participants while it left
great patches of shadow on their faces—so that they
looked as if they had been half-eaten by the rats which
one could hear scrambling among the rafters of this
wretched tenement. It was a house of child prostitutes,
and there in the dimness, clad in ludicrous biblical night-
shirts, with rouged lips, arch bead fringes and cheap
rings, stood a dozen fuzzy-haired girls who could not have
been much above ten years of age; the peculiar innocence
of childhood which shone out from under the fancy-dress
was in startling contrast to the barbaric adult figure of
the French sailor who stood in the centre of the room
on flexed calves, his ravaged and tormented face thrust
out from the neck towards Justine who stood with her
half-profile turned towards us. What he had just shouted
had expired on the silence but the force with which the
words had been uttered was still visible in the jut of the
chin and the black corded muscles which held his head
upon his shoulders. As for Justine, her face was lit by a

sort of painful academic precision. She held a bottle
raised in one hand, and it was clear that she had never
thrown one before, for she held it the wrong way.

On a rotting sofa in one corner of the room, magneti-
cally lit by the warm shadow reflected from the walls, lay
one of the children horribly shrunk up in its nightshirt
in an attitude which suggested death. The wall above the
sofa was covered in the blue imprints of juvenile hands—
the talisman which in this part of the world guards a
house against the evil eye. It was the only decoration in
the room; indeed the commonest decoration of the whole
Arab quarter of the city.

We stood there, Nessim and I, for a good half-second,
astonished by the scene which had a sort of horrifying
beauty—like some hideous colored engraving for a Victorian penny bible, say, whose subject matter had somehow become distorted and displaced. Justine was breathing harshly in a manner which suggested that she was
on the point of tears.

We pounced on her, I suppose, and dragged her out
into the street; at any rate I can only remember the three
of us reached the sea and driving the whole length of
the Corniche in clean bronze moonlight, Nessim's sad
and silent face reflected in the driving-mirror, and the
figure of his silent wife seated beside him, gazing out at
the crashing silver waves and smoking the cigarette
which she had burrowed from the pockets of his jacket.
Later in the garage, before we left the car, she kissed
Nessim tenderly on the eyes.

*   *   *   *   *

All this I have come to regard as a sort of overture to
that first real meeting face to face, when such understanding as we had enjoyed until then—a gaiety and friendship founded in tastes which were common to the three
of us—disintegrated into something which was not love

—how could it have been?—but into a sort of mental
possession in which the bonds of a ravenous sexuality
played the least part. How did we let it come about—
matched as we were so well in experience, weathered and
seasoned by the disappointments of love in other places?

In autumn the female bays turn to uneasy phosphorus
and after the long chafing days of dust one feels the first
palpitations of the autumn, like the wings of a butterfly
fluttering to unwrap themselves. Mareotis turns lemon-
mauve and its muddy flanks are starred by sheets of ra-
diant anemones, growing through the quickened plaster-
mud of the shore. One day while Nessim was away in
Cairo I called at the house to borrow some books and to
my surprise found Justine alone in the studio, darning an
old pullover. She had taken the night train back to
Alexandria, leaving Nessim to attend some business con-
ference. We had tea together and then, on a sudden impulse took our bathing things and drove out through the
rusty slag-heaps of Mex towards the sand-beaches off
Bourg El Arab, glittering in the mauve-lemon light of
the fast-fading afternoon. Here the open sea boomed
upon the carpets of fresh sand the colour of oxidized
mercury; its deep melodious percussion was the background to such conversation as we had. We walked ankle
deep in the spurge of those shallow dimpled pools,
choked here and there with sponges torn up by the roots
and flung ashore. We passed no one on the road I remember save a gaunt Bedouin youth carrying on his head a
wire crate full of wild birds caught with lime-twigs.
Dazed quail.

We lay for a long time, side by side in our wet bathing
costumes to take the last pale rays of the sun upon our
skins in the delicious evening coolness. I lay with half-
shut eyes while Justine (how clearly I see her!) was up
on one elbow, shading her eyes with the palm of one
hand and watching my face. Whenever I was talking she

had the habit of gazing at my lips with a curious half-mocking, an almost impertinent intentness, as if she were waiting for me to mispronounce a word. If indeed it all began at this point I have forgotten the context, but I remember the hoarse troubled voice saying something like: "And if it should happen to us—what would you say?" But before I could say anything she leaned down and kissed me—I should say derisively, antagonistically, on the mouth. This seemed so much out of character that I turned with some sort of half-formulated reproach on my lips—but from here on her kisses were like tremendous soft breathless stabs punctuating the savage laughter which seemed to well up in her—a jeering unstable laughter. It struck me then that she was like someone who had had a bad fright. If I said now: "It must not happen to us," she must have replied: "But let us *suppose*. What if it did?" Then—and this I remember clearly—the mania for self-justification seized her (we spoke French: language creates national character) and between those breathless half-seconds when I felt her strong mouth on my own and those worldly brown arms closing upon mine: "I would not mistake it for gluttony or self-indulgence. We are too worldly for that: simply we have something to learn from each other. What is it?"

What was it? "And is this the way?" I remember asking as I saw the tall toppling figure of Nessim upon the evening sky. "I do not know," she said with a savage, obstinate, desperate expression of humility upon her face, "I do not know"; and she pressed herself upon me like someone pressing upon a bruise. It was as if she wished to expunge the very thought of me, and yet in the fragile quivering context of every kiss found a sort of painful surcease—like cold water on a sprain. How well I recognized her now as a child of the city, which decrees that its women shall be the voluptuaries not of pleasure but of pain, doomed to hunt for what they least dare to find!

She got up now and walked away down the long curving perspective of the beach crossing the pools of lava
slowly, her head bent; and I thought of Nessim's handsome face smiling at her from every mirror in the room.
The whole of the scene which we had just enacted was
invested in my mind with a dream-like improbability. It
was curious in an objective sort of way to notice how my
hands trembled as I lit a cigarette and rose to follow
her.

But when I overtook her and halted her the face she
turned to me was that of a sick demon. She was in a tow-
ering rage. "You thought I simply wanted to make love?
God! haven't we had enough of that? How is it that you
do not *know* what I feel for once? How is it?" She
stamped her foot in the wet sand. It was not merely that
a geological fault had opened in the ground upon which
we had been treading with such self-confidence. It was as
if some long-disused mineshaft in my own character had
suddenly fallen in. I recognized that this barren traffic
in ideas and feelings had driven a path through towards
the denser jungles of the heart; and that here we became
bondsmen in the body, possessors of an enigmatic knowledge which could only be passed on—received, deci-
phered, understood—by those rare complementaries of
ours in the world. (How few they were, how seldom one
found them!) "After all," I remember her saying, "this
has nothing to do with sex," which tempted me to laugh
though I recognized in the phrase her desperate attempt
to dissociate the flesh from the message it carried. I suppose this sort of thing always happens to bankrupts when
they fall in love. I saw then what I should have seen long
before: namely that our friendship had ripened to a
point when we had already become in a way part-owners
of each other.

I think we were both horrified by the thought; for exhausted as we were we could not help but quail before

such a relationship. We did not say any more but walked
back along the beach to where we had left our clothes,
speechless and hand in hand. Justine looked utterly exhausted. We were both dying to get away from each other,
in order to examine our own feelings. We did not speak
to each other again. We drove into the city and she
dropped me at the usual corner near my flat. I snapped
the door of the car closed and she drove off without a
word or a glance in my direction.

As I opened the door of my room I could still see the
imprint of Justine's foot in the wet sand. Melissa was
reading, and looking up at me she said with characteristic
calm foreknowledge: "Something has happened—
what is it?" I could not tell her since I did not myself
know. I took her face in my hands and examined it silently, with a care and attention, with a sadness and
hunger I don't ever remember feeling before. She said:
"It is not me you are seeing, it is someone else." But in
truth I was seeing Melissa for the first time. In some para-
doxical way it was Justine who was now permitting me
to see Melissa as she really was—and to recognize my
love for her. Melissa smilingly reached for a cigarette and
said: "You are falling in love with Justine"; and I answered as sincerely, as honestly, as painfully as I could:
"No, Melissa, it is worse than that"—though I could not
for the life of me have explained how or why.

When I thought of Justine I thought of some great
freehand composition, a cartoon of a woman represent-
ing someone released from bondage in the male. "Where
the carrion is," she once quoted proudly from Boehme,
speaking of her native city, "there the eagles will gather."
Truly she looked and seemed an eagle at this moment.
But Melissa was a sad painting from a winter landscape
contained by dark sky; a window-box with a few flower-
ing geraniums lying forgotten on the window-sill of a
cement-factory.

There is a passage in one of Justine's diaries which comes to mind here. I translate it here because though it must have referred to incidents long preceding those which I have recounted yet nevertheless it almost exactly expresses the curiously ingrown quality of a love which I have come to recognize as peculiar to the city rather than to ourselves. "Idle," she writes, "to imagine falling in love as a correspondence of minds, of thoughts; it is a simultaneous firing of two spirits engaged in the autonomous act of growing up. And the sensation is of something having noiselessly exploded inside each of them. Around this event, dazed and preoccupied, the lover moves examining his or her own experience; her gratitude alone, stretching away towards a mistaken donor, creates the illusion that she communicates with her fellow, but this is false. The loved object is simply one that has shared an experience at the same moment of time, narcissistically; and the desire to be near the beloved object is at first not due to the idea of possessing it, but simply to let the two experiences compare themselves, like reflections in different mirrors. All this may precede the first look, kiss, or touch; precede ambition, pride or envy; precede the first declarations which mark the turning point—for from here love degenerates into habit, possession, and back to loneliness." How characteristic and how humourless a delineation of the magical gift: and yet how true . . . of Justine!

"Every man," she writes elsewhere, and here I can hear the hoarse and sorrowful accents of her voice repeating the words as she writes them: "Every man is made of clay and daimon, and no woman can nourish both."

That afternoon she went home to find that Nessim had arrived by the afternoon plane. She complained of feeling feverish and went early to bed. When he came to sit by her side and take her temperature she said something which struck him as interesting enough to remem-

ber—for long afterwards he repeated it to me: "This is
nothing of medical interest—a small chill. Diseases are
not interested in those who want to die." And then with
one of those characteristic swerves of association, like a
swallow turning in mid-air she added, "Oh! Nessim, I
have always been so strong. Has it prevented me from
being truly loved?"

* * * * *

It was through Nessim that I first began to move with
any freedom in the great cobweb of Alexandrian society; my own exiguous earnings did not even permit
me to visit the night-club where Melissa danced. At first
I was a trifle ashamed of being forever on the receiving
end of Nessim's hospitality, but we were soon such fast
friends that I went everywhere with them and never
gave the matter a thought. Melissa unearthed an ancient
dinner-jacket from one of my trunks and refurbished it.
It was in their company that I first visited the club where
she danced. It was strange to sit between Justine and
Nessim and watch the flaky white light suddenly blaze
down upon a Melissa I could no longer recognize under
a layer of paint which gave her gentle face an air of gross
and precocious unimaginativeness. I was horrified too at
the banality of her dancing, which was bad beyond
measure; yet watching her make those gentle and ineffectual movements of her slim hands and feet (the air
of a gazelle harnessed to a water-wheel) I was filled with
tenderness at her mediocrity, at the dazed and self-depre-
cating way she bowed to the lukewarm applause. Afterwards she was made to carry a tray round and take up a
collection for the orchestra, and this she did with a hopeless timidity, coming to the table where I sat with
lowered eyes under those ghastly false lashes, and with
trembling hands. My friends did not know at that time of
our relationship; but I noticed Justine's curious and

mocking glance as I turned out my pockets and found a
few notes to thrust into the tray with hands that shook
not less than Melissa's—so keenly did I feel her embarrassment.

Afterwards when I got back to the flat a little tipsy and
exhilarated from dancing with Justine I found her still
awake, boiling a kettle of water over the electric ring:
"Oh why," she said, "did you put all that money into the
collecting tray? A whole week's wages: are you mad?
What will we eat tomorrow?"

We were both hopelessly improvident in money matters, yet somehow we managed better together than
apart. At night, walking back late from the night-club,
she would pause in the alley outside the house and if she
saw my light still burning give a low whistle: and I, hearing the signal, would put down the book I was reading
and creep quietly down the staircase, seeing in my mind's
eye her lips pursed about that low liquid sound, as if to
take the soft imprint of a brush. At the time of which I
write she was still being followed about and importuned
by the old man or his agents. Without exchanging a
word we would join hands and hurry down the maze of
alleys by the Polish Consulate, pausing from time to time
in a dark doorway to see if there was anyone on our trail.
At last, far down where the shops tailed away into the
blue we would step out into the sea-gleaming milk-
white Alexandrian midnight—our preoccupations sliding from us in that fine warm air; and we would walk
towards the morning star which lay throbbing above the
dark velvet breast of Montaza, touched by the wind and
the waves.

In these days Melissa's absorbed and provoking gentleness had all the qualities of a rediscovered youth. Her
long uncertain fingers—I used to feel them moving over
my face when she thought I slept, as if to memorize the
happiness we had shared. In her there was a pliancy, a

resilience which was Oriental—a passion to serve. My shabby clothes—the way she picked up a dirty shirt seemed to engulf it with an overflowing solicitude; in the morning I found my razor beautifully cleaned and even the toothpaste laid upon the brush in readiness. Her care for me was a goad, provoking me to give my life some sort of shape and style that might match the simplicity of hers. Of her experiences in love she would never speak, turning from them with a weariness and distaste which suggested that they had been born of necessity rather than desire. She paid me the compliment of saying: "For the first time I am not afraid to be lightheaded or foolish with a man."

Being poor was also a deep bond. For the most part our excursions were the simple excursions that all provincials make in a sea-side town. The little tin tram bore us with the clicking of its wheels to the sand-beaches of Sidi Bishr, or we spent Shem El Nessim in the gardens of Nouzha, camped on the grass under the oleanders among some dozens of humble Egyptian families. The inconvenience of crowds brought us both distraction and great intimacy. By the rotting canal watching the children dive for coins in the ooze, or eating a fragment of watermelon from a stall we wandered among the other idlers of the city, anonymously happy. The very names of the tram stops echoed the poetry of these journeys: Chatby, Camp de César, Laurens, Mazarita, Glymenopoulos, Sidi Bishr. . . .

Then there was the other side: coming back late at night to find her asleep with her red slippers kicked off and the little hashish-pipe beside her on the pillow . . . I would know that one of her depressions had set in. At such times there was nothing to be done with her; she would become pale, melancholy, exhausted-looking, and would be unable to rouse herself from her lethargy for several days together. She talked much to herself, and would spend hours listening to the radio and yawning, or going negligently through a bundle of old film magazines. At such times when the *cafard* of the city seized her I was at my wits' end to devise a means of rousing her. She would lie with far-seeing eyes like a sibyl, stroking my face and repeating over and over again: "If you knew how I have lived you would leave me. I am not the woman for you, for any man. I am exhausted. Your kindness is wasted." If I protested that it was not kindness but love she might say with a grimace: "If it were love you would poison me rather than let me go on like this." Then she would begin to cough with her uncollapsed lung and, unable to bear the sound, I would go for a walk in the dark Arab-smudged street, or visit the British Council library to consult reference books; and here, where the general impression of British culture suggested parsimony, indigence, intellectual strap-hanging—here I would pass the evening alone, glad of the studious rustle and babble around me.

But there were other times too: those sun-tormented afternoons—"honey-sweating," as Pombal called them —when we lay together bemused by the silence, watching the yellow curtains breathing tenderly against the light— the quiet respirations of the wind off Mareotis which matched our own. Then she might rise and consult the clock after giving it a shake and listening to it intently: sit naked at the dressing-table to light a cigarette—looking so young and pretty, with her slender arm raised to show the cheap bracelet I had given her. ("Yes, I am looking at myself, but it helps me to think about you.") And turning aside from this fragile mirror-worship she would swiftly cross to the ugly scullery which was my only bath-room, and standing at the dirty iron sink would wash herself with deft swift movements, gasping at the coldness of the water, while I lay inhaling the warmth and sweetness of the pillow upon which her dark head had been resting: watching the long bereft Greek face, with its sane pointed nose and candid eyes, the satiny skin that is given only to the thymus-dominated, the mole upon the slender stalk of the neck. These are the moments which are not calculable, and cannot be assessed in words; they live on in the solution of memory, like wonderful creatures, unique of their kind, dredged up from the floors of some unexplored ocean.

*   *   *   *   *

That summer Pombal decided to let his flat to Purse-warden, much to my annoyance. I disliked this literary figure for the contrast he offered to his own work—poetry and prose of real grace. I did not know him well but he was financially successful as a novelist which made me envious, and through years of becoming social practice had developed a sort of *savoir faire* which I felt should never become part of my own equipment. He was little, fattish and blond and gave the impression of a young man lying becalmed in his mother. I cannot say that he was not kind or good, for he was both—but the incon-venience of living in the flat with someone I did not like was galling. However it would have involved greater in-convenience to move so I accepted the box-room at the end of the corridor at a reduced rent, and did my wash-ing in the grimy little scullery.

Pursewarden could afford to be convivial and about twice a week I was kept up by the noise of drinking and laughter from the flat. One night quite late there came a knock at the door. In the corridor stood Pursewarden, looking pale and rather perky—as if he had just been fired out of a gun into a net. Beside him stood a stout naval stoker of unprepossessing ugliness—looking like all naval stokers; as if he had been sold into slavery as a child. "I say," said Pursewarden shrilly, "Pombal told me you were a doctor; would you come and take a look

at somebody who is ill?" I had once told Georges of the
year I spent as a medical student with the result that for
him I had become a fully-fledged doctor. He not only
confided all his own indispositions to my care—which included frequent infestations of body-crabs—but he once
went so far as to try and persuade me to perform an abor-
tion for him on the dining-room table. I hastened to tell
Pursewarden that I was certainly not a doctor, and ad-
vised him to telephone for one: but the phone was out
of order, and the *boab* could not be roused from his
sleep: so more in the spirit of disinterested curiosity than
anything I put on a mackintosh over my pyjamas and
made my way along the corridor.

Opening the door I was immediately blinded by the
glare and smoke. The party did not seem to be of the
usual kind, for the guests consisted of three or four
maimed-looking naval cadets, and a prostitute from
Golfo's tavern, smelling of briny paws and *taphia*.*
Improbably enough, too, she was bending over a figure
seated on the end of a couch—the figure which I now
recognize as Melissa, but which then seemed like a cata-
strophic Greek comic mask. Melissa appeared to be rav-
ing, but soundlessly for her voice had gone—so that she
looked like a film of herself without a sound-track. Her
features were a cave. The older woman appeared to be
panic-stricken, and was boxing her ears and pulling her
hair; while one of the naval cadets was splashing water
rather inexpertly upon her from a heavily decorated
chamber-pot which was one of Pombal's dearest treasures
and which bore the royal arms of France on its under-
side. Somewhere out of sight someone was being slowly,
unctuously sick. Pursewarden stood beside me surveying
the scene, looking rather ashamed of himself.

Melissa was pouring with sweat, and her hair was
glued to her temples; as we broke the circle of her tor-
mentors she sank back into an expressionless quivering

silence, with this permanently engraved shriek on her face. It would have been wise to try and find out where she had been and what she had been eating and drinking, but a glance at the maudlin, jabbering group around me showed that it would be impossible to get any sense out of them. Nevertheless, seizing the boy nearest me I started to interrogate him when the hag from Golfo's who was herself in a state of hysterics, and was only restrained by a naval stoker (who had her pinioned from behind), began to shout in a hoarse chewed voice, "Spanish fly. He gave it to her." And darting out of the arms of her captor like a rat she seized her handbag and fetched one of the sailors a resounding crack over the head. The bag must have been full of nails for he went down swimming and came up with fragments of shattered crockery in his hair.

She now began to sob in a voice which wore a beard and call for the police. Three sailors converged upon her with blunt fingers extended advising, exhorting, imploring her to desist. Nobody wanted a brush with the naval police. But neither did anyone relish a crack from that Promethean handbag, bulging with french letters and belladonna bottles. She retreated carefully step by step. (Meanwhile I took Melissa's pulse, and ripping off her blouse listened to her heart. I began to be alarmed for her, and indeed for Pursewarden who had taken up a strategic position behind an armchair and was making eloquent gestures at everyone.) By now the fun had started, for the sailors had the roaring girl cornered— but unfortunately against the decorative Sheraton cupboard which housed Pombal's cherished collection of pottery. Reaching behind her for support her hands encountered an almost inexhaustible supply of ammunition, and letting go her handbag with a hoarse cry of triumph she began to throw china with a single-mindedness and accuracy I have never seen equalled. The air

was all at once full of Egyptian and Greek tear-bottles,
Ushabti, and Sèvres. It could not be long now before
there came the familiar and much-dreaded banging of
hob-nailed boots against the door-lintels, as lights were
beginning to go on all round us in the building. Pursewarden's alarm was very marked indeed; as a resident
and moreover a famous one he could hardly afford the
sort of scandal which the Egyptian press might make out
of an affray like this. He was relieved when I motioned to
him and started to wrap the by now almost insensible
figure of Melissa in the soft Bokhara rug. Together we
staggered with her down the corridor and into the blessed
privacy of my box-room where, like Cleopatra, we un-
rolled her and placed her on the bed.

I had remembered the existence of an old doctor, a
Greek, who lived down the street, and it was not long
before I managed to fetch him up the dark staircase,
stumbling and swearing in a transpontine demotic, dropping catheters and stethoscopes all the way. He pronounced Melissa very ill indeed but his diagnosis was
ample and vague—in the tradition of the city. "It is
everything," he said, "malnutrition, hysteria, alcohol,
hashish, tuberculosis, Spanish fly . . . help yourself,"
and he made the gesture of putting his hand in his
pocket and fetching it out full of imaginary diseases
which he offered us to choose from. But he was also prac-
tical, and proposed to have a bed ready for her in the
Greek Hospital next day. Meanwhile she was not to be
moved.

I spent that night and the next on the couch at the
foot of the bed. While I was out at work she was confided to the care of one-eyed Hamid, the gentlest of Ber-
berines. For the first twelve hours she was very ill indeed,
delirious at times, and suffered agonizing attacks of
blindness—agonizing because they made her so afraid.
But by being gently rough with her we managed between

us to give her courage enough to surmount the worst,
and by the afternoon of the second day she was well
enough to talk in whispers. The Greek doctor pronounced himself satisfied with her progress. He asked
her where she came from and a haunted expression came
into her face as she replied "Smyrna"; nor would she
give the name and address of her parents, and when he
pressed her she turned her face to the wall and tears of
exhaustion welled slowly out of her eyes. The doctor
took up her hand and examined the wedding-finger.
"You see," he said to me with a clinical detachment,
pointing out the absence of a ring. "That is why. Her
family has disowned her and turned her out of doors. It
is so often these days . . ." and he shook a shaggy com-
miserating head over her. Melissa said nothing, but when
the ambulance came and the stretcher was being prepared to take her away she thanked me warmly for my
help, pressed Hamid's hand to her cheek, and surprised
me by a gallantry to which my life had unaccustomed
me: "If you have no girl when I come out, think of me.
If you call me I will come to you."* I do not know how to
reduce the gallant candour of the Greek to English.

So I had lost sight of her for a month or more; and indeed I did not think of her, having many other preoccupations at this time. Then, one hot blank afternoon,
when I was sitting at my window watching the city un-
wrinkle from sleep I saw a different Melissa walk down
the street and turn into the shadowy doorway of the
house. She tapped at my door and walked in with her
arms full of flowers, and all at once I found myself separated from that forgotten evening by centuries. She had
in her something of the same diffidence with which I
later saw her take up a collection for the orchestra in the
night-club. She looked like a statue of pride hanging its
head.

A nerve-racking politeness beset me. I offered her a
chair and she sat upon the edge of it. The flowers were
for me, yes, but she had not the courage to thrust the
bouquet into my arms, and I could see her gazing dis-
tractedly around for a vase into which she might put
them. There was only an enamel washbasin full of half-
peeled potatoes. I began to wish she had not come. I
would have liked to offer her some tea but my electric
ring was broken and I had no money to take her out—
at this time I was sliding ever more steeply into debt. Besides, I had sent Hamid out to have my only summer suit
ironed and was clad in a torn dressing-gown. She for her
part looked wonderfully, intimidatingly smart, with a
new summer frock of a crisp vine-leaf pattern and a straw
hat like a great gold bell. I began to pray passionately
that Hamid would come back and create a diversion. I
would have offered her a cigarette but my packet was
empty and I was forced to accept one of her own from
the little filigree cigarette-case she always carried. This
I smoked with what I hoped was an air of composure
and told her that I had accepted a new job near
Sidi Gabr, which would mean a little extra money. She
said she was going back to work; her contract had been
renewed: but they were giving her less money. After a
few minutes of this sort of thing she said that she must
be leaving as she had a tea-appointment. I showed her
out on the landing and asked her to come again whenever she wished. She thanked me, still clutching the flowers which she was too timid to thrust upon me and
walked slowly downstairs. After she had gone I sat on the
bed and uttered every foul swear-word I could remember
in four languages—though it was not clear to me whom
I was addressing. By the time one-eyed Hamid came
shuffling in I was still in a fury and turned my anger
upon him. This startled him considerably: it was a long
time since I had lost my temper with him, and he retired

into the scullery muttering and shaking his head and invoking the spirits to help him.

After I had dressed and managed to borrow some money from Pursewarden—while I was on my way to post a letter—I saw Melissa again sitting in the corner of a coffee shop, alone, with her hands supporting her chin. Her hat and handbag lay beside her and she was staring into her cup with a wry reflective air of amusement. Impulsively I entered the place and sat down beside her. I had come, I said, to apologize for receiving her so badly, but . . . and I began to describe the circumstances which had preoccupied me, leaving nothing out. The broken electric-ring, the absence of Hamid, my summer-suit. As I began to enumerate the evils by which I was beset they began to seem to me slightly funny, and altering my angle of approach I began to recount them with a lugubrious exasperation which coaxed from her one of the most delightful laughs I have ever heard. On the subjects of my debts I frankly exaggerated, though it was certainly a fact that since the night of the affray Pursewarden was always ready to lend me small sums of money without hesitation. And then to cap it all, I said, she had appeared while I was still barely cured of a minor but irritating venereal infection—the fruit of Pombal's solicitude—contracted no doubt from one of the Syrians he had thoughtfully left behind him. This was a lie but I felt impelled to relate it in spite of myself. I had been terrified I said at the thought of having to make love again before I was quite well. At this she put out her hand and placed it on mine while she laughed, wrinkling up her nose: laughing with such candour, so lightly and effortlessly, that there and then I decided to love her.

We idled arm in arm by the sea that afternoon, our conversations full of the débris of lives lived without forethought, without architecture. We had not a taste

in common. Our characters and predispositions were
wholly different, and yet in the magical ease of
this friendship we felt something promised us. I like, also,
to remember that first kiss by the sea, the wind blowing
up a flake of hair at each white temple—a kiss broken
off by the laughter which beset her as she remembered
my account of the trials I was enduring. It symbolized
the passion we enjoyed, its humour and lack of intense-
ness: its charity.

* * * * *

Two subjects upon which it was fruitless to question
Justine too closely: her age, her origins. Nobody—pos-
sibly not even Nessim himself—knew all about her with
any certainty. Even the city's oracle Mnemjian seemed
for once at loss, though he was knowledgeable about her
recent love affairs. Yet the violet eyes narrowed as he
spoke of her and hesitantly he volunteered the information that she came from the dense Attarine Quarter, and
had been born of a poor Jewish family which had since
emigrated to Salonika. The diaries are not very helpful
either since they lack clues—names, dates, places—and
consist for the most part of wild flights of fancy punctuated by bitter little anecdotes and sharp line-drawings
of people whose identity is masked by a letter of the alphabet. The French she writes in is not very correct, but
spirited and highly-flavoured; and carries the matchless
quality of that husky speaking-voice. Look: "Clea speaking of her childhood: thinking of mine, passionately
thinking. The childhood of my race, my time. . . . Blows
first in the hovel behind the Stadium; the clock-mend-
er's shop. I see myself now caught in the passionate concentration of watching a lover's sleeping face as I so
often saw him bent over a broken timepiece with the
harsh light pouring down noiselessly over him. Blows and
curses, and printed everywhere on the red mud walls

(like the blows struck by conscience) the imprint of blue
hands, fingers outstretched, that guarded us against the
evil eye. With these blows we grew up, aching heads,
flinching eyes. A house with an earthen floor alive with
rats, dim with wicks floating upon oil. The old money-
lender drunk and snoring, drawing in with every breath
the compost-odours, soil, excrement, the droppings of
bats; gutters choked with leaves and breadcrumbs soft-
ened by piss; yellow wreaths of jasmine, heady, meretricious. And then add screams in the night behind other
shutters in that crooked street: the *bey* beating his
wives because he was impotent. The old herb-woman
selling herself every night on the flat ground among the
razed houses—a sulky mysterious whining. The soft *palm*
noise of bare black feet passing on the baked mud street,
late at night. Our room bulging with darkness and pesti-
lence, and we Europeans in such disharmony with the
fearful animal health of the blacks around us. The
copulations of boabs shaking the house like a palm-tree.
Black tigers with gleaming teeth. And everywhere the
veils, the screaming, the mad giggle under the pepper-
trees, the insanity and the lepers. Such things as children
see and store up to fortify or disorient their lives. A
camel has collapsed from exhaustion in the street outside the house. It is too heavy to transport to the
slaughter-house so a couple of men come with axes
and cut it up there and then in the open street, alive.
They hack through the white flesh—the poor creature
looking ever more pained, more aristocratic, more puzzled as its legs are hacked off. Finally there is the head
still alive, the eyes open, looking round. Not a scream of
protest, not a struggle. The animal submits like a palm-
tree. But for days afterwards the mud street is soaked in
its blood and our bare feet are printed by the moisture.

"Money falling into the tin bowls of beggars. Fragments of every language—Armenian, Greek, Amharic,

Moroccan Arabic; Jews from Asia Minor, Pontus, Georgia: mothers born in Greek settlements on the Black Sea; communities cut down like the branches of trees, lacking a parent body, dreaming of Eden. These are the poor quarters of the white city; they bear no resemblance to those lovely streets built and decorated by foreigners where the brokers sit and sip their morning papers. Even the harbour does not exist for us here. In the winter, sometimes, rarely, you can hear the thunder of a siren—but it is another country. Ah! the misery of harbours and the names they conjure when you are going nowhere. It is like a death—a death of the self uttered in every repetition of the word *Alexandria, Alexandria.*"

* * * * *

Rue Bab-el-Mandeb, Rue Abou-el-Dardar, Minet-el-Bassal (streets slippery with discarded fluff from the cotton marts), Nouzha (the rose-garden, some remembered kisses) or bus stops with haunted names like Saba Pacha, Mazloum, Zizinia Bacos, Schutz, Gianaclis. A city becomes a world when one loves one of its inhabitants.

* * * * *

One of the consequences of frequenting the great house was that I began to be noticed and to receive the attention of those who considered Nessim influential and presumed that if he spent his time with me I must also in some undiscovered fashion, be either rich or distinguished. Pombal came to my room one afternoon while I was dozing and sat on my bed: "Look here," he said, "you are beginning to be noticed. Of course a *cicisbeo* is a normal enough figure in Alexandrian life, but things are going to become socially very boring for you if you go out with those two so much. Look!" And he handed me a large and florid piece of pasteboard with a printed

invitation on it for cocktails at the French Consulate. I
read it uncomprehendingly. Pombal said: "This is very
silly. My chief, the consul-general, is impassionated by
Justine. All attempts to meet her have failed so far. His
spies tell him that you have an entrée into the family circle, indeed that you are . . . I know, I know. But he is
hoping to displace you in her affections." He laughed
heavily. Nothing sounded more preposterous to me at
this time. "Tell the consul-general," I said . . . and uttered a forcible remark or two which caused Pombal to
click his tongue reprovingly and shake his head. "I
would love to," he said. "But *mon cher* there is a Pecking
Order among diplomats as there is among poultry. I depend upon him for my little cross."

Heaving his bulk round he next produced from his
pocket a battered little yellow-covered novelette and
placed it on my knees. "Here is something to interest you.
Justine was married when she was very young to a
French national, Albanian by descent, a writer. This little book is about her—post-mortem on her; it is quite
decently done." I turned the novel over in my hands. It
was entitled *Moeurs* and it was by a certain Jacob
Arnauti. The flyleaf showed it to have enjoyed numerous
reprintings in the early thirties. "How do you know this?"
I asked, and Georges winked a large, heavy-lidded reptilian eye as he replied. "We have been making enquiries.
The Consul can think of nothing but Justine, and the
whole staff has been busy for weeks collecting information about her. *Vive la France!*"

When he had gone I started turning the pages of
Moeurs, still half-dazed by sleep. It was very well written
indeed, in the first person singular, and was a diary of
Alexandrian life as seen by a foreigner in the middle
thirties. The author of the diary is engaged on research
for a novel he proposes to do—and the day to day account of his life in Alexandria is accurate and penetrat-

ing; but what arrested me was the portrait of a young
Jewess he meets and marries: takes to Europe: divorces.
The foundering of this marriage on their return to
Egypt is done with a savage insight that throws into relief the character of Claudia, his wife. And what astonished and interested me was to see in her a sketch of Justine I recognized without knowing: a younger, a more
disoriented Justine, to be sure. But unmistakable. Indeed whenever I read the book, and this was often, I was
in the habit of restoring her name to the text. It fitted
with an appalling verisimilitude.

They met, where I had first seen her, in the gaunt vestibule of the Cecil, in a mirror. "In the vestibule of this
moribund hotel the palms splinter and refract their motionless fronds in the gilt-edged mirrors. Only the rich
can afford to stay permanently—those who live on in the
guilt-edged security of a pensionable old age. I am looking for cheaper lodgings. In the lobby tonight a small
circle of Syrians, heavy in their dark suits, and yellow in
their scarlet *tarbushes,* solemnly sit. Their hippopota-
mus-like womenfolk, lightly moustached, have jingled off
to bed in their jewelry. The men's curious soft oval faces
and effeminate voices are busy upon jewel-boxes—for
each of these brokers carries his choicest jewels with
him in a casket; and after dinner the talk has turned to
male jewelry. It is all the Mediterranean world has left
to talk about; a self-interest, a narcissism which comes
from sexual exhaustion expressing itself in the possessive
symbol: so that meeting a man you are at once informed
what he is worth, and meeting his wife you are told in the
same breathless whisper what her dowry was. They croon
like eunuchs over the jewels, turning them this way and
that in the light to appraise them. They flash their sweet
white teeth in little feminine smiles. They sigh. A white-
robed waiter with a polished ebony face brings coffee.
A silver hinge flies open upon heavy white (like the

thighs of Egyptian women) cigarettes each with its few
flecks of *hashish*. A few grains of drunkenness before
bedtime. I have been thinking about the girl I met last
night in the mirror: dark on marble-ivory white: glossy
black hair: deep suspiring eyes in which one's glances
sink because they are nervous, curious, turned to sexual
curiosity. She pretends to be a Greek, but she must be
Jewish. It takes a Jew to smell out a Jew; and neither of
us has the courage to confess our true race. I have told
her I am French. Sooner or later we shall find one another out.

"The women of the foreign communities here are
more beautiful than elsewhere. Fear, insecurity domi-
nates them. They have the illusion of foundering in the
ocean of blackness all around. This city has been built
like a dyke to hold back the flood of African darkness;
but the soft-footed blacks have already started leaking
into the European quarters: a sort of racial osmosis is
going on. To be happy one would have to be a Moslem,
an Egyptian woman—absorbent, soft, lax, overblown;
given to veneers; their waxen skins turn citron-yellow or
melon-green in the naphtha-flares. Hard bodies like
boxes. Breasts apple-green and hard—a reptilian coldness of the outer flesh with its bony outposts of toes and
fingers. Their feelings are buried in the pre-conscious.
In love they give out nothing of themselves, having no
self to give, but enclose themselves around you in an
agonized reflection—an agony of unexpressed yearning
that is at the opposite pole from tenderness, pleasure. For
centuries now they have been shut in a stall with the
oxen, masked, circumcised. Fed in darkness on jams and
scented fats they have become tuns of pleasure, rolling on
paper-white blue-veined legs.

Walking through the Egyptian quarter the smell of
flesh changes—ammoniac, sandal-wood, saltpetre, spice,
fish. She would not let me take her home—no doubt be-

cause she was ashamed of her house in these slums.
Nevertheless she spoke wonderfully about her childhood. I have taken a few notes: returning home to find
her father breaking walnuts with a little hammer on the
table by the light of an oil-lamp. I can see him. He is no
Greek but a Jew from Odessa in fur cap with greasy ring-
lets. Also the kiss of the Berberin, the enormous rigid
penis like an obsidian of the ice age; leaning to take her
underlip between beautiful unfiled teeth. We have left
Europe behind here and are moving towards a new spiritual latitude. She gave herself to me with such contempt
that I was for the first time in my life surprised at the
quality of her anxiety; it was as if she were desperate,
swollen with disaster. And yet these women belonging to
these lost communities have a desperate bravery very
different to ours. They have explored the flesh to a degree which makes them true foreigners to us. How am I
to write about all this? Will she come, or has she disappeared forever? The Syrians are going to bed with little
cries, like migrating birds."

She comes. They talk. ("Under the apparent provincial sophistication and mental hardness I thought I detected an inexperience, not of the world to be sure but
of society. I was interesting, I realized, as a foreigner
with good manners—and she turned upon me now the
shy-wise regard of an owl from those enormous brown
eyes whose faintly bluish eyeballs and long lashes threw
into relief the splendour of the pupils, glittering and
candid.")

It may be imagined with what breathless, painful anxiety I first read this account of a love-affair with Justine;
and truly after many re-readings the book, which I now
know almost by heart, has always remained for me a
document, full of personal pain and astonishment. "Our
love," he writes in another, much later, "was like a syl-
logism to which the true premises were missing: I mean

regard. It was a sort of mental possession which trapped us both and set us to drift upon the shallow tepid waters of Mareotis like spawning frogs, a prey to instincts based in lassitude and heat. . . . No, that is not the way to put it. It is not very just. Let me try again with these infirm and unstable tools to sketch Claudia. Where shall we begin?

"Well: her talent for situations had served her well for twenty years of an erratic and unpunctual life. Of her origins I learned little, save that she had been very poor. She gave me the impression of someone engaged in giving a series of savage caricatures of herself—but this is common to most lonely people who feel that their true self can find no correspondence in another. The speed with which she moved from one milieu to another, from one man, place, date to another, was staggering. But her instability had a magnificence that was truly arresting. The more I knew her the less predictable she seemed; the only constant was this frantic struggle to break through the barrier of her autism. And every action ended in error, guilt, repentance. How often I remember—'Darling, this time it will be different. I promise you.'

"Later, when we went abroad: at the Adlon, the pollen of the spotlights playing upon the Spanish dancers fuming in the smoke of a thousand cigarettes; by the dark waters of Buda, her tears dropping hotly among the quietly flowing dead leaves; riding on the gaunt Spanish plains, the silence pock-marked by the sound of our horses' hooves: by the Mediterranean lying on some forgotten reef. It was never her betrayals that upset me —for with Justine the question of male pride in possession became somehow secondary. I was bewitched by the illusion that I could really come to know her; but I see now that she was not really a woman but the incarnation of Woman admitting no ties in the society we inhabited. 'I hunt everywhere for a life that is worth living. Perhaps if I could die or go mad it would provide a focus for all the feelings I have which find no proper outlet. The doctor I loved told me I was a nymphomaniac—but there is no gluttony or self-indulgence in my pleasure, Jacob. It is purely wasted from that point of view. The waste, my dear, the waste! You speak of taking pleasure sadly, like the puritans do. Even there you are unjust to me. I take it tragically, and if my medical friends want a compound word to describe the heartless creature I seem, why they will have to admit that what I lack of heart I make up in soul. That is where the trouble lies.' These are not, you see, the sort of distinctions of which women are usually capable. It was as if somehow her world lacked a dimension, and love had become turned inwards into a kind of idolatry. At first I mistook this for a devastating and self-consuming egotism, for she seemed so ignorant of the little prescribed loyalties which constitute the foundations of affection between men and women. This sounds pompous, but never mind. But now, remembering the panics and exaltations which she endured, I wonder whether I was right. I am thinking of those tiresome dramas—scenes in furnished bedrooms, with Justine turning on the taps to drown the noise of her own crying. Walking up and down, hugging her arms in her armpits, muttering to herself, she seemed to smoulder like a tar-barrel on the point of explosion. My indifferent health and poor nerves—but above all my European sense of humour—seemed at such times to goad her beyond endurance. Suffering, let us say, from some imagined slight at a dinner-party she would patrol the strip of carpet at the foot of the bed like a panther. If I fell asleep she might become enraged and shake me by the shoulders, crying: 'Get up, Jacob. I am suffering, can't you see?' When I declined to take a part in this charade she would perhaps break something upon the dressing-table in order to have an excuse to ring the bell. How many fearful faces of night-maids have I not seen confronted by this wild figure in a silver or gold evening-dress, saying with a terrifying po-liteness: 'Oblige me by clearing up the dressing-table. I have clumsily broken something.' Then she would sit smoking cigarette after cigarette. 'I know exactly what this is,' I told her once. 'I expect that every time you are unfaithful to me and consumed by guilt you would like to provoke me to beat you up and give a sort of remis-sion for your sins. My dear, I simply refuse to pander to your satisfactions. You must carry your own burdens. You are trying hard to get me to use a stockwhip on you. But I only pity you.' This, I must confess, made her very thoughtful for a moment and involuntarily her hands strayed to touch the smooth surface of the legs she had so carefully shaved that afternoon. . . .

"Latterly, too, when I began to weary of her, I found this sort of abuse of the emotions so tiresome that I took to insulting her and laughing at her. One night I called her a tiresome hysterical Jewess. Bursting into those ter-rible hoarse sobs which I so often heard that even now in memory the thought of them (their richness, their melodious density) hurts me, she flung herself down to her own bed to lie, limbs loose and flaccid, played upon by the currents of her hysteria like jets from a hose.

"Did this sort of thing happen so often or is it that my memory has multiplied it? Perhaps it was only once, and the echoes have misled me. At any rate I seem to hear so often the noise she made unstopping the bottle of sleeping-tablets, and the small sound of the tablets fall-ing into the glass. Even when I was dozing I would count, to see that she did not take too many. All this was much later, of course; in the early days I would ask her to come into my bed and self-conscious, sullen, cold, she would obey me. I was foolish enough to think that I could thaw her out and give her the physical peace upon which—I thought—mental peace must depend. I was wrong. There was some unresolved inner knot which she wished to untie and which was quite beyond my skill as a lover or a friend. Of course. Of course. I knew as much as could be known of the psychopathology of hysteria at that time. But there was some other quality which I thought I could detect behind all this. In a way she was not looking for life but for some integrating revelation which would give it point.

"I have already described how we met—in the long mirror of the Cecil, before the open door of the ballroom, on a night of carnival. The first words we spoke were spoken, symbolically enough, in the mirror. She was there with a man who resembled a cuttle-fish and who waited while she examined her dark face attentively. I stopped to adjust an unfamiliar bow-tie. She had a hungry natural candour which seemed proof against any suggestion of forwardness as she smiled and said: 'There is never enough light.' To which I responded without thought: 'For women perhaps. We men are less exigent.' We smiled and I passed her on my way to the ballroom, ready to walk out of her mirror-life forever, without a thought. Later the hazards of one of those awful English dances, called the Paul Jones I believe, left me facing her for a waltz. We spoke a few disjointed words—I dance badly; and here I must confess that her beauty made no impression on me. It was only later when she began her trick of drawing hasty ill-defined designs round my character, throwing my critical faculties into disorder by her sharp penetrating stabs: ascribing to me qualities which she invented on the spur of the moment out of that remorseless desire to capture my attention. Women must attack writers—and from the moment she learned I was a writer she felt disposed to make herself interesting by dissecting me. All this would have been most flattering to my *amour propre* had some of her observations been further from the mark. But she was acute, and I was too feeble to resist this sort of game—the mental ambuscades which constitute the opening gambits of a flirtation.

"From here I remember nothing more until that night —that marvellous summer night on the moon-drenched balcony above the sea with Justine pressing a warm hand on my mouth to stop me talking and saying something like: 'Quick. *Engorge-moi*. From desire to revulsion—let's get it over.' She had, it seemed, already exhausted me in her own imagination. But the words were spoken with such weariness and humility—who could forbear to love her?

"It is idle to go over all this in a medium as unstable as words. I remember the edges and corners of so many meetings, and I see a sort of composite Justine, concealing a ravenous hunger for information, for power through self-knowledge, under a pretence of feeling. Sadly I am driven to wonder whether I ever really moved her—or existed simply as a laboratory in which she could work. She learned much from me: to read and reflect. She had achieved neither before. And perhaps what I took to be love was merely a gratitude. Among the thousand discarded people, impressions, subjects of study— somewhere I see myself drifting, floating, reaching out arms. Strangely enough it was never in the *lover* that I really met her but in the *writer*. Here we clasped hands —in that amoral world of suspended judgements where curiosity and wonder seem greater than order—the syllogistic order imposed by the mind. This is where one waits in silence, holding one's breath, lest the pane should cloud over. I watched over her like this. I was mad about her.

"She had of course many secrets being a true child of the Mouseion, and I had to guard myself desperately against jealousy or the desire to intrude upon the hidden side of her life. I was almost successful in this and if I spied upon her it was really from curiosity to know what she might be doing or thinking when she was not with me. There was, for example, a woman of the town whom she visited frequently, and whose influence on her was profound enough to make me suspect an illicit relationship; there was also a man to whom she wrote long letters, though as far I could see he lived in the city. Perhaps he was bedridden? I made inquiries, but my spies always brought me back uninteresting information. The woman was a fortune-teller, elderly, a widow. The man to whom she wrote—her pen shrilling across the cheap notepaper—turned out to be a doctor who held a small part-time post on a local consulate. He was not bedridden; but he was a homosexual, and dabbled in hermetic philosophy which is now so much in vogue. Once she left a particularly clear impression on my blotting-pad and in the mirror (the mirror again!) I was able to read:—'my life there is a sort of Unhealed Place as you call it which I try to keep full of people, accidents, diseases, anything that comes to hand. You are right when you say it is an apology for better living, wiser living. But while I respect your disciplines and your knowledge I feel that if I am ever going to come to terms with myself I must work *through* the dross in my own character and burn it up. Anyone could solve my problem artificially by placing it in the lap of a priest. We Alexandrians have more pride than that—and more respect for religion. It would not be fair to God, my dear sir, and whoever else I fail (I see you smile) I am determined not to fail Him whoever He is.'

"It seemed to me then that if this was part of a love-letter it was the kind of love-letter one could only address to a saint; and again I was struck, despite the clumsiness and incorrectness of the writing, by the fluency with which she could dissociate between ideas of different categories. I began to see her in an altered light; as somebody who might well destroy herself in an excess of wrong-headed courage and forfeit the happiness which she, in common with all the rest of us, desired and lived only to achieve. These thoughts had the effect of qualifying my love for her, and I found myself filled sometimes by disgust for her. But what made me afraid was that after quite a short time I found to my horror that I could not live without her. I tried. I took short journeys away from her. But without her I found life full of consuming boredom which was quite insupportable. I had fallen *in love*. The very thought filled me with an inexplicable despair and disgust. It was as if I unconsciously realized that in her I had met my evil genius. To come to Alexandria heart-whole and to discover an *amor fati*—it was a stroke of ill-luck which neither my health nor my nerves felt capable of supporting. Looking in the mirror I reminded myself that I had turned forty and already there was a white hair or two at my temples! I thought once of trying to end this attachment, but in every smile and kiss of Justine I felt my resolutions founder. Yet with her one felt all around the companionship of shadows which invaded life and filled it with a new resonance. Feeling so rich in ambiguities could not be resolved by a sudden act of the will. I had at times the impression of a woman whose every kiss was a blow struck on the side of death. When I discovered, for example (what I knew) that she had been repeatedly unfaithful to me, and at times when I had felt myself to be closest to her, I felt nothing very sharp in outline: rather a sinking numbness such as one might feel on leaving a friend in hospital, to enter a lift and fall six floors in silence, standing beside a uniformed automaton whose breathing one could hear. The silence of my room deafened me. And then, thinking about it, gather-

ing my whole mind about the fact I realized that what
she had done bore no relation to myself: it was an attempt to free herself for me: to give me what she
knew belonged to me. I cannot say that this sounded any
better to my ears than a sophistry. Nevertheless my heart
seemed to know the truth of this and dictated a tactful
silence to me to which she responded with a new warmth,
a new ardour, of gratitude added to love. This again disgusted me somewhat.

"Ah! but if you had seen her then as I did in
her humbler, gentler moments, remembering that she
was only a child, you would not have reproached me for
cowardice. In the early morning, sleeping in my arms,
her hair blown across that smiling mouth, she looked like
no other woman I could remember: indeed like no
woman at all, but some marvellous creature caught in
the Pleistocene stage of her development. And later
again, thinking about her as I did and have done these
past few years I was surprised to find that though I loved
her wholly and knew that I should never love anyone
else—yet I shrank from the thought that she might return. The two ideas co-existed in my mind without displacing one another. I thought to myself with relief,
'Good. I *have* really loved at last. That is something
achieved'; and to this my alter ego added: 'Spare me the
pangs of love *requited* with Justine.' This enigmatic
polarity of feeling was something I found completely unexpected. If this was love then it was a variety of the
plant which I have never seen before. ('Damn the word,'
said Justine once, 'I would like to spell it backwards as
you say the Elizabethans did God. Call it *evol* and make
it a part of "evolution" or "revolt." Never use the word
to me.')"

*   *   *   *   *

These later extracts I have taken from the section of
the *diary* which is called *Posthumous Life* and is an at-

tempt the author makes to sum up and evaluate these
episodes. Pombal finds much of this banal and even dull;
but who, knowing Justine, could fail to be moved by it?
Nor can it be said that the author's intentions are not
full of interest. He maintains for example that real people can only exist in the imagination of an artist strong
enough to contain them and give them form. "Life, the
raw material, is only lived *in potentia* until the artist
deploys it in his work. Would that I could do this service
of love for poor Justine." (I mean, of course, "Claudia.")
"I dream of a book powerful enough to contain the ele-
ments of her—but it is not the sort of book to which we
are accustomed these days. For example, on the first page
a synopsis of the plot in a few lines. Thus we might dis-
pense with the narrative articulation. What follows
would be drama freed from the burden of form. *I would
set my own book free to dream.*"

But of course one cannot escape so easily from the pattern which he regards as imposed but which in fact grows
up organically within the work and appropriates it.
What is missing in his work—but this is a criticism of all
works which do not reach the front rank—is a sense of
play. He bears down so hard upon his subject-matter; so
hard that it infects his style with some of the unbalanced
ferocity of Claudia herself. Then, too, everything which
is a fund of emotion becomes of equal importance to
him: a sign uttered by Claudia among the oleanders of
Noussha, the fireplace where she burnt the manuscript
of his novel about her ("For days she looked at me as if
she were trying to read my book in me"), the little room
in the Rue Lepsius with its creaking cane chair. . . .
He says of his characters: "All bound by time in a dimension which is not reality *as we would wish it to be*—but
is created by the needs of the work. For all drama creates
bondage, and the actor is only significant to the degree
that he is bound."

But setting these reservations aside, how graceful and accurate a portrait of Alexandria he manages to convey; Alexandria and its women. There are sketches here of Leonie, Gaby, Fosca*—the pale rose-coloured one, the gold, the bitumen. Some one can identify quite easily from his pages. Clea, who still lives in that high studio, a swallow's nest made of cobwebs and old cloth—he has her unmistakably. But for the most part these Alexandrian girls are distinguished from women in other places only by a terrifying honesty and world-weariness. He is enough of a writer to have isolated these true qualities in the city of the Soma. One could not expect more from an intruder of gifts who almost by mistake pierced the hard banausic shell of Alexandria and discovered himself.

As for Justine herself, there are few if any references to Arnauti in the heavily armoured pages of her diary. Here and there I have traced the letter A, but usually in passages abounding with the purest introspection. Here is one where the identification might seem plausible:

"What first attracted me in A was his room. There always seemed to me some sort of ferment going on there behind the heavy shutters. Books lay everywhere with their jackets turned inside out or covered in white drawing-paper—as if to hide their titles. A huge litter of newspapers with holes in them, as if a horde of mice had been feasting in them—A's cuttings from 'real life' as he called it, the abstraction which he felt to be so remote from his own. He would sit down to his newspapers as if to a meal in a patched dressing-gown and velvet slippers, snipping away with a pair of blunt nail-scissors. He puzzled over 'reality' in the world outside his work like a child; it was presumably a place where people could be happy, laugh, bear children."

A few such sketches comprise the whole portrait of the author of *Moeurs*; it seems a meagre and disappointing

reward for so much painstaking and loving observation;
nor can I trace one word about their separation after this
brief and fruitless marriage. But it was interesting to
see from his book how he had made the same judgements
upon her character as we were later to make, Nessim and
I. The compliance she extorted from us all was the astonishing thing about her. It was as if men knew at once
that they were in the presence of someone who could not
be judged according to the standards they had hitherto
employed in thinking about women. Clea once said of
her (and her judgements were seldom if ever charita-
ble): "The true whore is man's real darling—like Justine; she alone has the capacity to wound men. But of
course our friend is only a shallow twentieth-century re-
production of the great *Hetairae* of the past, the type to
which she belongs without knowing it, Lais, Charis and
the rest. . . . Justine's role has been taken from her and
on her shoulders society has placed the burden of guilt
to add to her troubles. It is a pity. For she is truly Alexandrian."

For Clea too the little book of Arnauti upon Justine
seemed shallow and infected by the desire to explain
everything. "It is our disease," she said, "to want to contain everything within the frame of reference of a psy-
chology or a philosophy. After all Justine cannot be
justified or excused. She simply and magnificently *is*; we
have to put up with her, like original sin. But to call her
a nymphomaniac or to try and Freudianise her, my
dear, takes away all her mythical substance—the only
thing she really is. Like all amoral people she verges on
the Goddess. If our world were a world there would be
temples to accommodate her where she would find the
peace she was seeking. Temples where one could outgrow the sort of inheritance she has: not these damn
monasteries full of pimply little Catholic youths who
have made a bicycle saddle of their sexual organs."

She was thinking of the chapters which Arnauti has
entitled *The Check,* and in which he thinks he has found
the clue to Justine's instability of heart. They may be, as
Clea thinks, shallow, but since everything is susceptible
of more than one explanation they are worth considera-
tion. I myself do not feel that they explain Justine, but to
a degree they do illuminate her actions—those immense
journeys they undertook together across the length and
breadth of Europe. "In the very heart of passion," he
writes, adding in parentheses, " (passion which to her
seemed the most facile of gifts; there was a check—some
great impediment of feeling which I became aware of
only after many months. It rose up between us like a
shadow and I recognized, or thought I did, the true
enemy of the happiness which we longed to share and
from which we felt ourselves somehow excluded. What
was it?

"She told me one night as we lay in that ugly great
bed in a rented room—a gaunt rectangular room of a
vaguely French-Levantine shape and flavour: a stucco
ceiling covered with decomposing cherubs and posies of
vine-leaves. She told me and left me raging with a jealousy I struggled to hide—but a jealousy of an entirely
novel sort. Its object was a man who though still alive,
no longer existed. It is perhaps what the Freudians
would call a screen-memory of incidents in her earliest
youth. She had (and there was no mistaking the force of
this confession for it was accompanied by floods of tears,
and I have never seen her weep like that before or since):
she had been raped by one of her relations. One cannot
help smiling at the commonplaceness of the thought. It
was impossible to judge at what age. Nevertheless—and
here I thought I had penetrated to the heart of The
Check: from this time forward she could obtain no satisfaction in love unless she mentally re-created these incidents and re-enacted them. For her we, her lovers, had

become only mental substitutes for this first childish act
—so that love, as a sort of masturbation, took on all the
colours of neurasthenia; she was suffering from an imagination dying of anaemia, for she could possess no one
thoroughly in the flesh. She could not appropriate to
herself the love she felt she needed, for her satisfactions
derived from the crepuscular corners of a life she was no
longer living. This was passionately interesting. But
what was even more amusing was that I felt this blow to
my *amour propre* as a man exactly as if she had
confessed to an act of deliberate unfaithfulness. What!
Every time she lay in my arms she could find no satisfaction save through this memory? In a way, then, I could
not possess her: had never done so. I was merely a
dummy. Even now as I write I cannot help smiling to
remember the strangled voice in which I asked who the
man was, and where he was. (What did I hope to do?
Challenge him to a duel?) Nevertheless there he was,
standing squarely between Justine and me; between Justine and the light of the sun.

"But here too I was sufficiently detached to observe how
much love feeds upon jealousy, for as a woman out of
my reach yet in my arms, she became ten times more desirable, more necessary. It was a heartbreaking predicament for a man who had no intention of falling in
love, and for a woman who only wished to be delivered
of an obsession and set free to love. From this something
else followed: if I could break The Check I could possess
her truly, as no man had possessed her. I could step into
the place of the shadow and receive her kisses truly; now
they fell upon a corpse. It seemed to me that I understood everything now.

"This explains the grand tour we took, hand in hand
so to speak, in order to overcome this succubus together
with help of science. Together we visited the book-lined
cell of Czechnia, where the famous mandarin of psychol-

ogy sat, gloating pallidly over his specimens. Basle,
Zurich, Baden, Paris—the flickering of steel rails over
the arterial systems of Europe's body: steel ganglia meeting and dividing away across mountains and valleys.
Confronting one's face in the pimpled mirrors of the
Orient Express. We carried her disease backwards and
forwards over Europe like a baby in a cradle until I began to despair, and even to imagine that perhaps Justine
did not wish to be cured of it. For to the involuntary
check of the psyche she added another—of the will. Why
this should be I cannot understand; but she would tell
no one his name, the shadow's name. A name which by
now could mean everything or nothing to her. After all,
somewhere in the world he must be now, his hair thinning and greying from business worries or excesses,
wearing a black patch over one eye as he did always after
an attack of ophthalmia. (If I can describe him to you it
is because once I actually saw him.) 'Why should I tell
people his name?' Justine used to cry. 'He is nothing to
me now—has never been. He has completely forgotten
these incidents. Don't you see he is dead? When I see
him . . .' This was like being stung by a serpent. 'So you
do see him?' She immediately withdrew to a safer position. 'Every few years, passing in the street. We just nod.'

"So this creature, this pattern of ordinariness, was still
breathing, still alive! How fantastic and ignoble jealousy
is. But jealousy for a figment of a lover's imagination borders on the ludicrous.

"Then once, in the heart of Cairo, during a traffic jam,
in the breathless heat of a midsummer night, a taxi drew
up beside ours and something in Justine's expression
drew my gaze in the direction of hers. In that palpitant
moist heat, dense from the rising damps of the river and
aching with the stink of rotten fruit, jasmine and sweating black bodies, I caught sight of the very ordinary man
in the taxi next to us. Apart from the black patch over

one eye there was nothing to distinguish him from the
thousand other warped and seedy business men of this
horrible city. His hair was thinning, his profile sharp, his
eye beady: he was wearing a grey summer suit. Justine's
expression of suspense and anguish was so marked however that involuntarily I cried: 'What is it?'; and as the
traffic block lifted and the cab moved off she replied with
a queer flushed light in her eye, an air almost of
drunken daring: 'The man you have all been hunting
for.' But before the words were out of her mouth I had
understood and as if in a bad dream stopped our own
taxi and leaped out into the road. I saw the red tail light
of his taxi turning into Suleiman Pacha, too far away for
me even to be able to distinguish its colour or number.
To give chase was impossible for the traffic behind us was
dense once more. I got back into the taxi trembling and
speechless. So this was the man for whose name Freud
had hunted with all the great might of his loving detachment. For this innocent middle-aged man Justine had
lain suspended, every nerve tense as if in the act of levita-
tion, while the thin steely voice of Magnani had repeated
over and over again: 'Tell me his name; you must tell
me his name'; while from the forgotten prospects where
her memory lay confined her voice repeated like an
oracle of the machine-age: 'I cannot remember. I cannot
remember.'

"It seemed to me clear then that in some perverted
way she did not wish to conquer The Check, and certainly all the power of the physicians could not persuade
her. This was the bare case without orchestration, and
here lay the so-called nymphomania with which these
reverend gentlemen assured me that she was afflicted.
At times I felt convinced that they were right; at others
I doubted. Nevertheless it was tempting to see in her behaviour the excuse that every man held out for her the
promise of a release in her passional self, release from

this suffocating self-enclosure where sex could only be fed by the fat flames of fantasy.

"Perhaps we did wrong in speaking of it openly, of treating it as a problem, for this only invested her with a feeling of self-importance and moreover contributed a nervous hesitation to her which until then had been missing. In her passional life she was direct—like an axe falling. She took kisses like so many coats of paint. I am puzzled indeed to remember how long and how vainly I searched for excuses which might make her amorality if not palatable at least understandable. I realize now how much time I wasted in this way; instead of enjoying her and turning aside from these preoccupations with the thought, 'She is as untrustworthy as she is beautiful. She takes love as plants do water, lightly, thoughtlessly.' Then I could have walked arm in arm with her by the rotting canal, or sailed on sundrenched Mareotis, enjoying her as she was, taking her as she was. What a marvellous capacity for unhappiness we writers have! I only know that this long and painful examination of Justine succeeded not only in making her less sure of herself, but also more consciously dishonest; worst of all, she began to look upon me as an enemy who watched for the least misconstruction, the least word or gesture which might give her away. She was doubly on her guard, and indeed began to accuse me of an insupportable jealousy. Perhaps she was right. I remember her saying: 'You live now among my imaginary intimacies. I was a fool to tell you everything, to be so honest. Look at the way you question me now. Several days running the same questions. And at the slightest discrepancy you are on me. You know I never tell a story the same way twice. Does that mean that I am lying?'

"I was not warned by this but redoubled my efforts to penetrate the curtain behind which I thought my adversary stood, a black patch over one eye. I was still in correspondence with Magnani and tried to collect as much evidence as possible which might help him elucidate the mystery, but in vain. In the thorny jungle of guilty impulses which constitute the human psyche who can find a way—even when the subject wishes to co-operate? The time we wasted upon futile researches into her likes and dislikes! If Justine had been blessed with a sense of humour what fun she could have had with us. I remember a whole correspondence based upon the confession that she could not read the words 'Washington D.C.' on a letter without a pang of disgust! It is a matter of deep regret to me now that I wasted this time when I should have been loving her as she deserved. Some of these doubts must also have afflicted old Magnani for I recall him writing: 'and my dear boy we must never forget that this infant science we are working at, which seems so full of miracles and promises, is at best founded on much that is as shaky as astrology. After all, these important *names* we give to things! Nymphomania may be considered another form of virginity if you wish; and as for Justine, she may never have been in love. Perhaps one day she will meet a man before whom all these tiresome chimeras will fade into innocence again. You must not rule this thought out.' He was not, of course, trying to hurt me—for this was a thought I did not care to admit to myself. But it penetrated me when I read it in this wise old man's letter."

* * * * *

I had not read these pages of Arnauti before the afternoon at Bourg El Arab when the future of our relationship was compromised by the introduction of a new element—I do not dare to use the word love, for fear of hearing that harsh sweet laugh in my imagination: a laugh which would somewhere be echoed by the diarist. Indeed so fascinating did I find his analysis of his subject,

and so closely did our relationship echo the relationship
he had enjoyed with Justine that at times I too felt like
some paper character out of *Moeurs*. Moreover, here I
am, attempting to do the same sort of thing with her in
words—though I lack his ability and have no pretensions
to being an artist. I want to put things down simply and
crudely, without style—the plaster and whitewash; for
the portrait of Justine should be rough-cast, with the
honest stonework of the predicament showing through.

After the episode of the beach we did not meet for
some small time, both of us infected by a vertiginous uncertainty—or at least I was. Nessim was called away to
Cairo on business but though Justine was, as far as I
knew, at home alone, I could not bring myself to visit
the studio. Once as I passed I heard the Bluthner and
was tempted to ring the bell—so sharply defined was the
image of her at the black piano. Then once passing the
garden at night I saw someone—it must have been she—
walking by the lily-pond, shading a candle in the palm
of one hand. I stood for a moment uncertainly before
the great doors wondering whether to ring or not. Melissa at this time also had taken the occasion to visit a
friend in Upper Egypt. Summer was growing apace,
and the town was sweltering. I bathed as often as my
work permitted, travelling to the crowded beaches in the
little tin tram.

Then one day while I was lying in bed with a
temperature brought on by an overdose of the sun Justine walked into the dank calm of the little flat, dressed
in a white frock and shoes, and carrying a rolled towel
under one arm with her handbag. The magnificence of
her dark skin and hair glowed out of all this whiteness
with an arresting quickness. When she spoke her voice
was harsh and unsteady, and it sounded for a moment
as if she had been drinking—perhaps she had. She put
one hand out and leaned upon the mantelshelf as she

said: "I want to put an end to all this as soon as possible. I feel as if we've gone too far to go back." As for me I was consumed by a terrible sort of desirelessness, a luxurious anguish of body and mind which prevented me from saying anything, thinking anything. I could not visualize the act of love with her, for somehow the emotional web we had woven about each other stood between us: an invisible cobweb of loyalties, ideas, hesitations which I had not the courage to brush aside. As she took a step forward I said feebly: "This bed is so awful and smelly. I have been drinking. I tried to make love to myself but it was no good—I kept thinking about you." I felt myself turning pale as I lay silent upon my pillows, all at once conscious of the silence of the little flat which was torn in one corner by the dripping of a leaky tap. A taxi brayed once in the distance, and from the harbour, like the stifled roar of a minotaur, came a single dark whiff of sound from a siren. Now it seemed we were completely alone together.

The whole room belonged to Melissa—the pitiful dressing-table full of empty powder-boxes and photos: the graceful curtain breathing softly in that breathless afternoon air like the sail of a ship. How often had we not lain in one another's arms watching the slow intake and recoil of that transparent piece of bright linen? Across all this, as across the image of someone dearly loved, held in the magnification of a gigantic tear moved the brown harsh body of Justine naked. It would have been blind of me not to notice how deeply her resolution was mixed with sadness. We lay eye to eye for a long time, our bodies touching, hardly communicating more than the animal lassitude of that vanishing afternoon. I could not help thinking then as I held her lightly in the crook of an arm how little we own our bodies. I thought of the words of Arnauti when he says: "It dawned on me then that in some fearful way this girl

had shorn me of all my *force morale*. I felt as if I had had
my head shaved." But the French, I thought, with their
endless gravitation between *bonheur* and *chagrin* must
inevitably suffer when they come up against something
which does not admit of *préjugés;* born for tactics and
virtuosity, not for staying-power, they lack the little
touch of crassness which armours the Anglo-Saxon mind.
And I thought: "Good. Let her lead me where she will.
She will find me a match for her. And there'll be no talk
of *chagrin* at the end." Then I thought of Nessim,
who was watching us (though I did not know) as if
through the wrong end of an enormous telescope: seeing
our small figures away on the skyline of his own hopes
and plans. I was anxious that he should not be hurt.

But she had closed her eyes—so soft and lustrous now,
as if polished by the silence which lay so densely all
around us. Her trembling fingers had become steady and
at ease upon my shoulder. We turned to each other, closing like the two leaves of a door upon the past, shutting
out everything, and I felt her happy spontaneous kisses
begin to compose the darkness around us like successive
washes of a colour. When we had made love and lay once
more awake she said: "I am always so bad the first time,
why is it?"

"Nerves perhaps. So am I."

"You are a little afraid of me."

Then rising on an elbow as if I had suddenly woken
up I said: "But Justine, what on earth are we going to
make of all this? If this is to be—" But she became absolutely terrified now and put her hand over my
mouth, saying: "For Godsake no justifications! Then I
shall know we are wrong! For nothing can justify it,
nothing. And yet it has got to be like this." And getting
out of bed she walked over to the dressing-table with its
row of photos and powder-boxes and with a single blow
like that of a leopard's paw swept it clean. *"That,"* she

said, "is what I am doing to Nessim and you to Melissa! It would be ignoble to try and pretend otherwise." This was more in the tradition that Arnauti had led me to expect and I said nothing. She turned now and started kissing me with such a hungry agony that my burnt shoulders began to throb until tears came into my eyes. "Ah!" she said softly and sadly: "You are crying. I wish I could. I have lost the knack."

I remember thinking to myself as I held her, tasting the warmth and sweetness of her body, salt from the sea —her ear-lobes tasted of salt—I remember thinking: "Every kiss will take her near Nessim, but separates me further from Melissa." But strangely enough I experienced no sense of despondency or anguish; and for her part she must have been thinking along the same lines for she suddenly said: "Balthazar says that the natural traitors—like you and I—are really Caballi. He says we are dead and live this life as a sort of limbo. Yet the living can't do without us. We infect them with a desire to experience more, to grow."

I tried to tell myself how stupid all this was—a banal story of an adultery which was among the cheapest commonplaces of the city: and how it did not deserve romantic or literary trappings. And yet somewhere else, at a deeper level, I seemed to recognize that the experience upon which I had embarked would have the deathless finality of a lesson learned. "You are too serious," I said, with a certain resentment, for I was vain and did not like the sensation of being carried out of my depth. Justine turned her great eyes on me. "O no!" she said softly, as if to herself: "It would be silly to spread so much harm as I have done and not to realize that it is my role. Only in this way, by knowing what I am doing, can I ever outgrow myself. It isn't easy to be me. I *so much* want to be responsible for myself. Please never doubt that."

We slept, and I was only woken by the dry click of Hamid's key turning in the lock and by his usual evening performance. For a pious man, whose little prayer mat lay rolled and ready to hand on the kitchen balcony, he was extraordinarily superstitious. He was as Pombal said, "djinn-ridden," and there seemed to be a djinn in every corner of the flat. How tired I had become of hearing his muttered "Destoor, destoor," as he poured slops down the kitchen sink—for here dwelt a powerful djinn and its pardon had to be invoked. The bathroom too was haunted by them, and I could always tell when Hamid used the outside lavatory (which he had been forbidden to do) because whenever he sat on the water-closet a hoarse involuntary invocation escaped his lips ("Permission O ye blessed ones!") which neutralized the djinn which might otherwise have dragged him down into the sewage system. Now I heard him shuffling round the kitchen in his old felt slippers like a boa-constrictor muttering softly.

I woke Justine from a troubled doze and explored her mouth and eyes and fine hair with the anguished curiosity which for me has always been the largest part of sensuality. "We must be going," I said. "Pombal will be coming back from the Consulate in a little while."

I recall the furtive languour with which we dressed and silent as accomplices made our way down the gloomy staircase into the street. We did not dare to link arms, but our hands kept meeting involuntarily as we walked, as if they had not shaken off the spell of the afternoon and could not bear to be separated. We parted speechlessly too, in the little square with its dying trees burnt to the colour of coffee by the sun; parted with only one look—as if we wished to take up emplacements in each other's minds forever.

It was as if the whole city had crashed about my ears; I walked about in it aimlessly as survivors must walk about the streets of their native city after an earthquake, amazed to find how much that had been familiar was changed. I felt in some curious way deafened and remember nothing more except that much later I ran into Pursewarden and Pombal in a bar, and that the former recited some lines from the old poet's famous "The City" which struck me with a new force—as if the poetry had been newly minted: though I knew them well. And when Pombal said: "You are abstracted this evening. What is the matter?" I felt like answering him in the words of the dying Amr:* "I feel as if heaven lay close upon the earth and I between them both, breathing through the eye of a needle."

To HAVE WRITTEN so much and to have said nothing about Balthazar is indeed an omission—for in a sense he is one of the keys to the City. The key: Yes, I took him very much as he was in those days and now in my memory I feel that he is in need of a new evaluation. There was much that I did not understand then, much that I have since learned. I remember chiefly those interminable evenings spent at the Café Al Aktar playing backgammon while he smoked his favourite Lakadif in a pipe with a long stem. If Mnemjian is the archives of the City, Balthazar is its Platonic *daimon*—the mediator between its Gods and its men. It sounds far-fetched, I know.

I see a tall man in a black hat with a narrow brim. Pombal christened him "the botanical goat." He is thin, stoops slightly, and has a deep croaking voice of great beauty, particularly when he quotes or recites. In speaking to you he never looks at you directly—a trait which I have noticed in many homosexuals. But in him this does not signify inversion of which he is not only not ashamed, but to which he is actually indifferent; his yellow goat-eyes are those of a hypnotist. In not looking at you he is sparing you from a regard so pitiless that it would discountenance you for an evening. It is a mystery how he can have, suspended from his trunk, hands of such monstrous ugliness. I would long since have cut them off and thrown them into the sea. Under his chin he has one dark spur of hair growing, such as one sometimes sees upon the hoof of a sculptured Pan.

Several times in the course of those long walks we took together, beside the sad velvet broth of the canal, I found myself wondering what was the quality in him which arrested me. This was before I knew anything about the Cabal. Though he reads widely Balthazar's conversation is not heavily loaded with the kind of material that might make one think him bookish: like Pursewarden. He loves poetry, parable, science and sophistry—but there is a lightness of touch and a judgement behind his thinking. Yet underneath the lightness there is something else—a resonance which gives his thinking density. His vein is aphoristic, and it sometimes gives him the touch of a minor oracle. I see now that he was one of those rare people who had found a philosophy for himself and whose life was occupied in trying to live it. I think this is the unanalysed quality which gives his talk cutting-edge.

As a doctor he spends much of his working-time in the government clinic for venereal disease. (He once said dryly: "I live at the centre of the city's life—its genito-urinary system: it is a sobering sort of place.") Then, too, he is the only man whose paederasty is somehow no qualification of his innate masculinity of mind. He is neither a puritan nor its opposite. Often I have entered his little room in the Rue Lepsius—the one with the creaking cane chair—and found him asleep in bed with a sailor. He has neither excused himself at such a time nor even alluded to his bedfellow. While dressing he will sometimes turn and tenderly tuck the sheet round his partner's sleeping form. I take this naturalness as a compliment.

He is a strange mixture; at times I have heard his voice tremble with emotion as he alludes to some aspect of the Cabal which he has been trying to make comprehensible to the study-group. Yet once when I spoke enthusiastically of some remarks he had made he sighed and said, with that perfect Alexandrian scepticism which somehow underlay an unquestionable belief in and devotion to the Gnosis: "We are all hunting for rational reasons for believing in the absurd." At another time after a long and tiresome argument with Justine about heredity and environment he said: "Ah! my dear, after all the work of the philosophers on his soul and the doctors on his body, what can we say we really know about man? That he is, when all is said and done, just a passage for liquids and solids, a pipe of flesh."

He was a fellow-student and close friend of the old poet, and of him he speaks with such warmth and penetration that what he has to say always moves me. "I sometimes think that I learned more from studying him than I did from studying philosophy. His exquisite balance of irony and tenderness would have put him among the saints had he been a religious man. He was by divine choice only a poet and often unhappy but with him one had the feeling that he was catching every minute as it flew and turning it upside down to expose its happy side. He was really using himself up, his inner self, in living. Most people lie and let life play upon them like the tepid discharges of a douche-bag. To the Cartesian proposition: 'I think therefore I am,' he opposed his own, which must have gone something like this: 'I imagine, therefore I belong and am free.'"

Of himself Balthazar once said wryly: "I am a Jew, with all the Jew's bloodthirsty interest in the ratiocinative faculty. It is the clue to many of the weaknesses in my thinking, and which I am learning to balance up with the rest of me—through the Cabal chiefly."

* * * * *

I remember meeting him, too, one bleak winter evening, walking along the rain-swept Corniche, dodging the sudden gushes of salt water from the conduits which lined it. Under the black hat a skull ringing with Smyrna, and the Sporades where his childhood lay. Under the

black hat too the haunting illumination of a truth which
he afterwards tried to convey me in an English not the
less faultless for having been learned. We had met before, it is true, but glancingly: and would have perhaps
passed each other with a nod had not his agitation made
him stop me and take my arm. "Ah! you can help me!"
he cried, taking me by the arm. "Please help me." His
pale face with its gleaming goat-eyes lowered itself towards mine in the approaching dusk.

The first wet blank lamps had begun to stiffen the wet
paper background of Alexandria. The sea-wall with its
lines of cafés swallowed in the spray glowed with a
smudged and trembling phosphorescence. The wind
blew dead south. Mareotis crouched among her reeds,
stiff as a crouching sphinx. He was looking, he said, for
the key to his watch—the beautiful gold pocket-watch
which had been made in Munich. I thought afterwards
that behind the urgency of his expression he masked
the symbolic meaning that this watch had for him: sig-
nifying the unbound time which flowed through his
body and mine, marked off for so many years now by
this historic timepiece. Munich, Zagreb, the Carpathians.
. . . The watch had belonged to his father. A tall Jew,
dressed in furs, riding in a sledge. He had crossed into
Poland lying in his mother's arms, knowing only that
the jewels she wore in that snowlit landscape were icy
cold to the touch. The watch had ticked softly against
his father's body as well as his own—like time ferment-
ing in them. It was wound by a small key in the shape of
an *ankh* which he kept attached to a strip of black rib-
bon on his key-ring. "Today is Saturday," he said
hoarsely, "in Alexandria." He spoke as if a different sort
of time obtained here, and he was not wrong. "If I don't
find the key it will stop." In the last gleams of the wet
dusk he tenderly drew the watch from its silk-lined waistcoat pocket. "I have until Monday evening. It will stop."

Without the key it was useless to open the delicate golden leaf and expose the palpitating viscera of time itself stirring. "I have been over the ground three times. I must have dropped it between the café and the hospital." I would gladly have helped him, but night was falling fast; and after we had walked a short distance examining the interstices of the stones we were forced to give up the search. "Surely," I said, "you can have another key cut for it?" He answered impatiently, "Yes. Of course. But you don't understand. It belonged to this watch. It was part of it."

We went, I remember, to a café on the sea-front and sat despondently before a black coffee while he croaked on about this historic watch. It was during this conversation that he said: "I think you know Justine. She has spoken to me warmly of you. She will bring you to the Cabal." "What is that?" I asked. "We study the Cabbala," he said almost shyly; "we are a sort of small lodge. She said you knew something about it and would be interested." This astonished me for I had never, as far as I knew, mentioned to Justine the line of study which I was pursuing—in between long bouts of lethargy and self-disgust. And as far as I knew the little suitcase containing the Hermetica and other books of the kind had always been kept under my bed locked. I said nothing however. He spoke now of Nessim, saying: "Of all of us he is the most happy in a way because he has no preconceived idea of what he wants in return for his love. And to love in such an unpremeditated way is something that most people have to re-learn after fifty. Children have it. So has he. I am serious."

"Did you know the writer Arnauti?"

"Yes. The author of *Moeurs*."

"Tell me about him."

"He intruded on us, but he did not see the spiritual city underlying the temporal one. Gifted, sensitive, but very French. He found Justine too young to be more than hurt by her. It was ill luck. Had he found another a little older—all our women are Justines, you know, in different styles—he might have—I will not say written better, for his book is well written: but he might have found in it a sort of resolution which would have made it more truly a work of art."

He paused and took a long pull at his pipe before adding slowly: "You see in his book he avoided dealing with a number of things which he knew to be true of Justine, but which he ignored for purely artistic purposes—like the incident of her child. I suppose he thought it smacked of melodrama."

"What child was this?"

"Justine had a child, by whom I do not know. It was kidnapped and disappeared one day. About six years old. A girl. These things do happen quite frequently in Egypt as you know. Later she heard that it had been seen or recognized and began a frantic hunt for it through the Arab quarter of every town, through every house of ill-fame, since you know what happens to parentless children in Egypt. Arnauti never mentioned this, though he often helped her follow up clues, and he must have seen how much this loss contributed to her unhappiness."

"Who did Justine love before Arnauti?"

"I cannot remember. You know many of Justine's lovers remained her friends; but more often I think you could say that her truest friends were never lovers. The town is always ready to gossip."

But I was thinking of a passage in *Moeurs* where Justine comes to meet him with a man who is her lover. Arnauti writes: "She embraced this man, her lover, so warmly in front of me, kissing him on the mouth and eyes, his cheeks, even his hands, that I was puzzled. Then it shot through me with a thrill that it was really *me* she was kissing in her imagination."

Balthazar said quietly: "Thank God I have been spared an undue interest in love. At least the invert escapes this fearful struggle to give oneself to another. Lying with one's own kind, enjoying an experience, one can still keep free the part of one's mind which dwells in Plato, or gardening, or the differential calculus. Sex has left the body and entered the imagination now; that is why Arnauti suffered so much with Justine, because she preyed upon all that he might have kept separate—his artist-hood if you like. He is when all is said and done a sort of minor Antony, and she a Cleo. You can read all about it in Shakespeare. And then, as far as Alexandria is concerned, you can understand why this is really a city of incest—I mean that here the cult of Serapis was founded. For this etiolation of the heart and reins in love-making must make one turn inwards upon one's sister. The lover mirrors himself like Narcissus in his own family; there is no exit from the predicament."

All this was not very comprehensible to me, yet vaguely I felt a sort of correspondence between the associations he employed; and certainly much of what he said seemed to—not explain, but to offer a frame to the picture of Justine—the dark, vehement creature in whose direct and energetic handwriting I had first read this quotation from Laforgue: "Je n'ai pas une jeune fille qui saurait me goûter. Ah! oui, une garde-malade! Une garde-malade pour l'amour de l'art, ne donnant ses baisers qu'à des mourants, des gens *in extremis*. . . ." Under this she wrote: "Often quoted by A. and at last discovered by accident in Laforgue."

"Have you fallen out of love with Melissa?" said Balthazar suddenly. "I do not know her. I have only seen her. Forgive me. I have hurt you."

It was at this time that I was becoming aware of how much Melissa was suffering. But not a word of reproach ever escaped her lips, nor did she ever speak of Justine. But she had taken on a lacklustre, unloved colour—her very flesh; and paradoxically enough though I could hardly make love to her without an effort, yet I felt myself at this time to be more deeply in love with her than ever. I was gnawed by a confusion of feelings and a sense of frustration which I had never experienced before; it made me sometimes angry with her.

It was so different from Justine, who was experiencing much the same confusion as myself between her ideas and her intentions, when she said: "Who invented the human heart, I wonder? Tell me, and then show me the place where he was hanged."

* * * * *

Of the Cabal itself, what is there to be said? Alexandria is a town of sects and gospels. And for every ascetic she has always thrown up one religious libertine—Carpocrates, Anthony—who was prepared to founder in the senses as deeply and truly as any desert father in the mind. "You speak slightingly of syncretism," said Balthazar once, "but you must understand that to work here at all—and I am speaking now as a religious maniac not a philosopher—one must try to reconcile two extremes of habit and behaviour which are not due to the intellectual disposition of the inhabitants, but to their soil, air, landscape. I mean extreme sensuality and intellectual asceticism. Historians always present syncretism as something which grew out of a mixture of warring intellectual principles; that hardly states the problem. It is not even a question of mixed races and tongues. It is the national peculiarity of the Alexandrians to seek a reconciliation between the two deepest psychological traits of which they are conscious. That is why we are hysterics and extremists. That is why we are the incomparable lovers we are."

This is not the place to try and write what I know of the Cabbala, even if I were disposed to try and define "The unpredicated ground of that Gnosis"; no aspiring hermetic could—for these fragments of revelation have their roots in the Mysteries. It is not that they are not to be revealed. They are raw experiences which only initiates can share.

I have dabbled in these matters before in Paris, conscious that in them I might find a pathway which could lead me to a deeper understanding of myself—the self which seemed to be only a huge, disorganised and shapeless society of lusts and impulses. I regarded this whole field of study as productive for my inner man, though a native and inborn scepticism kept me free from the toils of any denominational religion. For almost a year I had studied under Mustapha, a Sufi, sitting on the rickety wooden terrace of his house every evening listening to him talk in that soft cobweb voice. I had drunk sherbet with a wise Turkish Moslem. So it was with a sense of familiarity that I walked beside Justine through the twisted warren of streets which crown the fort of Kom El Dick, trying with one half of my mind to visualize how it must have looked when it was a Park sacred to Pan, the whole brown soft hillock carved into a pine-cone. Here the narrowness of the streets produced a sort of sense of intimacy, though they were lined only by verminous warrens and benighted little cafés lit by flickering rush-lamps. A strange sense of repose invested this little corner of the city giving it some of the atmosphere of a delta village. Below on the amorphous brown-violet *meidan* by the Railway Station, forlorn in the fading dusk little crowds of Arabs gathered about groups of sportsmen playing at single-stick, their shrill cries muffled in the fading dusk. Southward gleamed the tarnished platter of Mareotis. Justine walked with her customary swiftness, and in silence, impatient of my

tendency to lag behind and peer into the doorways on
to those scenes of domestic life which (lighted like toy
theatres) seemed filled with a tremendous dramatic significance.

The Cabal met at this time in what resembled a dis-
used curator's wooden hut, built against the red earth
walls of an embankment, very near to Pompey's Pillar.
I suppose the morbid sensitivity of the Egyptian Police
to political meetings dictated the choice of such a *venue*.
One crossed the wilderness of trenches and parapets
thrown up by the archaeologist and followed a muddy
path through the stone gate; then turning sharply at
right angles one entered this large inelegant shack, one
of whose walls was the earth side of an embankment
and whose floor was of tamped earth. The interior
was strongly lit by two petrol lamps and furnished with
chairs of wicker.

The gathering consisted of about twenty people
drawn from various parts of the city. I noticed with some
surprise the lean bored figure of Capodistria in one corner. Nessim was there, of course, but there were very few
representatives of the richer or more educated sections
of the city. There was, for example, an elderly clock-
maker I knew well by sight—a graceful silver-haired
man whose austere features had always seemed to me to
demand a violin under them in order to set them off. A
few nondescript elderly ladies. A chemist. Balthazar sat
before them in a low chair with his ugly hands lying in
his lap. I recognized him at once as if in an entirely new
context as the habitué of the Café Al Aktar with whom
I had once played backgammon. A few desultory minutes
passed in gossip while the Cabal waited upon its later
members; then the old clock-maker stood up and suggested that Balthazar should open proceedings, and my
friend settled back in his chair, closed his eyes and in
that harsh croaking voice which gradually gathered an

extraordinary sweetness began to talk. He spoke, I remember, of the *fons signatus* of the psyche and of its
ability to perceive an inherent order in the universe
which underlay the apparent formlessness and arbitrari-
ness of phenomena. Disciplines of mind could enable
people to penetrate behind the veil of reality and to discover harmonies in space and time which corresponded
to the inner structure of their own psyches. But the study
of the Cabbala was both a science and a religion. All this
was of course familiar enough. But throughout Balthazar's expositions extraordinary fragments of thought
would emerge in the form of pregnant aphorisms which
teased the mind long after one had left his presence. I
remember him saying, for example, "None of the great
religions have done more than exclude, throw out a
long range of prohibitions. But prohibitions create the
desire they are intended to cure. We of this Cabal say:
indulge but refine. We are enlisting everything in order
to make man's wholeness match the wholeness of the
universe—even pleasure, the destructive granulation of
the mind in pleasure."

The constitution of the Cabal consisted of an inner
circle of initiates (Balthazar would have winced at the
word, but I do not know how else to express it) and an
outer circle of students to which Nessim and Justine belonged. The inner circle consisted of twelve members
who were widely scattered over the Mediterranean—in
Beirut, Jaffa, Tunis and so on. In each place there was
a small academy of students who were learning to use
the strange mental-emotional calculus which the Cabbala has erected about the idea of God. The members of
the inner Cabal corresponded frequently with one another, using the curious old form of writing, known as
the *boustrophedon;* that is to say a writing which is read
from right to left and from left to right in alternate
lines. But the letters used in their alphabet were ideo-

grams for mental or spiritual states. I have said enough.

On that first evening Justine sat there between us, her arms linked lightly in ours, listening with a humility and concentration that were touching. At times the speaker's eye rested on her for a moment with a glance of affectionate familiarity. Did I know then—or was it afterwards I discovered—that Balthazar was perhaps her only friend and certainly the only confidant she had in the city? I do not remember. ("Balthazar is the only man to whom I can tell everything. He only laughs. But somehow he helps me to dispel the hollowness I feel in everything I do.") And it was to Balthazar that she would always write those long self-tortured letters which interested the curious mind of Arnauti. In the diaries she recorded how one moonlight night they gained access to the Museum and sat for an hour among the statues "sightless as nightmares" listening to him talk. He said many things which struck her then but later when she came to try and write them down they had vanished. Yet she did remember him saying in a quiet reflective voice something about "those of us who are bound to submit our bodies to the ogres," and the thought penetrated her marrow as a reference to the sort of life she was leading. As for Nessim, I remember him telling me that once, when he was in a great agony of mind about Justine, Balthazar remarked dryly to him: *"Omnis ardentior amator propriae uxoris adulter est."* Adding as he did so: "I speak now as a member of the Cabal, not as a private person. Passionate love even for a man's own wife is also adultery."

*   *   *   *   *

Alexandria Main Station: midnight. A deathly heavy dew. The noise of wheels cracking the slime-slithering pavements. Yellow pools of phosphorous light, and corridors of darkness like tears in the dull brick façade of a stage set. Policemen in the shadows. Standing against an insanitary brick wall to kiss her goodbye. She is going for a week, but in the panic, half-asleep I can see that she may never come back. The soft resolute kiss and the bright eyes fill me with emptiness. From the dark platform comes the crunch of rifle-butts and the clicking of Bengali. A detail of Indian troops on some routine transfer to Cairo. It is only as the train begins to move, and as the figure at the window, dark against the darkness, lets go of my hand, that I feel Melissa is really leaving; feel everything that is inexorably denied—the long pull of the train into the silver light reminds me of the sudden long pull of the vertebrae of her white back turning in bed. "Melissa," I call out but the giant sniffing of the engine blots out all sound. She begins to tilt, to curve and slide; and quick as a scene-shifter the station packs away advertisement after advertisement, stacking them in the darkness. I stand as if marooned on an iceberg. Beside me a tall Sikh shoulders the rifle he has stopped with a rose. The shadowy figure is sliding away down the steel rails into the darkness; a final lurch and the train pours away down a tunnel, as if turned to liquid.

I walk about Moharrem-Bey that night, watching the moon cloud over, preyed upon by an inexpressible anxiety.

Intense light behind cloud; by four o'clock a thin pure drizzle like needles. The poinsettias in the Consulate garden stark with silver drops standing on their stamens. No birds singing in the dawn. A light wind making the palm trees sway their necks with a faint dry formal clicking. The wonderful hushing of rain on Mareotis.

Five o'clock. Walking about in her room, studying inanimate objects with intense concentration. The empty powder-boxes. The depilatories from Sardis. The

smell of satin and leather. The horrible feeling of some
great impending scandal. . . .

I write these lines in very different circumstances and
many months have elapsed since that night; here, under
this olive-tree, in the pool of light thrown by an oil lamp,
I write and relive that night which has taken its place
in the enormous fund of the city's memories. Somewhere
else, in a great study hung with tawny curtains Justine
was copying into her diary the terrible aphorisms of
Herakleitos. The book lies beside me now. On one page
she has written: "It is hard to fight with one's heart's desire; whatever it wishes to get, it purchases at the cost
of soul." And lower down in the margin: "Night-walkers,
Magians, Bakchoi, Lenai and the *initiated*. . . ."

* * * * *

Was it about this time that Mnemjian startled me by
breathing into my ear the words: "Cohen is dying, you
know?" The old furrier had drifted out of sight for some
months past. Melissa had heard that he was in hospital
suffering from uraemia. But the orbit we once described
about the girl had changed; the kaleidoscope had tilted
once more and he had sunk out of sight like a vanished
chip of coloured glass. Now he was dying? I said nothing as I sat exploring the memories of those early days
—the encounters at street-corners and bars. In the long
silence that ensued Mnemjian scraped my hairline clean
with a razor and began to spray my head with bay-rum.
He gave a little sigh and said: "He has been asking for
your Melissa. All night, all day."

"I will tell her," I said, and the little memory man
nodded with a mossy conspiratorial look in his eyes.
"What a horrible disease," he said under his breath, "he
smells so. They scrape his tongue with a spatula. Pfui!"
And he turned the spray upwards towards the roof as if

to disinfect the memory: as if the smell had invaded the shop.

Melissa was lying on the sofa in her dressing-gown with her face turned to the wall. I thought at first she was asleep, but as I came in she turned and sat up. I told her Mnemjian's news. "I know," she said. "They sent me word from the hospital. But what can I do? I cannot go and see him. He is nothing to me, never was, never will be." Then getting up and walking the length of the room she added in a rage which hovered on the edge of tears. "He has a wife and children. What are they doing?" I sat down and once more confronted the memory of that tame seal staring sadly into a human wineglass. Melissa took my silence for criticism I suppose for she came to me and shook me gently by the shoulders, rousing me from my thoughts. "But if he is dying?" I said. The question was addressed as much to myself as to her. She cried out suddenly and kneeling down placed her head on my knees. "O it is so disgusting! Please do not make me go."

"Of course not."

"But if you think I should I will have to."

I said nothing. Cohen was in a sense already dead and buried. He had lost his place in our history, and an expenditure of emotional energy on him seemed to me useless. It had no relation to the real man who lay among the migrating fragments of his old body in a whitewashed ward. For us he had become merely an historic figure. And yet here he was, obstinately trying to insist on his identity, trying to walk back into our lives at another point in the circumference. What could Melissa give him now? What could she deny him?

"Would you like me to go?" I said. The sudden irrational thought had come into my mind that here, in the death of Cohen, I could study my own love and its death. That someone *in extremis,* calling for help to an old lover, could only elicit a cry of disgust—this terrified me.

It was too late for the old man to awake compassion or even interest in my lover, who was already steeped in new misfortunes against the backcloth of which the old had faded, rotted. And in a little time perhaps, if she should call on me or I on her? Would we turn from each other with a cry of emptiness and disgust? I realized then the truth about all love: that it is an absolute which takes all or forfeits all. The other feelings, compassion, tenderness and so on, exist only on the periphery and belong to the constructions of society and habit. But she herself—austere and merciless Aphrodite—is a pagan. It is not our brains or instincts which she picks—but our very bones. It terrified me to think that this old man, at such a point in his life, had been unable to conjure up an instant's tenderness by the memory of anything he had said or done: tenderness from one who was at heart the most tender and gentle of mortals.

To be forgotten in this way was to die the death of a dog. "I shall go and see him for you," I said, though my heart quailed in disgust at the prospect; but Melissa had already fallen asleep with her dark head upon my knees. Whenever she was upset about anything she took refuge in the guileless world of sleep, slipping into it as smoothly and easily as a deer or a child. I put my hands inside the faded kimono and gently rubbed her shallow ribs and flanks. She stirred half-awake and murmured something inaudible as she allowed me to lift her and carry her gently back to the sofa. I watched her sleeping for a long time.

It was already dark and the city was drifting like a bed of seaweed towards the lighted cafés of the upper town. I went to Pastroudi and ordered a double whisky which I drank slowly and thoughtfully. Then I took a taxi to the hospital.

I followed a duty-nurse down the long anonymous green corridors whose oil-painted walls exuded an atmosphere of damp. The white phosphorescent bulbs which punctuated our progress wallowed in the gloom like swollen glow-worms.

They had put him in the little ward with the single curtained bed which was, as I afterwards learned from Mnemjian, reserved for critical cases whose expectation of life was short. He did not see me at first, for he was watching with an air of shocked exhaustion while a nurse disposed his pillows for him. I was amazed at the masterful, thoughtful reserve of the face which stared up from the mattress, for he had become so thin as almost to be unrecognizable. The flesh had sunk down upon his cheek-bones exposing the long slightly curved nose to its very roots and throwing into relief the carved nostrils. This gave the whole mouth and jaw a buoyancy, a spirit which must have characterized his face in earliest youth. His eyes looked bruised with fever and a dark stubble shaded his neck and throat, but under this the exposed lines of the face were as clean as those on the face of a man of thirty. The images of him which I had so long held in my memory—a sweaty porcupine, a tame seal— were immediately dissolved and replaced by this new face, this new man who looked like—one of the beasts of the Apocalypse. I stood for a long minute in astonishment watching an unknown personage accepting the ministration of the nurses with a dazed and regal exhaustion. The duty-nurse was whispering in my ear: "It is good you have come. Nobody will come and see him. He is delirious at times. Then he wakes and asks for people. You are a relation?"

"A business associate," I said.

"It will do him good to see a face he knows."

But would he recognize me, I wondered? If I had changed only half as much as he had we would be complete strangers to one another. He was lying back now, the breath whistling harshly through that long vulpine

nose which lay resting against his face like the proud
figurehead of an abandoned ship. Our whispers had disturbed him, for he turned upon me a vague but nevertheless pure and thoughtful eye which seemed to belong
to some great bird of prey. Recognition did not come
until I moved forward a few paces to the side of the bed.
Then all at once his eyes were flooded with light—a
strange mixture of humility, hurt pride, and innocent
fear. He turned his face to the wall. I blurted out the
whole of my message in one sentence. Melissa was away,
I said, and I had telegraphed her to come as quickly
as possible; meanwhile I had come to see if I could help
him in any way. His shoulders shook, and I thought that
an involuntary groan was about to burst from his lips;
but presently in its place came the mockery of a laugh,
harsh, mindless and unmusical. As if directed at the dead
carcass of a joke so rotten and threadbare that it could
compel nothing beyond this ghastly *rictus* gouged out
in his taut cheeks.

"I know she is here," he said, and one of his hands
came running over the counterpane like a frightened
rat to grope for mine. "Thank you for your kindness."
And with this he suddenly seemed to grow calm, though
he kept his face turned away from me. "I wanted," he
said slowly, as if he were collecting himself in order to
give the phrase its exactest meaning, "I wanted to close
my account honourably with her. I treated her badly,
very badly. She did not notice, of course; she is too sim-
ple-minded, but good, such a good girl." It sounded
strange to hear the phrase *"bonne copine"* on the lips of
an Alexandrian, and moreover pronounced in the
chipped trailing sing-song accent common to those educated here. Then he added, with considerable effort, and
struggling against a formidable inner resistance. "I
cheated her over her coat. It was really sealskin. Also
the moths had been at it. I had it relined. Why should I

do such a thing? When she was ill I would not pay for
her to see the doctor. Small things, but they weigh
heavy." Tears crowded up into his eyes and his throat
tightened as if choked by the enormity of such thoughts.
He swallowed harshly and said: "They were not really
in my character. Ask any business man who knows me.
Ask anyone."

But now confusion began to set in, and holding me
gently by the hand he led me into the dense jungle of
his illusions, walking among them with such surefooted-
ness and acknowledging them so calmly that I almost
found myself keeping company with them too. Unknown
fronds of trees arched over him, brushing his face, while
cobbles punctuated the rubber wheels of some dark
ambulance full of metal and other dark bodies, whose
talk was of limbo—a repulsive yelping streaked with
Arabic objurgations. The pain, too, had begun to reach
up at his reason and lift down fantasies. The hard white
edges of the bed turned to boxes of coloured bricks, the
white temperature chart to a boatman's white face.

They were drifting, Melissa and he, across the shallow
blood-red waters of Mareotis, in each other's arms, towards the rabble of mud-huts where once Rhakotis
stood. He reproduced their conversations so perfectly
that though my lover's share was inaudible I could
nevertheless hear her cool voice, could deduce her questions from the answers he gave her. She was desperately
trying to persuade him to marry her and he was tem-
porizing, unwilling to lose the beauty of her person and
equally unwilling to commit himself. What interested
me was the extraordinary fidelity with which he reproduced this whole conversation which obviously in his
memory ranked as one of the great experiences of his
life. He did not know then how much he loved her; it
had remained for me to teach him the lesson. And con-
versely how was it that Melissa had never spoken to me

of marriage, had never betrayed to me the depth of her weakness and exhaustion as she had to him? This was deeply wounding. My vanity was gnawed by the thought that she had shown him a side of her nature which she had kept hidden from me.

Now the scene changed again and he fell into a more lucid vein. It was as if in the vast jungle of unreason we came upon clearings of sanity where he was emptied of his poetic illusions. Here he spoke of Melissa with feeling but coolly, like a husband of a king. It was as if now that the flesh was dying the whole funds of his inner life, so long dammed up behind the falsities of a life wrongly lived, burst through the dykes and flooded the foreground of his consciousness. It was not only Melissa either, for he spoke of his wife—and at times confused their names. There was also a third name, Rebecca, which he pronounced with a deeper reserve, a more passionate sorrow than either of the others. I took this to be his little daughter, for it is the children who deliver the final *coup de grâce* in all these terrible transactions of the heart.

Sitting there at his side, feeling our pulses ticking in unison and listening to him as he talked of my lover with a new magistral calm I could not help but see how much there was in the man which Melissa might have found to love. By what strange chance had she missed the real person? For far from being an object of contempt (as I had always taken him to be) he seemed to be now a dangerous rival whose powers I had been unaware of; and I was visited by a thought so ignoble that I am ashamed to write it down. I felt glad that Melissa had not come to see him die lest seeing him, as I saw him now, she might at a blow rediscover him. And by one of those paradoxes in which love delights I found myself more jealous of him in his dying than I had ever been during his life. These were horrible thoughts for one who had been so long a patient and attentive student of love, but I recognized once more in them the austere mindless primitive face of Aphrodite.

In a sense I recognized in him, in the very resonance of his voice when he spoke her name, a maturity which I lacked; for he had surmounted his love for her without damaging or hurting it, and allowed it to mature as all love should into a consuming and depersonalized friendship. So far from fearing to die, and importuning her for comfort, he wished only to offer her, from the inexhaustible treasury of his dying, a last gift.

The magnificent sable lay across a chair at the end of the bed wrapped in tissue paper; I could see at a glance that it was not the sort of gift for Melissa, for it would throw her scant and shabby wardrobe into confusion, outshining everything. "I was always worried about money," he said felicitously, "while I was alive. But when you are dying you suddenly find yourself in funds." He was able for the first time in his life to be almost light-hearted. Only the sickness was there like some patient and cruel monitor.

He passed from time to time into a short confused sleep and the darkness hummed about my tired ears like a hive of bees. It was getting late and yet I could not bring myself to leave him. A duty-nurse brought me a cup of coffee and we talked in whispers. It was restful to hear her talk, for to her illness was simply a profession which she had mastered and her attitude to it was that of a journeyman. In her cold voice she said: "He deserted his wife and child for *une femme quelconque*. Now neither the wife nor the woman who is his mistress wants to see him. Well!" She shrugged her shoulders. These tangled loyalties evoked no feeling of compassion in her, for she saw them simply as despicable weaknesses. "Why doesn't the child come? Has he not asked for her?" She picked a front tooth with the nail of her little finger

and said: "Yes. But he does not want to frighten her by
letting her see him sick. It is you understand not pleasant for a child." She picked up an atomizer and lan-
guidly squirted some disinfectant into the air above us,
reminding me sharply of Mnemjian. "It is late," she
added, "are you going to stay the night?"

I was about to make a move, but the sleeper awoke
and clutched at my hand once more. "Don't go," he said
in a deep fragmented but sane voice, as if he had overheard the last few phrases of our conversation. "Stay a
little while. There is something else I have been thinking over and which I must reveal to you." Turning
to the nurse he said quietly but distinctly, "Go!"
She smoothed the bed and left us alone once more. He
gave a great sigh which, if one had not been watching his
face, might have seemed a sigh of plenitude, happiness.
"In the cupboard," he said, "you will find my clothes."
There were two dark suits hanging up, and under his
direction I detached a waistcoat from one of them, in
the pockets of which I burrowed until my fingers came
upon two rings. "I had decided to offer to marry Melissa
now if she wished. That is why I sent for her. After all
what use am I? My name?" He smiled vaguely at the
ceiling. "And the rings—" he held them lightly, rever-
ently in his fingers like a communion wafer. "These are
rings she chose for herself long ago. So now she must
have them. Perhaps. . . ." He looked at me for a long
moment with pained, searching eyes, "But no," he said,
"you will not marry her. Why should you? Never mind.
Take them for her, and the coat."

I put the rings into the shallow breast-pocket of my
coat and said nothing. He sighed once more and then to
my surprise, in a small gnome's tenor muffled almost to
inaudibility sang a few bars of a popular song which had
once been the rage of Alexandria, *Jamais de la vie,* and
to which Melissa still danced at the cabaret. "Listen to

the music!" he said, and I thought suddenly of the dying Antony in the poem of Cavafy—a poem he had never read, would never read. Sirens whooped suddenly from the harbour like planets in pain. Then once more I heard this gnome singing softly of *chagrin* and *bonheur,* and he was singing not to Melissa but to Rebecca. How different from the great heart-sundering choir that Antony heard—the rich poignance of strings and voices which in the dark street welled up—Alexandria's last bequest to those who are her exemplars. Each man goes out to his own music, I thought, and remembered with shame and pain the clumsy movements that Melissa made when she danced.

He had drifted now to the very borders of sleep and I judged that it was time to leave him. I took the coat and put it in the bottom drawer of the cupboard before tiptoeing out and summoning the duty-nurse. "It is very late," she said.

"I will come in the morning," I said. I meant to.

Walking slowly home through the dark avenue of trees, tasting the brackish harbour wind, I remembered Justine saying harshly as she lay in bed: "We use each other like axes to cut down the ones we really love."

* * * * *

We have been told so often that history is indifferent, but we always take its parsimony or plenty as somehow planned; we never really listen. . . .

Now on this tenebrous peninsula shaped like a plane-leaf, fingers outstretched (where the winter rain crackles like straw among the rocks), I walk stiffly sheathed in wind by a sealine choked with groaning sponges: hunting for the meaning to the pattern.

As a poet of the historic consciousness I suppose I am bound to see landscape as a field dominated by the human wish—tortured into farms and hamlets,

ploughed into cities. A landscape scribbled with the sig-
natures of men and epochs. Now, however, I am beginning to believe that the wish is inherited from the site;
that man depends for the furniture of the will upon his
location in place, tenant of fruitful acres or a perverted
wood. It is not the impact of his freewill upon nature
which I see (as I thought) but the irresistible growth,
through him, of nature's own blind unspecified doctrines
of variation and torment. She has chosen this poor
forked thing as an exemplar. Then how idle it seems for
any man to say, as I once heard Balthazar say: "The mis-
sion of the Cabal, if it has one, is so to ennoble function
that even eating and excreting will be raised to the rank
of arts." You will see in all this the flower of a perfect
scepticism which undermines the will to survive. Only
love can sustain one a little longer.

I think, too, that something of this sort must have
been in Arnauti's mind when he wrote: "For the writer
people as psychologies are finished. The contemporary
psyche has exploded like a soap-bubble under the investigations of the mystagogues. What now remains to
the writer?"

Perhaps it was the realization of this which made me
select this empty place to live for the next few years—
this sunburnt headland in the Cyclades. Surrounded by
history on all sides, this empty island alone is free from
every reference. It has never been mentioned in the an-
nals of the race which owns it. Its historic past is re-
funded, not into time, but into place—no temples,
groves, amphitheatres, to corrupt ideas with their false
comparisons. A shelf of coloured boats, a harbour over
the hills, and a little town denuded by neglect. That is
all. Once a month a steamer touches on its way to
Smyrna.

These winter evenings the sea-tempests climb the cliffs
and invade the grove of giant untended planes where I

walk, talking a sudden wild slang, slopping and tilting the schooner trees.

I walk here with those coveted intimations of a past which none can share with me; but which time itself cannot deprive me of. My hair is clenched back to my scalp and one hand guards the burning dottle of my pipe from the force of the wind. Above, the sky is set in a brilliant comb of stars. Antares guttering up there, buried in spray. . . . To have cheerfully laid down obedient books and friends, lighted rooms, fireplaces built for conversation—the whole parish of the civilized mind—is not something I regret but merely wonder at.

In this choice too I see something fortuitous, born of impulses which I am forced to regard as outside the range of my own nature. And yet, strangely enough, it is only here that I am at last able to re-enter, reinhabit the unburied city with my friends; to frame them in the heavy steel webs of metaphors which will last half as long as the city itself—or so I hope. Here at least I am able to see their history and the city's as one and the same phenomenon.

But strangest of all: I owe this release to Pursewarden —the last person I should ever have considered a possible benefactor. That last meeting, for example, in the ugly and expensive hotel bedroom to which he always moved on Pombal's return from leave . . . I did not recognize the heavy musty odour of the room as the odour of his impending suicide—how should I? I knew he was unhappy; even had he not been he would have felt obliged to simulate unhappiness. All artists today are expected to cultivate a little fashionable unhappiness. And being Anglo-Saxon there was a touch of maudlin self-pity and weakness which made him drink a bit. That evening he was savage, silly and witty by turns; and listening to him I remember thinking suddenly: "Here is someone who in farming his talent has neglected his sensibility, not by accident, but deliberately, for its self-expression might have brought him into conflict with the world, or his loneliness threatened his reason. He could not bear to be refused admittance, while he lived, to the halls of fame and recognition. Underneath it all he has been steadily putting up with an almost insupportable consciousness of his own mental poltroonery. And now his career has reached an interesting stage: I mean beautiful women, whom he always felt to be out of reach as a timid provincial would, are now glad to be seen out with him. In his presence they wear the air of faintly distracted Muses suffering from constipation. In public they are flattered if he holds a gloved hand for an instant longer than form permits. At first all this must have been balm to a lonely man's vanity; but finally it has only furthered his sense of insecurity. His freedom, gained through a modest financial success, has begun to bore him. He has begun to feel more and more wanting in true greatness while his name has been daily swelling in size like some disgusting poster. He has realized that people are walking the street with a Reputation now and not a man. They see him no longer—and all his work was done in order to draw attention to the lonely, suffering figure he felt himself to be. His name has covered him like a tombstone. And now comes the terrifying thought: perhaps there *is* no one left to see? Who, after all, is he?"

I am not proud of these thoughts, for they betray the envy that every failure feels for every success; but spite may often see as clearly as charity. And indeed, running as it were upon a parallel track in my mind went the words which Clea once used about him and which, for some reason, I remembered and reflected upon: "He is unlovely somewhere. Part of the secret is his physical ungainliness. Being wizened his talent has a germ of shyness in it. Shyness has laws: you can only give yourself,

tragically, to those who least understand. For to understand one would be to admit pity for one's frailty. Hence
the women he loves, the letters he writes to the women
he loves, stand as ciphers in his mind for the women he
thinks he wants, or at any rate deserves—*cher ami.*"
Clea's sentences always broke in half and ended in that
magical smile of tenderness—"am I my brother's
keeper?". . .

(What I most need to do is to record experiences, not
in the order in which they took place—for that is history—but in the order in which they first became significant for me.)

What, then, could have been his motive in leaving
me five hundred pounds with the sole stipulation that I
should spend them with Melissa? I thought perhaps that
he may have loved her himself but after deep reflection
I have come to the conclusion that he loved, not her, but
my love for her. Of all my qualities he envied me only
my capacity to respond warmly to endearments whose
value he recognized, perhaps even desired, but from
which he would be forever barred by self-disgust. Indeed this itself was a blow to my pride for I would have
liked him to admire—if not the work I have done—at
least the promise it shows of what I have yet to do. How
stupid, how limited we are—mere vanities on legs!

We had not met for weeks, for we did not habitually
frequent each other, and when we did it was in the little
tin *pissotière* in the main square by the tram-station. It
was after dark and we would never have recognized each
other had not the headlights of a car occasionally
drenched the foetid cubicle in white light like spray.
"Ah!" he said in recognition: unsteadily, thoughtfully,
for he was drunk. (Some time, weeks before, he had left
me five hundred pounds; in a sense he had summed me
up, judged me—though that judgement was only to reach
me from the other side of the grave.)

The rain cropped at the tin roof above us. I longed
to go home, for I had had a very tiring day, but I feebly
lingered, obstructed by the apologetic politeness I always
feel with people I do not really like. The slightly waver-
ing figure outlined itself upon the darkness before me.
"Let me," he said in a maudlin tone, "confide in you the
secret of my novelist's trade. I am a success, you a failure.
The answer, old man, is sex and plenty of it." He
raised his voice and his chin as he said, or rather de-
claimed, the word "sex": tilting his scraggy neck like a
chicken drinking and biting off the word with a half-
yelp like a drill-serjeant. "Lashings of sex," he repeated
more normally, "but remember," and he allowed his
voice to sink to a confidential mumble, *"stay buttoned up
tight.* Eternal grandma strong to save. You must stay
buttoned up and suffering. Try and look as if you had a
stricture, a book society choice. What is not permissible
is rude health, ordure, the natural and the funny.
That was all right for Chaucer and the Elizabethans but
it won't make the grade today—buttoned up tightly
with stout Presbyterian buttons." And in the very act of
shaking himself off he turned to me a face composed to
resemble a fly-button—tight, narrow and grotesque. I
thanked him but he waved aside the thanks in a royal
manner. "It's all free," he said, and leading me by the
hand he piloted me out into the dark street. We walked
towards the lighted centre of the town like bondsmen,
fellow writers, heavy with a sense of different failures.
He talked confidentially to himself of matters which interested him in a mumble which I could not interpret.
Once as we turned into the Rue des Soeurs he stopped
before the lighted door of a house of ill fame and pronounced: "Baudelaire says that copulation is the lyric
of the mob. Not any more alas! For sex is dying. In another century we shall lie with our tongues in each
other's mouths, silent and passionless as sea-fruit. O yes!

Indubitably so." And he quoted the Arabic proverb which he uses as an epigraph to his trilogy: "The world is like a cucumber—today it's in your hand, tomorrow up your arse." We then resumed our stitching, crab-like advance in the direction of his hotel, he repeating the word "indubitably" with obvious pleasure at the soft plosive sound of it.

He was unshaven and haggard, but in comparatively good spirits after the walk and we resorted to a bottle of gin which he kept in the commode by his bed. I commented on the two bulging suitcases which stood by the dressing-table ready packed; over a chair lay his rain-coat stuffed with newspapers, pyjamas, toothpaste, and so on. He was catching the night train for Gaza, he said. He wanted to slack off and pay a visit to Petra. The galley-proofs of his latest novel had already been corrected, wrapped up and addressed. They lay dead upon the marble top of the dressing-table. I recognized in his sour and dejected attitude the exhaustion which pursues the artist after he has brought a piece of work to completion. These are the low moments when the long flirtation with suicide begins afresh.

Unfortunately, though I have searched my mind, I can recall little of our actual conversation, though I have often tried to do so. The fact that this was our last meeting has invested it, in retrospect, with a significance which surely it cannot have possessed. Nor, for the purposes of this writing, has he ceased to exist; he has simply stepped into the quicksilver of a mirror as we all must—to leave our illnesses, our evil acts, the hornets' nest of our desires, still operative for good or evil in the real world—which is the memory of our friends. Yet the presence of death always refreshes experience thus—that is its function: to help us deliberate on the novelty of time. Yet at that moment we were both situated at points equidistant from death—or so I think. Perhaps

some quiet premeditation blossomed in him even then
—no matter. I cannot tell. It is not mysterious that any
artist should desire to end a life which he has exhausted
—(a character in the last volume exclaims: "For years
one has to put up with the feeling that people do not
care, really care, about one; then one day with growing
alarm, one realizes that it is God who does not care: and
not merely that he does not *care*, he does not care *one
way or the other*").

But this aside reminds me of one small fragment of
that drunken conversation. He spoke derisively of Balthazar, of his preoccupation with religion, of the Cabal
(of which he had only heard). I listened without inter-
rupting him and gradually his voice ran down like a
time-piece overcome by the weight of seconds. He stood
up to pour himself a drink and said: "One needs a tremendous ignorance to approach God. I have always
known too much I suppose."

These are the sort of fragments which tease the waking mind on evenings like these, walking about in the
wintry darkness; until at last I turn back to the crackling
fire of olive-wood in the old-fashioned arched hearth
where Justine lies asleep in her cot of sweet-smelling
pine.

How much of him can I claim to know? I realize that
each person can only claim one aspect of our character
as part of his knowledge. To every one we turn a different face of the prism. Over and over again I have found
myself surprised by observations which brought this
home to me. As for example when Justine said of Pombal, "one of the great primates of sex." To me my friend
had never seemed predatory; only self-indulgent to a
ludicrous degree. I saw him as touching and amusing,
faintly to be cherished for an inherent ridiculousness.
But she must have seen in him the great soft-footed cat
he was (to her).

And as for Pursewarden, I remember, too, that in the very act of speaking thus about religious ignorance he straightened himself and caught sight of his pale reflection in the mirror. The glass was raised to his lips, and now, turning his head he squirted out upon his own glittering reflection a mouthful of the drink. That remains clearly in my mind: a reflection liquefying in the mirror of that shabby, expensive room which seems now so appropriate a place for the scene which must have followed later that night.

* * * * *

Place Zagloul—silverware and caged doves. A vaulted cave lined with black barrels and choking with the smoke from flying whitebait and the smell of *retzinnato*. A message scribbled on the edge of a newspaper. Here I spilt wine on her cloak, and while attempting to help her repair the damage, accidentally touched her breasts. No word was spoken. While Pursewarden spoke so brilliantly of Alexandria and the burning library. In the room above a poor wretch screaming with meningitis. . . .

* * * * *

Today, unexpectedly, comes a squinting spring shower, stiffening the dust and pollen of the city, flailing the glass roof of the studio where Nessim sits over his *croquis* for his wife's portrait. He has captured her sitting before the fire with a guitar in her hands, her throat snatched up by a spotted scarf, her singing head bent. The noise of her voice is jumbled in the back of his brain like the sound-track of an earthquake run backwards. Prodigious archery over the parks where the palm-trees have been dragged back taut; a mythology of yellow-maned waves attacking the Pharos. At night the city is full of new sounds, the pulls and stresses of the wind, until you feel it has become a ship, its old timbers groaning and creaking with every assault of the weather.

This is the weather Scobie loves. Lying in bed he will fondle his telescope lovingly, turning a wistful eye on the blank wall of rotting mud-brick which shuts off his view of the sea.

Scobie is getting on for seventy and still afraid to die; his one fear is that he will awake one morning and find himself lying dead—Lieutenant-Commander Scobie, O.B.E. Consequently it gives him a severe shock every morning when the water-carriers shriek under his window before dawn, waking him up. For a moment, he says, he dare not open his eyes. Keeping them fast shut (for fear that they might open on the heavenly host or the cherubims hymning) he gropes along the cake-stand beside his bed and grabs his pipe. It is always loaded from the night before and an open matchbox stands beside it. The first whiff of seaman's plug restores both his composure and his eyesight. He breathes deeply, grateful for the reassurance. He smiles. He gloats. Drawing the heavy sheepskin which serves him as a bedcover up to his ears he sings his little triumphal paean to the morning, his voice crackling like tinfoil. *"Taisez-vous, petit babouin: laissez parler votre mère."*

His pendulous trumpeter's cheeks become rosy with the effort. Taking stock of himself he discovers that he has the inevitable headache. His tongue is raw from last night's brandy. But against these trifling discomforts the prospect of another day in life weighs heavily. *"Taisez-vous, petit babouin,"* and so on, pausing to slip in his false teeth. He places his wrinkled fingers to his chest and is comforted by the sound of his heart at work, maintaining a tremulous circulation in that venous system whose deficiencies (real or imaginary I do not know) are only offset by brandy in daily and all-but lethal doses. He is rather proud of his heart. If you ever visit him when he is in bed he is almost sure to grasp your hand in a horny mandible and ask you to feel it: "Strong as a bullock, what? Ticking over nicely," is the way he puts it, in spite of the brandy. Swallowing a little you shove your hand inside his cheap night-jacket to experience those sad, blunt, far-away little bumps of life—like a foetal heart in the seventh month. He buttons up his pyjamas with a touching pride and gives his imitation roar of animal health. "Bounding from my bed like a lion"—that is another of his phrases. You have not experienced the full charm of the man until you have actually seen him, bent double with rheumatism, crawling out from between his coarse cotton sheets like a derelict. Only in the warmest months of the year do his bones thaw out sufficiently to enable him to stand fully erect. In the summer afternoons he walks the Park, his little cranium glowing like a minor sun, his briar canted to heaven, his jaw set in a violent grimace of lewd health.

No mythology of the city would be complete without its Scobie, and Alexandria will be the poorer for it when his sun-cured body wrapped in a Union Jack is finally lowered into the shallow grave which awaits him at the Roman Catholic cemetery by the tram-line.

His exiguous nautical pension is hardly enough to pay for the one cockroach-infested room which he inhabits in the slum-area behind Tatwig Street; he ekes it out with an equally exiguous salary from the Egyptian Government which carries with it the proud title of Bimbashi in the Police Force. Clea has painted a wonderful portrait of him in his police uniform with the scarlet tarbush on his head, and the great fly-whisk, as thick as a horse's tail, laid gracefully across his bony knees.

It is Clea who supplies him with tobacco and I with admiration, company, and weather permitting, brandy. We take it in turns to applaud his health, and to pick him up when he has struck himself too hard on the chest in enthusiastic demonstration of it. Origins he has none—his past proliferates through a dozen continents like a true subject of myth. And his presence is so rich with imaginary health that he needs nothing more—except perhaps an occasional trip to Cairo during Ramadan when his office is closed and when presumably all crime comes to a standstill because of the fast.

Youth is beardless, so is second childhood. Scobie tugs tenderly at the remains of a once handsome and bushy torpedo-beard—but very gently, caressingly, for fear of pulling it out altogether and leaving himself quite naked. He clings to life like a limpet, each year bringing its hardly visible sea-change. It is as if his body were being reduced, shrunk, by the passing of the winters; his cranium will soon be the size of a baby's. A year or two more and we will be able to squeeze it into a bottle and pickle it forever. The wrinkles become ever more heavily indented. Without his teeth his face is the face of an ancient ape; above the meagre beard his two cherry-red cheeks known affectionately as "port" and "starboard," glow warm in all weathers.

Physically he has drawn heavily on the replacement department; in nineteen hundred a fall from the mizzen threw his jaw two points west by south-west, and smashed the frontal sinus. When he speaks his denture behaves like a moving staircase, travelling upwards and round inside his skull in a jerky spiral. His smile is capricious; it might appear from anywhere, like that of the Cheshire Cat. In eighty-four he made eyes at another man's wife (so he says) and lost one of them. No one except Clea is supposed to know about this, but the replacement in this case was rather a crude one. In repose it is not very noticeable, but the minute he becomes animated a disparity between his two eyes becomes obvious. There is also a small technical problem: his own eye is almost permanently bloodshot. On the very first occasion when he treated me to a reedy rendering of "Watchman, What

of the Night?", while he stood in the corner of the room
with an ancient chamber-pot in his hand, I noticed that
his right eye moved a trifle slower than his left. It
seemed then to be a larger imitation of the stuffed eagle's
eye which lours so glumly from a niche in the public
library. In winter, however, it is the false eye and not the
true which throbs unbearably making him morose and
foul-mouthed until he has applied a little brandy to his
stomach.

Scobie is a sort of protozoic profile in fog and rain, for
he carries with him a sort of English weather, and he is
never happier than when he can sit over a microscopic
wood-fire in winter and talk. One by one his memories
leak through the faulty machinery of his mind until he
no longer knows them for his own. Behind him I see the
long grey rollers of the Atlantic at work, curling up over
his memories, smothering them in spray, blinding him.
When he speaks of the past it is in a series of short dim
telegrams—as if already communications were poor, the
weather inimical to transmission. In Dawson City the
ten who went up the river were frozen to death. Winter
came down like a hammer, beating them senseless:
whisky, gold, murder—it was like a new crusade north-
ward into the timberlands. At this time his brother fell
over the falls in Uganda; in his dream he saw the tiny
figure, like a fly, fall and at once get smoothed out by the
yellow claw of water. No: that was later when he was already staring along the sights of a carbine into the very
brain-box of a Boer. He tries to remember exactly *when*
it must have been, dropping his polished head into his
hands; but the grey rollers intervene, the long effortless tides patrol the barrier between himself and his
memory. That is why the phrase came to me: a *sea-
change* for the old pirate: his skull looks palped and
sucked down until only the thinnest integument separates his smile from the smile of the hidden skeleton. Ob-

serve the brain-case with its heavy indentations: the twigs
of bone inside his wax fingers: the rods of tallow which
support his quivering shins. . . . Really, as Clea has
remarked, old Scobie is like some little old experimental
engine left over from the last century, something as
pathetic and friendly as Stephenson's first Rocket.

He lives in his little sloping attic like an anchorite.
"An anchorite!" that is another favourite phrase; he will
pop his cheek vulgarly with his finger as he utters it, allowing his rolling eye to insinuate all the feminine in-
dulgences he permits himself in secret. This is for Clea's
benefit, however; in the presence of "a perfect lady," he
feels obliged to assume a protective colouring which he
sheds the moment she leaves. The truth is somewhat sad-
der. "I've done quite a bit of scout-mastering," he ad-
mits to me *sotto voce,* "with the Hackney Troop. That
was after I was invalided out. But I had to keep out of
England, old boy. The strain was too much for me. Every
week I expected to see a headline in the *News of the
World,* 'Another youthful victim of scoutmaster's dirty
wish.' Down in Hackney things didn't matter so much.
My kids were experts in woodcraft. Proper young
Etonians I used to call them. The scoutmaster before me
got twenty years. It's enough to make one have Doubts.
These things made you think. Somehow I couldn't settle
down in Hackney. Mind you, I'm a bit past everything
now, but I do like to have my peace of mind—just in
case. And somehow in England one doesn't feel free any
more. Look at the way they are pulling up clergymen,
respected churchmen and so on. I used to lie awake
worrying. Finally I came abroad as a private tooter
—Toby Mannering, his father was an M.P., wanted an
excuse to travel. They said he had to have a tooter. He
wanted to go into the navy. That's how I fetched up
here. I saw at once it was nice and free-and-easy here. Got
a job right off with the Vice Squad under Nimrod Pasha.

And here I am, dear boy. And no complaints do you
see? Looking from east to west over this fertile Delta
what do I see? Mile upon mile of angelic little blacks."

The Egyptian Government, with the typical generous
quixotry the Levant lavishes on any foreigner who shows
a little warmth and friendliness, had offered him a
means to live on in Alexandria. It is said that after his
appointment to the Vice Squad vice assumed such
alarming proportions that it was found necessary to up-
grade and transfer him; but he himself always main-
tained that his transfer to the routine C.I.D. branch of
the police had been a deserved promotion—and I for
my part have never had the courage to tease him on the
subject. His work is not onerous. For a couple of hours
every morning he works in a ramshackle office in the
upper quarter of the town, with the fleas jumping out of
the rotten woodwork of his old-fashioned desk. He
lunches modestly at the Lutetia and, funds permitting,
buys himself an apple and a bottle of brandy for his
evening meal there. The long fierce summer afternoons
are spent in sleep, in turning over the newspapers which
he borrows from a friendly Greek newsvendor. (As he
reads the pulse in the top of his skull beats softly.) Ripe-
ness is all.

The furnishing of his little room suggests a highly
eclectic spirit; the few objects which adorn the anchorite's life have a severely personal flavour, as if together they composed the personality of their owner.
That is why Clea's portrait gives such a feeling of com-
pleteness, for she has worked into the background the
whole sum of the old man's possessions. The shabby little crucifix on the wall behind the bed, for example; it
is some years since Scobie accepted the consolations of
the Holy Roman Church against old age and those defects of character which had by this time become second
nature. Nearby hangs a small coloured print of the Mona

Lisa whose enigmatic smile has always reminded Scobie of his mother. (For my part the famous smile has always seemed to me to be the smile of a woman who has just dined off her husband.) However this too has somehow incorporated itself into the existence of Scobie, established a special and private relationship. It is as if his Mona Lisa were like no other; it is a deserter from Leonardo.

Then, of course, there is the ancient cake-stand which serves as his commode, bookcase and escritoire in one. Clea has accorded it the ungrudging treatment it deserves, painting it with a microscopic fidelity. It has four tiers, each fringed with a narrow but elegant bevel. It cost him ninepence farthing in the Euston Road in 1911, and it has travelled twice round the world with him. He will help you admire it without a trace of humour or self-consciousness. "Fetching little thing, what?" he will say jauntily, as he takes a cloth and dusts it. The top tier, he will explain carefully, was designed for buttered toast: the middle for shortbreads: the bottom tier is for "two kinds of cake." At the moment, however, it is fulfilling another purpose. On the top shelf lies his telescope, compass and Bible; on the middle tier lies his correspondence which consists only of his pension envelope; on the bottom tier, with tremendous gravity lies a chamber-pot which is always referred to as "the heirloom," and to which is attached a mysterious story which he will one day confide to me.

The room is lit by one weak electric-light bulb and a cluster of rush lights standing in a niche which also houses an earthenware jar full of cool drinking water. The one uncurtained window looks blindly out upon a sad peeling wall of mud. Lying in bed with the smoky feeble glare of the night-lights glinting in the glass of his compass—lying in bed after midnight with the brandy throbbing in his skull he reminds me of some ancient wedding-cake, waiting only for someone to lean forward and blow out the candles!

His last remark at night, when one has seen him safely to bed and tucked him in—apart from the vulgar "Kiss Me Hardy" which is always accompanied by a leer and a popped cheek—is more serious. "Tell me honestly," he says. "Do I look my age?"

Frankly Scobie looks anybody's age; older than the birth of tragedy, younger than the Athenian death. Spawned in the Ark by a chance meeting and mating of the bear and the ostrich; delivered before term by the sickening grunt of the keel on Ararat. Scobie came forth from the womb in a wheel chair with rubber tyres, dressed in a deer-stalker and a red flannel binder. On his prehensile toes the glossiest pair of elastic-sided boots. In his hand a ravaged family Bible whose fly-leaf bore the words "Joshua Samuel Scobie 1870. Honour thy father and thy mother." To these possessions were added eyes like dead moons, a distinct curvature of the pirate's spinal column, and a taste for quinqueremes. It was not blood which flowed in Scobie's veins but green salt water, deep-sea stuff. His walk is the slow rolling grinding trudge of a saint walking on Galilee. His talk is a green-water jargon swept up in five oceans—an antique shop of polite fable bristling with sextants, astrolabes, porpentines and isobars. When he sings, which he so often does, it is in the very accents of the Old Man of the Sea. Like a patron saint he has left little pieces of his flesh all over the world, in Zanzibar, Colombo, Togoland, Wu Fu: the little deciduous morsels which he has been shedding for so long now, old antlers, cuff-links, teeth, hair. . . . Now the retreating tide has left him high and dry above the speeding currents of time, Joshua the insolvent weather-man, the islander, the anchorite.

*   *   *   *   *

Clea, the gentle, lovable, unknowable Clea is Scobie's greatest friend, and spends much of her time with the old pirate; she deserts her cobweb studio to make him tea and to enjoy those interminable monologues about a life which has long since receded, lost its vital momentum, only to live on vicariously in the labyrinths of memory.

As for Clea herself: is it only my imagination which makes it seem so difficult to sketch her portrait? I think of her so much—and yet I see how in all this writing I have been shrinking from dealing directly with her. Perhaps the difficulty lies here: that there does not seem to be an easy correspondence between her habits and her true disposition. If I should describe the outward structure of her life—so disarmingly simple, graceful, self-contained—there is a real danger that she might seem either a nun for whom the whole range of human passions had given place to an absorbing search for her subliminal self, or a disappointed and ingrown virgin who had deprived herself of the world because of some psychic instability, or some insurmountable early wound.

Everything about her person is honey-gold and warm in tone; the fair, crisply-trimmed hair which she wears rather long at the back, knotting it simply at the downy nape of her neck. This focuses the candid face of a minor muse with its smiling grey-green eyes. The calmly disposed hands have a deftness and shapeliness which one only notices when one sees them at work, holding a paintbrush perhaps or setting the broken leg of a sparrow in splints made from match-ends.

I should say something like this: that she had been poured, while still warm, into the body of a young grace: that is to say, into a body born without instincts or desires.

To have great beauty; to have enough money to construct an independent life; to have a skill—these are the

factors which persuade the envious, the dispirited to regard her as undeservedly lucky. But why, ask her critics
and observers, has she denied herself marriage?

She lives in modest though not miserly style, inhabiting
a comfortable attic-studio furnished with little beyond
an iron bed and a few ragged beach chairs which in the
summer are transferred bodily to her little bathing cabin
at Sidi Bishr. Her only luxury is a glittering tiled bathroom in the corner of which she has installed a minute
stove to cope with whatever cooking she feels inclined to
do for herself; and a bookcase whose crowded shelves indicate that she denies it nothing.

She lives without lovers or family ties, without malices
or pets, concentrating with single-mindedness upon her
painting which she takes seriously, but not too seriously.
In her work, too, she is lucky; for these bold yet elegant
canvases radiate clemency and humour. They are full of
a sense of play—like children much-beloved.

But I see that I have foolishly spoken of her as "denying herself marriage." How this would anger her: for I
remember her once saying: "If we are to be friends you
must not think or speak about me as someone who is
denying herself something in life. My solitude does not
deprive me of anything, nor am I fitted to be other than
I am. I want you to see how successful I am and not imagine me full of inner failings. As for love itself—*cher
ami*—I told you already that love interested me only very
briefly—and men more briefly still; the few, indeed the
one, experience which marked me was an experience
with a woman. I am still living in the happiness of that
perfectly *achieved* relationship: any physical substitute
would seem today horribly vulgar and hollow. But do
not imagine me as suffering from any fashionable form
of broken heart. No. In a funny sort of way I feel that our
love has really gained by the passing of the love-object;
it is as if the physical body somehow stood in the way of

love's true growth, its self-realization. Does that sound calamitous?" She laughed.

We were walking, I remember, along the rainswept Corniche in autumn, under a darkening crescent of clouded sky; and as she spoke she put her arm affectionately through mine and smiled at me with such tenderness that a passer-by might have been forgiven for imagining that we ourselves were lovers.

"And then," she went on, "there is another thing which perhaps you will discover for yourself. There is something about love—I will not say defective for the defect lies in ourselves: but something we have mistaken about its nature. For example, the love you now feel for Justine is not a different love for a different object but the same love you feel for Melissa trying to work itself out through the medium of Justine. Love is horribly stable, and each of us is only allotted a certain portion of it, a ration. It is capable of appearing in an infinity of forms and attaching itself to an infinity of people. But it is limited in quantity, can be used up, become shop-worn and faded before it reaches its true object. For its destination lies somewhere in the deepest regions of the psyche where it will come to recognize itself as self-love, the ground upon which we build the sort of health of the psyche. I do not mean egoism or narcissism."

It was conversations like these: conversations lasting sometimes far into the night, which first brought me close to Clea, taught me that I could rely upon the strength which she had quarried out of self-knowledge and reflection. In our friendship we were able to share our private thoughts and ideas, to test them upon one another, in a way that would have been impossible had we been linked more closely by ties which, paradoxically enough, separate more profoundly than they join, though human illusion forbids us to believe this. "It is true," I remember her saying once, when I had men-

tioned this strange fact, "that in some senses I am closer
to you than either Melissa or Justine. You see, Melissa's
love is too confiding: it blinds her. While Justine's
cowardly monomania sees you through an invented picture of you, and this forbids you to do anything except
to be a demoniac like her. Do not look hurt. There is no
malice in what I say."

But apart from Clea's own painting, I should not forget to mention the work she does for Balthazar. She is
the clinic painter. For some reason or other my friend is
not content with the normal slipshod method of recording medical anomalies by photographs. He is pursuing
some private theory which makes him attach importance
to the pigmentation of the skin in certain stages of his pet
diseases. The ravages of syphilis, for example, in every
degree of anomaly, Clea has recorded for him in large
coloured drawings of terrifying lucidity and tenderness.
In a sense these are truly works of art; the purely utili-
tarian object has freed the painter from any compulsion
towards self-expression; she has set herself to record; and
these tortured and benighted human members which
Balthazar picks out daily from the long sad queue in the
out-patients' ward (like a man picking rotten apples from
a barrel) have all the values of depicted human faces—
abdomens blown like fuses, skin surfaces shrunken and
peeling like plaster, carcinomata bursting through the
rubber membranes which retain them. . . . I remember
the first time I saw her at work; I had called on Balthazar
at the clinic to collect a certificate for some routine matter in connection with the school at which I worked.
Through the glass doors of the surgery I caught a
glimpse of Clea, whom I did not then know, sitting under the withered pear-tree in the shabby garden. She was
dressed in a white medical smock, and her colours were
laid out methodically beside her on a slab of fallen marble. Before her, seated half-crouching upon a wicker

chair, was a big-breasted sphinx-faced *fellah* girl, with her
skirt drawn up above her waist to expose some choice object of my friend's study. It was a brilliant spring day,
and in the distance one could hear the scampering of the
sea. Clea's capable and innocent fingers moved back and
forth upon the white surface of the paper, surely, deftly,
with wise premeditation. Her face showed the rapt and
concentrated pleasure of a specialist touching in the colours of some rare tulip.

When Melissa was dying it was for Clea that she asked;
and it was Clea who spent whole nights at her bedside
telling her stories and tending her. As for Scobie—I do
not dare to say that their inversion constituted a hidden
bond—sunk like a submarine cable linking two continents—for that might do an injustice to both. Certainly
the old man is unaware of any such matter; and she for
her part is restrained by her perfect tact from showing
him how hollow are his boasts of love-making. They are
perfectly matched, and perfectly happy in their relationship, like a father and daughter. On the only occasion
when I heard him rally her upon not being married
Clea's lovely face became round and smooth as that of a
schoolgirl, and from the depths of an assumed serious-
ness which completely disguised the twinkle of the imp
in her grey eyes, she replied that she was waiting for the
right man to come along: at which Scobie nodded profoundly, and agreed that this was the right line of con-
duct.

It was from a litter of dusty canvases in one corner of
her studio that I unearthed a head of Justine one day—
a half profile, touched in impressionistically and obviously not finished. Clea caught her breath and gazed at
it with all the compassion a mother might show for a
child which she recognized as ugly, but which was none
the less beautiful for her. "It is ages old," she said; and
after much reflection gave it to me for my birthday. It

stands now on the old arched mantelshelf to remind me
of the breathless, incisive beauty of that dark and beloved head. She has just taken a cigarette from between
her lips, and she is about to say something which her
mind has already formulated but which has so far only
reached the eyes. The lips are parted, ready to utter it in
words.

* * * * *

A mania for self-justification is common both to those
whose consciences are uneasy and to those who seek a
philosophic rationale for their actions: but in either case
it leads to strange forms of thinking. The idea is not
spontaneous, but *voulue*. In the case of Justine this
mania led to a perpetual flow of ideas, speculations on
past and present actions, which pressed upon her mind
with the weight of a massive current pressing upon the
walls of a dam. And for all the wretched expenditure of
energy in this direction, for all the passionate con-
trivance in her self-examination, one could not help
distrusting her conclusions, since they were always changing, were never at rest. She shed theories about herself
like so many petals. "Do you not believe that love consists
wholly of paradoxes?" she once asked Arnauti. I remember her asking me much the same question in that turbid
voice of hers which somehow gave the question tenderness as well as a sort of menace. "Supposing I were to
tell you that I only allowed myself to approach you to
save myself from the danger and ignominy of falling
deeply in love with you? I felt I was saving Nessim with
every kiss I gave you." How could this, for example, have
constituted the true motive for that extraordinary scene
on the beach? No rest from doubt, no rest from doubt.
On another occasion she dealt with the problem from another angle, not perhaps less truthfully: "The moral is—
what is the moral? We were not simply gluttons, were

we? And how completely this love-affair has repaid all the promises it held out for us—at least for me. We met and the worst befell us, but the best part of us, our lovers. O! please do not laugh at me."

For my part I remained always stupefied and mum-chance at all the avenues opened up by these thoughts; and afraid, so strange did it seem to talk about what we were actually experiencing in such obituary terms. At times I was almost provoked like Arnauti, on a similar occasion, to shout: "For the love of God, stop this mania for unhappiness or it will bring us to disaster. You are exhausting our lives before we have a chance to live them." I knew of course the uselessness of such an exhortation. There are some characters in this world who are marked down for self-destruction, and to these no amount of rational argument can appeal. For my part Justine always reminded me of a somnambulist discovered treading the perilous leads of a high tower; any attempt to wake her with a shout might lead to disaster. One could only follow her silently in the hope of guiding her gradually away from the great shadowy drops which loomed up on every side.

But by some curious paradox it was these very defects of character—these vulgarities of the psyche—which constituted for me the greatest attraction of this weird kinetic personage. I suppose in some way they corresponded to weaknesses in my own character which I was lucky to be able to master more thoroughly than she could. I know that for us love-making was only a small part of the total picture projected by a mental intimacy which proliferated and ramified daily around us. How we talked! Night after night in shabby sea-front cafés (trying ineffectually to conceal from Nessim and other common friends an attachment for which we felt guilty). As we talked we insensibly drew nearer and nearer to each other until we were holding hands, or all but in each other's arms: not from the customary sensuality which afflicts lovers but as if the physical contact could ease the pain of self-exploration.

Of course this is the unhappiest love-relationship of which a human being is capable—weighed down by something as heartbreaking as the post-coital sadness which clings to every endearment, which lingers like a sediment in the clear waters of a kiss. "It is easy to write of kisses," says Arnauti, "but where passion should have been full of clues and keys it served only to slake our thoughts. It did not convey information as it usually does. There was so much else going on." And indeed in making love to her I too began to understand fully what he meant in describing The Check as "the parching sense of lying with some lovely statue which was unable to return the kisses of the common flesh which it touches. There was something exhausting and perverting about loving so well and yet loving so little."

The bedroom for example with its bronze phosphorous light, the pastels burning in the green Tibetan urn diffusing a smell of roses to the whole room. By the bed the rich poignant scent of her powder hanging heavy in the bed-curtains. A dressing-table with its stoppered cream and salves. Over the bed the Universe of Ptolemy! She has had it drawn upon parchment and handsomely framed. It will hang forever over her bed, over the eikons in their leather cases, over the martial array of philosophers. Kant in his nightcap feeling his way upstairs. Jupiter Tonans. There is somehow a heavy futility in this array of great ones—among whom she has permitted Pursewarden an appearance. Four of his novels are to be seen though whether she has put them there specially for the occasion (we are all dining together) I cannot say. Justine surrounded by her philosophers is like an invalid surrounded by medicines—empty capsules, bottles and syringes. "Kiss her," says Arnauti, "and you are aware that her eyes do not close but open more widely, with an increasing doubt and madness. The mind is so awake that it makes any gift of the body partial —a panic which will respond to nothing less than a *curette*. At night you can hear her brain ticking like a cheap alarm-clock."

On the far wall there is an idol the eyes of which are lit from within by electricity, and it is to this graven mentor that Justine acts her private role. Imagine a torch thrust through the throat of a skeleton to light up the vault of the skull from which the eyeless sockets ponder. Shadows thrown on the arch of the cranium flap there in imprisonment. When the electricity is out of order a stump of candle is soldered to the bracket: Justine then, standing naked on tip-toes to push a lighted match into the eyeball of the God. Immediately the furrows of the jaw spring into relief, the shaven frontal bone, the straight rod of the nose. She has never been tranquil unless this visitant from distant mythology is watching over her nightmares. Under it lie a few small inexpensive toys, a celluloid doll, a sailor, about which I have never had the courage to question her. It is to this idol that her most marvellous dialogues are composed. It is possible, she says, to talk in her sleep and be overheard by the wise and sympathetic mask which has come to represent what she calls her Noble Self—adding sadly, with a smile of misgiving, "It does exist you know."

The pages of Arnauti run through my mind as I watch her and talk to her. "A face famished by the inward light of her terrors. In the darkness long after I am asleep she wakes to ponder on something I have said about our relationship. I am always waking to find her busy with something, preoccupied; sitting before the mirror naked, smoking a cigarette, and tapping with her bare foot on the expensive carpet." It is strange that I should always see Justine in the context of this bedroom which she

could never have known before Nessim gave it to her. It
is always here that I see her undergoing those dreadful
intimacies of which he writes. "There is no pain compared to that of loving a woman who makes her body
accessible to one and yet who is incapable of delivering
her true self—because she does not know where to find
it." How often, lying beside her, I have debated these
observations which, to the ordinary reader, might pass
unnoticed in the general flux and reflux of ideas in
Moeurs.

She does not slide from kisses into sleep—a door into
a private garden—as Melissa does. In the warm bronze
light her pale skin looks paler—the red eatable flowers
growing in the cheeks where the light sinks and is held
fast. She will throw back her dress to unroll her stocking
and show you the dark cicatrice above the knee, lodged
between the twin dimples of the suspender. It is undes-
cribable the feeling I have when I see this wound—like
a character out of the book—and recall its terrible origin. In the mirror the dark head, younger and more
graceful now than the original it has outlived, gives back
a vestigial image of a young Justine—like the calcimined
imprint of a fern in chalk: the youth she believes she has
lost.

I cannot believe that she existed so thoroughly in some
other room; that the idol hung elsewhere, in another setting. Somehow I always see her walking up the long staircase, crossing the gallery with its *putti* and ferns, and
then entering the low doorway into this most private of
rooms. Fatma, the black Ethiopian maid, follows her.
Invariably Justine sinks on to the bed and holds out her
ringed fingers; as with an air of mild hallucination the
Negress draws them off the long fingers and places them
in a small casket on the dressing-table. The night on
which Pursewarden and I dined alone with her we were
invited back to the great house, and after examining the

great cold reception rooms Justine suddenly turned and led the way upstairs, in search of an ambience which might persuade my friend, whom she greatly admired and feared, to relax.

Pursewarden had been surly all evening, as he often was, and had busied himself with the drinks to the exclusion of anything else. The little ritual with Fatma seemed to free Justine from constraint; she was free to be natural, to move about with "that insolent unbalanced air, cursing her frock for catching in the cupboard door," or pausing to apostrophize herself in the great spade-shaped mirror. She told us of the mask, adding sadly, "It sounds cheap and rather theatrical, I know. I turn my face to the wall and talk to it. I forgive myself my trespasses as I forgive those who trespass against me. Sometimes I rave a little and beat on the wall when I remember the follies which must seem insignificant to others or to God—if there is a God. I speak to the person I always imagine inhabiting a green and quiet place like the Twenty-third Psalm." Then coming to rest her head upon my shoulder and put her arms round me, "That is why so often I ask you to be a little tender with me. The edifice feels as if it had cracked up here. I need little strokes and endearments like you give Melissa; I know it is she you love. Who could love me?"

Pursewarden was not, I think, proof against the naturalness and charm of the tones in which she said this, for he went to the corner of the room and gazed at her bookshelf. The sight of his own books made him first pale and then red, though whether with shame or anger I could not tell. Turning back he seemed at first about to say something, but changed his mind. He turned back once more with an air of guilty chagrin to confront that tremendous shelf. Justine said: "If you wouldn't consider it an impertinence I should so like you to autograph one for me," but he did not reply. He

stayed quite still, staring at the shelf, with his glass in
his hand. Then he wheeled about and all of a sudden
he appeared to have become completely drunk; he said
in a fierce ringing tone: "The modern novel! The
grumus merdae left behind by criminals upon the scene
of their misdeeds." And quietly falling sideways, but taking care to place his glass upright on the floor he passed
immediately into a magistral sleep.

The whole of the long colloquy which ensued took
place over this prostrate body. I took him to be asleep,
but in fact he must have been awake for he subsequently
reproduced much of Justine's conversation in a cruel
satirical short story, which for some reason amused Justine though it caused me great pain. He described her
black eyes shining with unshed tears as she said (sitting
at the mirror, the comb travelling through her hair,
crackling and sputtering like her voice): "When I first
met Nessim and knew that I was falling in love with him
I tried to save us both. I deliberately took a lover—a dull
brute of a Swede, hoping to wound him and force him to
detach himself from his feeling for me. The Swede's wife
had left him and I said (anything to stop him snivel-
ling): 'Tell me how she behaves and I will imitate her.
In the dark we are all meat and treacherous however
our hair kinks or skin smells. Tell me, and I will give you
the wedding-smile and fall into your arms like a mountain of silk.' And all the time I was thinking over and
over again: 'Nessim. Nessim.' "

I remember in this context, too, a remark of Purse-
warden's which summed up his attitude to our friends.
"Alexandria!" he said (it was on one of those long
moonlit walks), "Jews with their cafeteria mysticism!
How could one deal with it in words? Place and people?"
Perhaps then he was meditating this cruel short story and
casting about for ways and means to deal with us.
"Justine and her city are alike in that they both have

a strong flavour without having any real character."

I am recalling now how during that last spring (forever) we walked together at full moon, overcome by the soft dazed air of the city, the quiet ablutions of water and moonlight that polished it like a great casket. An aerial lunacy among the deserted trees of the dark squares, and the long dusty roads reaching away from midnight to midnight, bluer than oxygen. The passing faces had become gem-like, tranced—the baker at his machine making the staff of tomorrow's life, the lover hurrying back to his lodging, nailed into a silver helmet of panic, the six-foot cinema posters borrowing a ghastly magnificence from the moon which seemed laid across the nerves like a bow.

We turn a corner and the world becomes a pattern of arteries, splashed with silver and deckle-edged with shadow. At this far end of Kom El Dick not a soul abroad save an occasional obsessive policeman, lurking like a guilty wish in the city's mind. Our footsteps run punctually as metronomes along the deserted pavements: two men, in their own time and city, remote from the world, walking as if they were treading one of the lugubrious canals of the moon. Pursewarden is speaking of the book which he has always wanted to write, and of the difficulty which besets a city-man when he faces a work of art.

"If you think of yourself as a sleeping city for example . . . what? You can sit quiet and hear the processes going on, going about their business; volition, desire, will, cognition, passion, conation. I mean like the million legs of a centipede carrying on with the body powerless to do anything about it. One gets exhausted trying to circumnavigate these huge fields of experience. We are never free, we writers. I could explain it much more clearly if it was dawn. I long to be musical in body and mind. I want style, consort. Not the little mental squirts as if through the ticker-tape of the mind. It is the age's disease, is it not? It explains the huge waves of occultism lapping round us. The Cabal, now, and Balthazar. He will never understand that it is with God we must be the most careful; for He makes such a powerful appeal to what is *lowest* in human nature—our feeling of insufficiency, fear of the unknown, personal failings; above all our monstrous egotism which sees in the martyr's crown an athletic prize which is really hard to attain. God's real and subtle nature must be clear of distinctions: a glass of spring-water, tasteless, odourless, merely refreshing: and surely its appeal would be to the few, the very few, real contemplatives? As for the many it is already included in the part of their nature which they least wish to admit or examine. I do not believe that there is any system which can do more than pervert the essential idea. And then, all these attempts to circumscribe God in words or ideas. . . . No one thing can explain everything: though everything can illuminate something. God, I must be still drunk. If God were anything He would be an art. Sculpture or medicine. But the immense extension of knowledge in this our age, the growth of new sciences, makes it almost impossible for us to digest the available flavours and put them to use.

"Holding a candle in your hand, I mean, you can throw the shadow of the retinal blood-vessels on the wall. It isn't silent enough. It's never dead still in there: never quiet enough for the trismegistus to be fed. All night long you can hear the rush of blood in the cerebral arteries. The loins of thinking. It starts you going back along the cogs of historical action, cause and effect. You can't rest ever, you can't give over and begin to scry. You climb through the physical body, softly parting the muscle-schemes to admit you—muscle striped and unstriped; you examine the coil ignition of the guts in the abdomen, the sweetbreads, the liver choked with refuse like a sink-filter, the bag of urine, the red unbuckled belt of the intestines, the soft horny corridor of the oesophagus, the glottis with its mucilage softer than the pouch of a kangaroo. What do I mean? You are searching for a co-ordinating scheme, the syntax of a Will which might stabilize everything and take the tragedy out of it. The sweat breaks out on your face, a cold panic as you feel the soft contraction and expansion of the viscera busy about their job, regardless of the man watching them who is yourself. A whole city of processes, a factory for the pro-duction of excrement, my goodness, a daily sacrifice. An offering to the toilet for every one you make to the altar. Where do they meet? Where is the correspondence? Out-side in the darkness by the railway bridge the lover of this man waits for him with the same indescribable mag-gotry going on in her body and blood; wine swilling the conduits, the pylorus disgorging like a sucker, the incom-mensurable bacteriological world multiplying in every drop of semen, spittle, sputum, musk. He takes a spinal column in his arms, the ducts flooded with ammonia, the meninges exuding their pollen, the cornea glowing in its little crucible. . . ."

He begins now that shocking boyish laughter, throw-ing back his head until the moonlight plays upon his per-fect white teeth under the sad little blond moustache.

It was on such a night that our footsteps led us to Bal-thazar's door, and seeing his light on, we knocked. The same night, on the old horn gramophone (with an emo-tion so deep that it was almost horror) I heard some ama-teur's recording of the old poet reciting the lines which begin:

> *Ideal voices and much beloved*
> *Of those who died, of those who are*
> *Now lost for us like the very dead;*
> *Sometimes within a dream they speak*
> *Or in the ticking brain a thought revives them. . . .*

These fugitive memories explain nothing, illuminate nothing: yet they return again and again when I think of my friends as if the very circumstances of our habits had become impregnated with what he then felt, the parts we then acted. The slither of tyres across the waves of the desert under a sky blue and frost-bound in winter; or in summer a fearful lunar bombardment which turned the sea to phosphorus—bodies shining like tin, crushed in electric bubbles; or walking to the last spit of sand near Montaza, sneaking through the dense green darkness of the King's gardens, past the drowsy sentry, to where the force of the sea was suddenly crippled and the waves hobbled over the sand-bar. Or walking arm-in-arm down the long gallery, already gloomy with an unusual yellow winter fog. Her hand is cold so she has slipped it in my pocket. Today because she has no emotion whatsoever she tells me that she is in love with me—something she has always refused to do. At the long windows the rain hisses down suddenly. The dark eyes are cool and amused. A centre of blackness in things which trembles and changes shape. "I am afraid of Nessim these days. He has changed." We are standing before the Chinese paintings from the Louvre. "The meaning of space," she says with disgust. There is no form, no pigment, no lens any more—simply a gaping hole into which the infinite drains slowly into the room: a blue gulf where the tiger's body was, emptying itself into the preoccupied atmosphere of the studios. Afterwards we walk up the dark staircase to the top floor to see Sveva, to put on the gramophone and dance. The little model pretends that she is heartbroken because Pombal has cast her off after a "whirlwind romance" lasting nearly a month.

My friend himself is a little surprised at the force of an attachment which could make him think of one woman for so long a time. He has cut himself while shav-

ing and his face looks grotesque with a moustache of surgical tape stuck to it. "It is a city of aberrations," he repeats angrily. "I very nearly married her. It is infuriating. Thank God that the veil lifted when it did. It was
seeing her naked in front of the mirror. All of a sudden
I was disgusted—though I mentally admitted a sort of
Renaissance dignity in the fallen breasts, the waxy skin,
the sunken belly and the little peasant paws. All of a
sudden I sat up in bed and said to myself, 'My God!
She is an elephant in need of a coat of whitewash!' "

Now Sveva is quietly sniffing into her handkerchief as
she recounts the extravagant promises which Pombal
has made her, and which will never be fulfilled. "It was
a curious and dangerous attachment for an easy-going
man" (hear Pombal's voice explaining). "It felt as if her
cool murderous charity had eaten away my locomotive
centres, paralysed my nervous system. Thank God I am
free to concentrate on my work once more."

He is troubled about his work. Rumours of his habits
and general outlook have begun to get back to the Consulate. Lying in bed he plans a campaign which will get
him crucified and promoted to a post with more scope.
"I have decided that I simply must get my cross. I am going to give several skilfully graded parties. I shall count
on you: I shall need a few shabby people at first in order to give my boss the feeling that he can patronize me
socially. He is a complete *parvenu* of course and rose on
his wife's fortune and judicious smarming of powerful
people. Worst of all he has a distinct inferiority complex
about my own birth and family background. He has still
not quite decided whether to do me down or not; but
he has been taking soundings at the Quai d'Orsay to see
how well padded I am there. Since my uncle died, of
course, and my godfather the bishop was involved in
that huge scandal over the brothel in Reims, I find myself rather less steady on my feet. I shall have to make the

brute feel protective, feel that I need encouraging and bringing out. Pouagh! First a rather shabby party with one celebrity only. O why did I join the service? Why have I not a small fortune of my own?"

Hearing all this in Sveva's artificial tears and then walking down the draughty staircase again arm in arm thinking not of Sveva, not of Pombal, but of the passage in Arnauti where he says of Justine: "Like women who think by biological precept and without the help of reason. To such women how fatal an error it is to give oneself; there is simply a small chewing noise, as when the cat reaches the backbone of the mouse."

The wet pavements are slick underfoot from the rain, and the air has become dense with the moisture so ardently longed for by the trees in the public gardens, the statues and other visitants. Justine is away upon another tack, walking slowly in her glorious silk frock with the dark lined cape, head hanging. She stops in front of a lighted shop-window and takes my arms so that I face her, looking into my eyes: "I am thinking about going away," she says in a quiet puzzled voice. "Something is happening to Nessim and I don't know what it is as yet." Then suddenly the tears come into her eyes and she says: "For the first time I am afraid, and I don't know why."

THAT second spring the khamseen was worse than I have even known it before or since. Before sunrise the skies of the desert turned brown as buckram, and then slowly darkened, swelling like a bruise and at last releasing the outlines of cloud, giant octaves of ochre which massed up from the Delta like the drift of ashes under a volcano. The city has shuttered itself tightly, as if against a gale. A few gusts of air and a thin sour rain are the forerunners of the darkness which blots out the light of the sky. And now unseen in the darkness of shuttered rooms the sand is invading everything, appearing as if by magic in clothes long locked away, books, pictures and teaspoons. In the locks of doors, beneath fingernails. The harsh sobbing air dries the membranes of throats and noses, and makes eyes raw with the configurations of conjunctivitis. Clouds of dried blood walk the streets like prophecies; the sand is settling into the sea like powder into the curls of a stale wig. Choked fountain-pens, dry lips—and along the slats of the Venetian shutters thin white drifts as of young snow. The ghastly feluccas passing along the canal are crewed by ghouls with wrapped heads. From time to time a cracked wind arrives from directly above and stirs the whole city round and round so that one has the illusion that everything—trees, minarets, monuments and people —has been caught in the final eddy of some great whirlpool and will pour softly back at last into the desert from which they rose, reverting once more to the anonymous wave-sculptured floor of dunes. . . .

I cannot deny that by this time we had both been seized by an exhaustion of spirit which had made us

desperate, reckless, impatient of discovery. Guilt always
hurries towards its complement, punishment: only there
does its satisfaction lie. A hidden desire for some sort of
expiation dictated Justine's folly which was greater than
mine; or perhaps we both dimly sensed that, bound as
we were hand and foot to each other, only an upheaval
of some sort could restore each to his vulgar right mind.
These days were full of omens and warnings upon which
our anxiety fed.

One-eyed Hamid told me one day of a mysterious
caller who had told him that he must keep careful watch
on his master as he was in great danger from some
highly-placed personage. His description of the man
might have been that of Selim, Nessim's secretary: but it
also might have been any of the 50,000 inhabitants of
the province. Meanwhile Nessim's own attitude to me
had changed, or rather deepened into a solicitous and
cloying sweetness. He shed his former reserve. When he
spoke to me he used unfamiliar endearments and took
me affectionately by the sleeve. At times as we spoke he
would flush suddenly: or tears would come into his eyes
and he would turn aside his head to hide them. Justine
watched this with a concern which was painful to observe. But the very humiliation and self-reproach we felt
at wounding him only drove us closer together as accomplices. At times she spoke of going away: at times I did
the same. But neither of us could move. We were forced
to await the outcome with a fatality and exhaustion that
was truly fearful to experience.

Nor were our follies diminished by these warnings;
rather did they multiply. A dreadful inadvertency
reigned over our actions, an appalling thoughtlessness
marked our behaviour. Nor did we (and here I realized
that I had lost myself completely) even hope to avert
whatever fate might be in store for us. We were only
foolishly concerned lest we might not be able to share it

—lest it might separate us! In this plain courting of mar-
tyrdom I realized that we showed our love at its hollow-
est, its most defective. "How disgusting I must seem to
you," said Justine once, "with my obscene jumble of con-
flicting ideas: all this sickly preoccupation with God and
a total inability to obey the smallest moral injunction
from my inner nature like being faithful to a man one
adores. I tremble for myself, my dear one, I tremble. If
only I could escape from the tiresome classical Jewess of
neurology. . . . If only I could peel it off."

During these months, while Melissa was away in Palestine on a cure (I had borrowed the money from Justine
in order for her to go) we had several narrow escapes.
For example, one day we were talking, Justine and I, in
the great bedroom of the house. We had come in from
bathing and had taken cold showers to get the salt off our
skins. Justine sat on the bed naked under the bathroom
towel which she had draped round her like a chiton.
Nessim was away in Cairo where he was supposed to
make a radio broadcast on behalf of some charity or
other. Outside the window the trees nodded their dusty
fronds in the damp summer air, while the faint huddle
of traffic on Rue Fuad could be heard.

Nessim's quiet voice came to us from the little black
radio by the bed, converted by the microphone into the
voice of a man prematurely aged. The mentally empty
phrases lived on in the silence they invaded until the
air seemed packed with commonplaces. But the voice
was beautiful, the voice of someone who had elaborately
isolated himself from feeling. Behind Justine's back the
door into the bathroom was open. Beyond it, a pane of
clinical whiteness, lay another door leading to an iron
fire-escape—for the house had been designed round a
central well so that its bathrooms and kitchens could be
connected by a cobweb of iron staircases such as span
the engine-room of a ship. Suddenly, while the voice was

still talking and while we listened to it, there came the light youthful patter of footsteps on the iron staircase outside the bathroom: a step unmistakably that of Nessim—or of any of the 50,000 inhabitants of the province. Looking over Justine's shoulder I saw developing on the glass panel of the frosted door, the head and shoulders of a tall slim man, with a soft felt hat pulled down over his eyes. He developed like a print in a photographer's developing-bowl. The figure paused with outstretched hand upon the knob of the door. Justine, seeing the direction of my glance, turned her head. She put one naked arm round my shoulders as both of us, with a feeling of complete calm whose core, like a heart beating, was a feverish impotent sexual excitement watched the dark figure standing there between two worlds, depicted as if on an X-ray screen. He would have found us absurdly posed, as if for a photograph, with an expression, not of fear but of guiltless relief upon our faces.

For a long time the figure stood there, as if in deep thought, perhaps listening. Then it shook its head once, slowly, and after a moment turned away with an air of perplexity to dissolve slowly on the glass. As it turned it seemed to slip something into the right-hand pocket of its coat. We heard the steps slowly diminishing—a dull descending scale of notes—on the iron ladder in the well. We neither of us spoke, but turned as if with deepened concentration to the little black radio from which the voice of Nessim still flowed with uninterrupted urbanity and gentleness. It seemed impossible that he could be in two places at once. It was only when the announcer informed us that the speech had been recorded that we understood. Why did he not open the door?

The truth is that he had been seized by the vertiginous uncertainty which, in a peaceable nature, follows upon a decision to act. Something had been building itself up inside him all this time, grain by grain, until the weight of it had become insupportable. He was aware of a profound interior change in his nature which had at last shaken off the long paralysis of impotent love which had hitherto ruled his actions. The thought of some sudden concise action, some determining factor for good or evil, presented itself to him as an intoxicating novelty. He felt (so he told me later) like a gambler about to stake the meagre remains of a lost fortune upon one desperate throw. But the nature of his action had not yet been decided upon. What form should it take? A mass of uneasy fantasies burst in.

Two major currents had reached their confluence in this desire to act; on the one hand the dossier which his agents had collected upon Justine had reached such proportions that it could not be ignored; on the other he was haunted by a new and fearful thought which for some reason had not struck him before—namely that Justine was really falling in love at last. The whole temper of her personality seemed to be changing; for the first time she had become reflective, thoughtful, and full of the echoes of a sweetness which a woman can always afford to spend upon the man she does not love. You see, he too had been dogging her steps through the pages of Arnauti.

"Originally I believed that she must be allowed to struggle towards me through the jungle of The Check. Whenever the wounding thought of her infidelity came upon me I reminded myself that she was not a pleasure-seeker, but a hunter of pain in search of herself—and me. I thought that if one man could release her from herself she would then become accessible to all men, and so to me who had most claim upon her. But when I began to see her melting like a summer ice-cap, a horrible thought came to me: namely that he who broke The Check must keep her forever, since the peace he gave her was precisely that for which she was hunting so frantically through our bodies and fortunes. For the first time my jealousy, helped forward by my fear, mastered me."

It has always seemed fantastic to me that even now he was jealous of everyone except the true author of Justine's present concern—myself. Despite the overwhelming mass of evidence he hardly dared to allow himself to suspect me. It is not love that is blind, but jealousy. It was a long time before he could bring himself to trust the mass of documentation his agents had piled up around us, around our meetings, our behaviour. But by now the facts had obtruded themselves so clearly that there was no possibility of error. The problem was how to dispose of me—"I do not mean in the flesh so much: you had become merely an image standing in my light. I saw you perhaps dying, perhaps going away. I did not know. The very uncertainty was itself exciting to the pitch of drunkenness."

But side by side with these preoccupations were others—the posthumous problems which Arnauti had been unable to solve and which Nessim had been following up with true Oriental curiosity over a period of years. He was now near to the man with the black patch over one eye—nearer than any of us had ever been. Here was another piece of knowledge which as yet he could not decide how best to use. If Justine was really ridding herself of him, however, what good would there be in revenging himself upon the true person of the mysterious being? On the other hand if I was about to step into the place vacated by the image? . . .

I asked Selim point-blank whether he had ever visited my flat to warn one-eyed Hamid. He did not reply but lowered his head and said under his breath, "My master is not himself these days."

Meanwhile my own fortunes had taken an absurd and unexpected turn. One night there came a banging on the door and I opened it to admit the dapper figure of

an Egyptian Army officer clad in resplendent boots and
tarbush, carrying under his arm a giant fly-whisk with an
ebony handle. Yussouf Bey spoke nearly perfect English,
allowing it to fall negligently from his lips, word by well-
chosen word, out of an earnest coal-black face fitted with
a dazzle of small perfect teeth like seed-pearls. He had
some of the endearing solemnity of a talking water-
melon just down from Cambridge. Hamid brought him
habitual coffee and a sticky liqueur, and over it he told
me that a great friend of mine in a high position very
much wished to see me. My thoughts at once turned to
Nessim; but this friend, the water-melon asserted, was an
Englishman, an official. More he could not say. His mis-
sion was confidential. Would I go with him and visit my
friend?

I was full of misgivings. Alexandria, outwardly so
peaceful, was not really a safe place for Christians. Only
last week Pombal had come home with a story of the
Swedish vice-consul whose car had broken down on the
Matrugh road. He had left his wife alone in it while he
walked to the nearest telephone-point in order to ring up
the consulate and ask them to send out another car. He
had arrived back to find her body sitting normally on the
back seat—without a head. Police were summoned and
the whole district was combed. Some Bedouin encamped
nearby were among those interrogated. While they were
busy denying any knowledge of the accident, out of the
apron of one of the women rolled the missing head.
They had been trying to extract the gold teeth which
had been such an unpleasant feature of her party-smile.
This sort of incident was not sufficiently uncommon to
give one courage in visiting strange quarters of the town
after dark, so it was with no feeling of jauntiness that I
followed the soldier into the back of a staff-car behind a
uniformed driver and saw myself being whirled towards
the seedier quarters of the town. Yussouf Bey stroked his

neat little brush-stroke moustache with the anticipatory
air of a musician tuning an instrument. It was useless
to question him further: I did not wish to betray any
of the anxiety I felt. So I made a sort of inner surrender
to the situation, lit a cigarette, and watched the long dissolving strip of the Corniche flow past us.

Presently the car dropped us and the soldier led me
on foot through a straggle of small streets and alleys
near the Rue des Soeurs. If the object here was to make
me lose myself it succeeded almost immediately. He
walked with a light self-confident step, humming under
his breath. Finally we debouched into a suburban street
full of merchants' stores and stopped before a great
carved door which he pushed open after having first rung
a bell. A courtyard with a stunted palm-tree; the path
which crossed it was punctuated by a couple of feeble
lanterns standing on the gravel. We crossed it and as-
cended some stairs to where a frosted electric light bulb
gleamed harshly above a tall white door. He knocked,
entered and saluted in one movement. I followed him
into a large, rather elegant and warmly-lighted room
with neat polished floors enhanced by fine Arab carpets.
In one corner seated at a high inlaid desk with the air of
a man riding a penny-farthing sat Scobie, with a scowl
of self-importance overlapping the smile of welcome with
which he greeted me. "My God," I said. The old pirate
gave a Drury Lane chuckle and said: "At last, old man,
at last." He did not rise however but sat on in his uncom-
fortable high-backed chair, tarbush on head, whisk on
knee, with a vaguely impressive air. I noticed an extra
pip on his shoulder, betokening heaven knows what increase of rank and power. "Sit down, old man," he said
with an awkward sawing movement of the hand which
bore a faint resemblance to a Second Empire gesture.
The soldier was dismissed and departed grinning. It
seemed to me that Scobie did not look very much at ease

in these opulent surroundings. He had a slightly defensive air. "I asked them to get hold of you," he said, sinking his voice to a theatrical whisper, "for a very special reason." There were a number of green files on his desk and a curiously disembodied-looking tea-cosy. I sat down.

He now rose quickly and opened the door. There was nobody outside. He opened the window. There was no one standing on the sill. He placed the tea-cosy over the desk telephone and reseated himself. Then, leaning forward and speaking carefully, he rolled his glass eye at me as with a conspiratorial solemnity he said: "Not a word to anyone, old man. Swear you won't say a word." I swore. *"They've made me head of the Secret Service."* The words fairly whistled in his dentures. I nodded in amazement. He drew a deep sucking breath as if he had been delivered of a weight and went on. "Old boy, there's going to be a war. Inside information." He pointed a long finger at his own temple. "There's going to be a war. The enemy is working night and day, old boy, right here among us." I could not dispute this. I could only marvel at the new Scobie who confronted me like a bad magazine illustration. "You can help us scupper them, old man," he went on with a devastating air of authority. "We want to take you on our strength." This sounded most agreeable. I waited for details. "The most dangerous gang of all is right here, in Alexandria," the old man creaked and boomed, "and you are in the centre of it. All friends of yours."

I saw through the knotted eyebrows and the rolling excited eye the sudden picture of Nessim, a brief flash, as of intuition, sitting at his huge desk in the cold steel-tube offices watching a telephone ring while the beads of sweat stood out on his forehead. He was expecting a message about Justine—one more twist of the knife. Scobie shook his head. "Not him so much," he said. "He's in it,

of course. The leader is a man called Balthazar. Look
what the censorship have been picking up."

He extracted a card from a file and passed it to me.
Balthazar writes an exquisite hand and the writing was
obviously his; but I could not help smiling when I saw
that the reverse of the postcard contained only the little
chessboard diagram of the *boustrophedon*. Greek letters
filled up the little squares. "He's got so much damn cheek
he sends them through the open post." I studied the diagram and tried to remember the little I had learned from
my friend of the calculus. "It's a nine-power system. I
can't read this one," Scobie added breathlessly. "They
have regular meetings, old man, to pool information. We
know this for a fact." I held the postcard lightly in my
fingers and seemed to hear the voice of Balthazar saying:
"The thinker's job is to be suggestive: that of the saint
to be silent about his discovery."

Scobie was leaning back in his chair now with uncon-
cealed self-satisfaction. He had puffed himself out like a
pouter-pigeon. He took his tarbush off his head, looked
at it with an air of complaisant patronage, and placed it
on the tea-cosy. Then he scratched his fissured skull with
bony fingers and went on—"We simply can't break the
code," he said. "We've got dozens of them"— he indicated a file full of photostatic reproductions of similar
postcards. "They've been round the code-rooms: even to
the Senior Wranglers in the Universities. No good, old
man." This did not surprise me. I laid the postcard on
the pile of photostats and returned to the contemplation
of Scobie. "That is where you come in," he said with a
grimace, "if you will come in, old man. We want you to
break the code however long it takes you. We'll put you
on a damn good screw, too. What do you say?"

- What could I say? The idea was too delightful to be
allowed to melt. Besides during the last months my
schoolwork had fallen off so much that I was sure my

contract was not going to be renewed at the end of the
present term. I was always arriving late from some meeting with Justine. I hardly bothered to correct papers any
more. I had become irritable and surly with my
colleagues and directors. Here was a chance to become
my own man. I heard Justine's voice in my head saying:
"Our love has become like some fearful misquotation in
a popular saying," as I leaned forward once more and
nodded my head. Scobie expelled a breath of relieved
pleasure and relaxed once more into the pirate. He confided his office to an anonymous Mustapha who apparently dwelt somewhere in the black telephone—Scobie
always looked into the mouthpiece as he spoke, as if into
a human eye. We left the building together and allowed
a staff car to take us down towards the sea. Further details
of my employment could be discussed over the little bottle of brandy in the bottom of the cake-stand by his bed.

We allowed ourselves to be dropped on the Corniche
and walked together the rest of the way by a brilliant
bullying moonlight, watching the old city dissolve and
reassemble in the graphs of evening mist, heavy with the
inertia of its surrounding desert, of the green alluvial
Delta which soaked into its very bones, informing its
values. Scobie talked inconsequently of this and that. I
remember him bemoaning the fact that he had been
left an orphan at an early age. His parents had been
killed together under dramatic circumstances which gave
him much food for reflection. "My father was an early
pioneer of motoring, old man. Early road races, flat out
at twenty miles an hour—all that sort of thing. He had
his own landau. I can see him now sitting behind the
wheel with a big moustache. Colonel Scobie, M.C. A
Lancer he was. My mother sat beside him, old man.
Never left his side, not even for road races. She used to
act as his mechanic. The newspapers always had pictures
of them at the start, sitting up there in bee-keeper's veils

—God knows why the pioneers always wore those huge veils. Dust, I suppose."

The veils had proved their undoing. Rounding a hairpin in the old London-Brighton road race his father's veil had been sucked into the front axle of the car they were driving. He had been dragged into the road, while his companion had careered on to smash headlong into a tree. "The only consolation is that that is just how he would have liked to go out. They were leading by quarter of a mile."

I have always been very fond of ludicrous deaths and had great difficulty in containing my laughter as Scobie described this misadventure to me with portentous rotations of his glass eye. Yet as he talked and I listened to this, half my thoughts were running upon a parallel track, busy about the new job I was to undertake, assessing it in terms of the freedom it offered me. Later that night Justine was to meet me near Montaza—the great car purring like a moth in the palm-cooled dusk of the road. What would she say to it? She would be delighted of course to see me freed from the shackles of my present work. But a part of her would groan inwardly at the thought that this relief would only create for us further chances to consort, to drive home our untruth, to reveal ourselves more fully than ever to our judges. Here was another paradox of love; that the very thing which brought us closer together—the *boustrophedon* —would, had we mastered the virtues which it illustrated, have separated us forever—I mean in the selves which preyed upon each other's infatuated images.

"Meanwhile," as Nessim was to say in those gentle tones so full of the shadowy sobriety which comes into the voice of those who have loved truly and failed to be loved in return, "meanwhile I was dwelling in the midst of a vertiginous excitement for which there was no relief except through an action the nature of which I could not discern. Tremendous bursts of self-confidence were succeeded by depressions so deep that it seemed I would never recover from them. With a vague feeling that I was preparing myself for a contest—as an athlete does— I began to take fencing lessons and learned to shoot with a pocket automatic. I studied the composition and effects of poisons from a manual of toxicology which I borrowed from Dr. Fuad Bey."

He had begun to harbour feelings which would not yield to analysis. The periods of intoxication were followed by others in which he felt, as if for the first time, the full weight of his loneliness: an inner agony of spirit for which, as yet, he could find no outward expression, either in paint or in action. He mused now incessantly upon his early years, full of a haunting sense of richness: his mother's shadowy house among the palms and poinsettias of Aboukir: the waters pulling and slithering among the old fort's emplacements, compiling the days of his early childhood in single condensed emotions born from visual memory. He clutched at these memories with a terror and clarity he had never experienced before. And all the time, behind the screen of nervous depression—for the incomplete action which he meditated lay within him like a *coitus interruptus*—there lived the germ of a wilful and uncontrolled exaltation. It was as if he were being egged on, to approach nearer and nearer . . . to what exactly? He could not tell; but here his ancient terror of madness stepped in and took possession of him, disturbing his physical balance, so that he suffered at times from attacks of vertigo which forced him to grope around himself like a blind man for something upon which to sit down—a chair or sofa. He would sit down, panting slightly and feeling the sweat beginning to start out on his forehead; but with relief that nothing of his interior struggle was visible to the casual onlooker. Now too he noticed that he involuntar-

ily repeated phrases aloud to which his conscious mind
refused to listen. "Good," she heard him tell one of his
mirrors, "so you are falling into a neurasthenia!" And
later as he was stepping out into the brilliant starlit air,
dressed in his well-cut evening clothes, Selim, at the
wheel of the car, heard him add: "I think this Jewish fox
has eaten my life."

At times, too, he was sufficiently alarmed to seek, if not
the help, at least the surcease of contact with other human beings: a doctor who left him with a phosphorous
tonic and a regimen he did not follow. The sight of a
column of marching Carmelites, tonsured like mandrils,
crossing Nebi Daniel drove him to renew his lapsed
friendship with Father Paul who in the past had seemed
so profoundly happy a man, folded into his religion like
a razor into its case. But now the kind of verbal consolations offered him by this lucky, happy, unimaginative
brute only filled him with nausea.

One night he knelt down beside his bed—a thing he
had not done since his twelfth year—and deliberately
set himself to pray. He stayed there a long time, mentally
spellbound, tongue-tied, with no words or thoughts shap-
ing themselves in his mind. He was filled by some ghastly
inhibition like a mental stroke. He stayed like this until
he could stand it no longer—until he felt that he was on
the point of suffocating. Then he jumped into bed and
drew the sheets over his head murmuring broken fragments of oaths and involuntary pleadings which he did
not recognize as emanating from any part of himself.

Outwardly however there were no signs of these strug-
gles to be seen; his speech remained dry and measured
despite the fever of the thoughts behind it. His doctor
complimented him on his excellent reflexes and assured
him that his urine was free from excess albumen. An
occasional headache only proved him to be a victim of

petit mal—or some other such customary disease of the rich and idle.

For his own part he was prepared to suffer thus as long as the suffering remained within the control of his consciousness. What terrified him only was the sensation of utter loneliness—a reality which he would never, he realized, be able to communicate either to his friends or to the doctors who might be called in to pronounce upon anomalies of behaviour which they would regard only as symptoms of disorder.

He tried feverishly to take up his painting again, but without result. Self-consciousness like a poison seemed to eat into the very paint, making it sluggish and dead. It was hard even to manipulate the brush with an invisible hand pulling at one's sleeve the whole time, hindering, whispering, displacing all freedom and fluidity of movement.

Surrounded as he was by this menacing twilight of the feelings he turned once more, in a vain effort to restore his balance and composure, to the completion of the Summer Palace—as it was jokingly called; the little group of Arab huts and stables at Abu Sir. Long ago, in the course of a ride to Benghazi along the lonely shoreline, he had come upon a fold in the desert, less than a mile from the sea, where a fresh spring suddenly burst through the thick sand pelt and hobbled a little way down towards the desolate beaches before it was overtaken and smothered by the dunes. Here the Bedouin, overtaken by the involuntary hunger for greenness which lies at the heart of all desert-lovers, had planted a palm and a fig whose roots had taken a firm subterranean grip upon the sandstone from which the pure water ran. Resting with the horses in the shade of these young trees, Nessim's eye had dwelt with wonder upon the distant view of the old Arab fort, and the long-drawn white scar of the empty beach where the waves pounded night and day. The dunes had folded themselves hereabouts into a long shapely valley which his imagination had already begun to people with clicking palm-trees and the green figs which, as always near running water, offer a shade so deep as to be like a wet cloth pressed to the skull. For a year he had allowed the spot to mature in his imagination, riding out frequently to study it in every kind of weather, until he had mastered its properties. He had not spoken of it to anyone, but in the back of his mind had lurked the idea of building a summer pleasure house for Justine—a miniature oasis where she could stable her three Arab thoroughbreds and pass the hottest season of the year in her favourite amusements, bathing and riding.

The spring had been dug out, channelled and gathered into the marble cistern which formed the centre-piece to the little courtyard, paved with rough sandstone, around which the house and stables were to stand. As the water grew so the green grew with it; shade created the prongy abstract shapes of cactus and the bushy exuberance of Indian corn. In time even a melon-bed was achieved—like some rare exile from Persia. A single severe stable in the Arab style turned its back upon the winter sea-wind, while in the form of an L grew up a cluster of store-rooms and small living-rooms with grilled windows and shutters of black iron.

Two or three small bedrooms, no larger than the cells of medieval monks, gave directly into a pleasant oblong central room with a low ceiling, which was both living-and dining-room; at one end a fireplace grew up massive and white, and with decorated lintels suggested by the designs of Arab ceramics. At the other end stood a stone table and stone benches reminiscent of some priory refectory used by desert fathers perhaps. The severity of the room was discountenanced by rich Persian rugs and some tremendous carved chests with gilt ornamentation writhing over their hooked clasps and leather-polished sides. It was all of a controlled simplicity which is the best sort of magnificence. On the severe white-washed walls, whose few grilled windows offered sudden magnificent slotted views of beach and desert, hung a few old trophies of hunting or meditation life: an Arab lance-pennon, a Buddhist *mandala*, a few assegais in exile, a longbow still used for hunting of hares, a yacht-burgee. There were no books save an old Koran with ivory covers and tarnished metal clasps, but several packs of cards lay about on the sills, including the Grand Tarot for amateur divination and a set of Happy Families. In one corner, too, there stood an old samovar to do justice to the one addiction from which they both suffered—tea-drinking.

The work went forward slowly and hesitantly, but when at last, unable to contain his secret any longer, he had taken Justine out to see it, she had been unable to contain her tears as she walked about it, from window to window of the graceful rooms, to snatch now a picture of the emerald sea rolling on the sand, now a sudden whorled picture of the dunes sliding eastward into the sky. Then she had sat down abruptly before the thorn fire in her habit and listened to the soft clear drumming of the sea upon the long beaches mingled with the cough and stamp of the horses in their new stalls beyond the courtyard. It was late autumn, then, and in the moist gathering darkness the fireflies had begun to snatch fitfully, filling them both with pleasure to think that already their oasis had begun to support other life than their own.

What Nessim had begun was now Justine's to complete. The small terrace under the palm-tree was extended towards the east and walled in to hold back the steady sand-drift which, after a winter of wind, would move forward and cover the stones of the courtyard in

six inches of sand. A windbreak of junipers contributed
a dull copper humus of leaf-mould which in time would
become firm soil nourishing first bushes and later other
and taller trees.

She was careful, too, to repay her husband's thoughtfulness by paying a tribute to what was then his ruling
passion—astronomy. At one corner of the L-shaped block
of buildings she laid down a small observatory which
housed a telescope of thirty magnifications. Here Nessim
would sit night after night in the winter, dressed in his
old rust-coloured *abba*, staring gravely at Betelgeuse, or
hovering over books of calculations for all the world like
some medieval soothsayer. Here too their friends could
look at the moon or by altering the angle of the barrel
catch sudden smoky glimpses of the clouds of pearl which
the city always seemed to exhale from afar.

All this, of course, began to stand in need of a
guardian, and it came as no surprise to them when Panayotis arrived and took up his residence in a tiny room
near the stables. This old man with his spade beard and
gimlet-eyes had been for twenty years a secondary schoolteacher at Damanhur. He had taken orders and spent
nine years at the monastery of St. Catherine in Sinai.
What brought him to the oasis it was impossible to tell
for at some stage in his apparently unadventurous life he
had had his tongue cut out of his head. From the signs
he made in response to questions it might seem that he
had been making a pilgrimage on foot to the little shrine
of St. Menas situated to the west when he had stumbled
upon the oasis. At any rate there seemed nothing
fortuitous about his decision to adopt it. He fitted it to
perfection, and for a small salary stayed there all the
year round as watchman and gardener. He was an able-
bodied little old man, active as a spider, and fearfully
jealous of the green things which owed their life to his
industry and care. It was he who coaxed the melon-bed

into life and at last persuaded a vine to start climbing beside the lintel of the central doorway. His laughter was an inarticulate clucking, and he had a shy habit of hiding his face in the tattered sleeve of his old beadle's soutane. His Greek loquacity, dammed up behind his disability, had overflowed into his eyes where it sparkled and danced at the slightest remark or question. What more could anyone ask of life, he seemed to say, than this oasis by the sea?

What more indeed? It was the question that Nessim asked himself repeatedly as the car whimpered towards the desert with hawk-featured Selim motionless at the wheel. Some miles before the Arab fort the road fetches away inland from the coast and to reach the oasis one must swerve aside off the tarmac along an outcrop of stiff flaky dune—like beaten white of egg, glittering and mica-shafted. Here and there where the swaying car threatens to sink its driving-wheels in the dune they always find purchase again on the bed of friable sandstone which forms the backbone to the whole promontory. It was exhilarating to feather this sea of white crispness like a cutter travelling before a following wind.

It had been in Nessim's mind for some time past—the suggestion had originally been Pursewarden's—to repay the devotion of old Panayotis with the only kind of gift the old man would understand and find acceptable: and he carried now in his polished brief-case a dispensation from the Patriarch of Alexandria permitting him to build and endow a small chapel to St. Arsenius in his house. The choice of saint had been, as it always should be, fortuitous. Clea had found an eighteenth-century ikon of him, in pleasing taste, lying among the lumber of a Muski stall in Cairo. She had given it to Justine as a birthday present.

These then were the treasures they unpacked before the restless bargaining eye of the old man. It took them

some time to make him understand for he followed
Arabic indifferently and Nessim knew no Greek. But
looking up at last from the written dispensation he
clasped both hands and threw up his chin with a smile;
he seemed about to founder under the emotions which
beset him. Everything was understood. Now he knew
why Nessim had spent such hours considering the empty
end-stable and sketching on paper. He shook his hands
warmly and made inarticulate clucking-noises. Nessim's
heart went out to him with a kind of malicious envy to
see how wholehearted his pleasure was at this act of
thoughtfulness. From deep inside the *camera obscura*
of the thoughts which filled his mind he studied the old
beadle carefully, as if by intense scrutiny to surprise the
single-heartedness which brought the old man happiness, peace of mind.

Here at least, thought Nessim, building something
with my own hands will keep me stable and unreflective
—and he studied the horny old hands of the Greek
with admiring envy as he thought of the time they had
killed for him, of the thinking they had saved him. He
read into them years of healthy bodily activity which
imprisoned thought, neutralized reflection. And yet . . .
who could say? Those long years of school-teaching: the
years in the monastery: and now the long winter solitude
which closed in around the oasis, when only the boom
and slither of the sea and the whacking of palm-fronds
were there to accompany one's thoughts. . . . There is
always time for spiritual crises, he thought, as he doggedly mixed cement and dry sand in a wooden mortar.

But even here he was not to be left alone for Justine,
with that maddening guilty solicitude which she had
come to feel for the man whom she loved, and yet was
trying to destroy, appeared with her trio of Arabs and
took up her summer quarters at the oasis. A restless,
moody, alert familiar. And then I, impelled by the fear-

ful pangs her absence created in me, smuggled a note to her telling her either that she must return to the city or persuade Nessim to invite me out to the Summer Palace. Selim duly arrived with the car and motored me out in a sympathetic silence into which he did not dare to inject the slightest trace of contempt.

For his part Nessim received me with a studied tenderness; in fact, he was glad to see us again at close quarters, to detach us from the fictitious framework of his agents' reports and to judge for himself if we were . . . what am I to say? "In love"? The word implies a totality which was missing in my mistress, who resembled one of those ancient Goddesses in that her attributes proliferated through her life and were not condensed about a single quality of heart which one could love or unlove. "Possession" is on the other hand too strong: we were human beings not Brontë cartoons. But English lacks the distinctions which might give us (as Modern Greek does) a word for passion-love.

Apart from all this, not knowing the content and direction of Nessim's thoughts I could in no way set his inmost fears at rest: by telling him that Justine was merely working out with me the same obsessive pattern she had followed out in the pages of Arnauti. She was creating a desire of the will which, since it fed secretly on itself, must be exhausted like a lamp—or blown out. I knew this with only a part of my mind: but there I detected the true lack in this union. It was not based on any repose of the will. And yet how magically she seemed to live—a mistress so full of wit and incantation that one wondered how one had ever managed to love before and be content in the quality of the loving.

At the same time I was astonished to realize that the side of me which clave to Melissa was living its own autonomous existence, quietly and surely belonging to her yet not wishing her back. The letters she wrote me were

gay and full and unmarred by any shadow of reproof or
self-pity; I found in all she wrote an enlargement of her
self-confidence. She described the little sanatorium where
she was lodged with humour and a nimble eye, describing the doctors and the other patients as a holidaymaker
might. On paper she seemed to have grown, to have become another woman. I answered her as well as I was
able but it was hard to disguise the shiftless confusion
which reigned in my life; it was equally impossible to
allude to my obsession with Justine—we were moving
through a different world of flowers and books and ideas,
a world quite foreign to Melissa. Environment had closed
the gates to her, not lack of sensibility. "Poverty is a
great cutter-off," said Justine once, "and riches a great
shutter-off." But she had gained admittance to both
worlds, the world of want and the world of plenty, and
was consequently free to live naturally.

But here at least in the oasis one had the illusion of a
beatitude which eluded one in town life. We rose early
and worked on the chapel until the heat of the day began, when Nessim retired to his business papers in the
little observatory and Justine and I rode down the feathery dunes to the sea to spend our time in swimming and
talking. About a mile from the oasis the sea had pushed
up a great coarse roundel of sand which formed a shal-
low-water lagoon beside which, tucked into the pectoral
curve of a dune, stood a reed hut roofed with leaves,
which offered the bather shade and a changing-place.
Here we spent most of the day together. The news of
Pursewarden's death was still fresh, I remember, and we
discussed him with a warmth and awe, as if for the first
time we were seriously trying to evaluate a character
whose qualities had masked its real nature. It was as if
in dying he had cast off from his earthly character, and
taken on some of the grandiose proportions of his own
writings, which swam more and more into view as the

memory of the man itself faded. Death provided a new
critical referent, and a new mental stature to the tiresome, brilliant, ineffectual and often tedious man with
whom we had had to cope. He was only to be seen now
through the distorting mirror of anecdote or the dusty
spectrum of memory. Later I was to hear people ask
whether Pursewarden had been tall or short, whether he
had worn a moustache or not: and these simple
memories were the hardest to recover and to be sure of.
Some who had known him well said his eyes had been
green, others that they had been brown. . . . It was
amazing how quickly the human image was dissolving
into the mythical image he had created of himself in
his trilogy GOD IS A HUMORIST.

Here, in these days of blinding sun-light, we talked of
him like people anxious to capture and fix the human
memory before it quite shaded into the growing myth;
we talked of him, confirming and denying and comparing, like secret agents rehearsing a cover story, for
after all the fallible human being had belonged to *us*,
the myth belonged to the world. It was now too that I
learned of him saying, one night to Justine, as they
watched Melissa dance: "If I thought there were any
hope of success I would propose marriage to her tomorrow. But she is so ignorant and her mind is so deformed
by poverty and bad luck that she would refuse out of
incredulity."

But step by step behind us Nessim followed with his
fears. One day I found the word "Beware" ($\Pi\rho\sigma\sigma\chi\tilde{\eta}$)
written in the sand with a stick at the bathing-place. The
Greek word suggested the hand of Panayotis but Selim
also knew Greek well.

This further warning was given point for me by an
incident which occurred very shortly afterwards when, in
search of a sheet of notepaper on which to write to Melissa, I strayed into Nessim's little observatory and rum-

maged about on his desk for what I needed. I happened
to notice that the telescope barrel had been canted down-
wards so that it no longer pointed at the sky but across
the dunes towards where the city slumbered in its misty
reaches of pearl cloud. This was not unusual, for trying
to catch glimpses of the highest minarets as the airs condensed and shifted was a favourite pastime. I sat on the
three-legged stool and placed my eye to the eye-piece, to
allow the faintly trembling and vibrating image of the
landscape to assemble for me. Despite the firm stone base
on which the tripod stood the high magnification of the
lens and the heat haze between them contributed a
feathery vibration to the image which gave the landscape the appearance of breathing softly and irregularly.
I was astonished to see—quivering and jumping, yet
pin-point clear—the little reed hut where not an hour
since Justine and I had been lying in each other's arms,
talking of Pursewarden. A brilliant yellow patch on the
dune showed up the cover of a pocket *King Lear* which
I had taken out with me and forgotten to bring back;
had the image not trembled so I do not doubt but that
I should have been able to read the title on the cover. I
stared at this image breathlessly for a long moment and
became afraid. It was as if, all of a sudden, in a dark but
familiar room one believed was empty a hand had suddenly reached out and placed itself on one's shoulder. I
tip-toed from the observatory with the writing pad and
pencil and sat in the arm-chair looking out at the sea,
wondering what I could say to Melissa.

* * * * *

That autumn, when we struck camp and returned to
the city for its winter season, nothing had been decided;
the feeling of crisis had even diminished. We were all
held there, so to speak, in the misty solution of every-
day life out of which futurity was to crystallize whatever

drama lay ahead. I was called upon to begin my new job for Scobie and addressed myself helplessly to the wretched *boustrophedon* upon which Balthazar continued to instruct me, in between bouts of chess. I admit that I tried to allay my pangs of conscience in the matter by trying at first to tell Scobie's office the truth—namely that the Cabal was a harmless sect devoted to Hermetic philosophy and that its activities bore no reference to espionage. In answer to this I was curtly told that I must not believe their obvious cover-story but must try to break the code. Detailed reports of the meetings were called for and these I duly supplied, typing out Balthazar's discourses on Ammon and Hermes Trismegistus with a certain peevish pleasure, imagining as I did so the jaded government servants who would have to wade through the stuff in damp basements a thousand miles away. But I was paid and paid well; for the first time I was able to send Melissa a little money and to make some attempt to pay Justine what I owed her.

It was interesting, too, to discover which of my acquaintances were really part of the espionage grape-vine. Mnemjian, for example, was one; his shop was a clearing-post for general intelligence concerning the city, and was admirably chosen. He performed his duties with tremendous care and discretion, and insisted on shaving me free of charge; it was disheartening to learn much later on that he patiently copied out his intelligence summaries in triplicate and sold copies to various other intelligence services.

Another interesting aspect of the work was that one had the power to order raids to be made on the house of one's friends. I enjoyed very much having Pombal's apartment raided. The poor fellow had a calamitous habit of bringing official files home to work on in the evening. We captured a whole set of papers which delighted Scobie for they contained detailed memoranda upon French in-

fluence in Syria, and a list of French agents in the city.
I noticed on one of these lists the name of the old furrier, Cohen.

Pombal was badly shaken by this raid and went about
looking over his shoulder for nearly a month afterwards,
convinced that he was being shadowed. He also developed the delusion that one-eyed Hamid had been paid
to poison him and would only eat food cooked at home
after I had first tasted it. He was still waiting for his cross
and his transfer and was very much afraid that the loss
of the files would prejudice both, but as we had thoughtfully left him the classification-covers he was able to return them to their series with a minute to say that they
had been burnt "according to instructions."

He had been having no small success lately with his
carefully graduated cocktail-parties—into which he occasionally introduced guests from the humbler spheres
of life like prostitution or the arts. But the expense and
boredom were excruciating and I remember him explaining to me once, in tones of misery, the origin of
these functions. "The cocktail-party—as the name itself
indicates—was originally invented by dogs. They are
simply bottom-sniffings raised to the rank of formal cere-
monies." Nevertheless he persevered in them and was
rewarded by the favours of his Consul-General whom,
despite his contempt, he still regarded with a certain
childish awe. He even persuaded Justine, after much
humourous pleading, to put in an appearance at one of
these functions in order to further his plans for crucifixion. This gave us a chance to study Pordre and the
small diplomatic circle of Alexandria—for the most part
people who gave the impression of being painted with
an air-brush, so etiolated and diffused did their official
personalities seem to me.

Pordre himself was a whim rather than a man. He was
born to be a cartoonist's butt. He had a long pale spoiled

face, set off by a splendid head of silver hair which he used to affect. But it was a lackey's countenance. The falseness of his gestures (his exaggerated solicitude and friendship for the merest acquaintances) grated disagreeably and enabled me to understand both the motto my friend had composed for the French Foreign Office and also the epitaph which he once told me should be placed on the tomb of his Chief. ("His mediocrity was his salvation.") All this, of course, was some years before Pordre became famous through his negotiations over the French Fleet. I cannot believe however that the person, such as it was, suffered any change: his character was as thin as a single skin of goldleaf—the veneer of culture which diplomats are in a better position to acquire than most men.

The party went off to perfection, and a dinner invitation from Nessim threw the old diplomat into a transport of pleasure which was not feigned. It was well known that the King was a frequent guest at Nessim's table and the old man was already writing a despatch in his mind which began with the words: "Dining with the King last week I brought the conversation round to the question of. . . . He said. . . . I replied. . . ." His lips began to move, his eyes to unfocus themselves, as he retired into one of those public trances for which he was famous, and from which he would awake with a start to astonish his interlocutors with a silly cod's smile of apology.

For my part I found it strange to revisit the little tank-like flat where I had passed nearly two years of my life; to recall that it was here, in this very room, that I had first encountered Melissa. It had undergone a great transformation at the hands of Pombal's latest mistress. She had insisted upon its being panelled and painted off-white with a maroon skirting-board. The old arm-chairs whose stuffing used to leak slowly out of the rents in their sides had been re-upholstered in some heavy damask material with a pattern of *fleur-de-lis* while the three ancient sofas had been banished completely to make floor-space. No doubt they had been sold or broken up. "Somewhere," I thought in quotation from a poem by the old poet, "somewhere those wretched old things must still be knocking about." How grudging memory is, and how bitterly she clutches the raw material of her daily work.

Pombal's gaunt bedroom had become vaguely *fin de siècle* and was as clean as a new pin. Oscar Wilde might have admitted it as a set for the first act of a play. My own room had reverted once more to a box-room, but the bed was still there standing against the wall by the iron sink. The yellow curtain had of course disappeared and had been replaced by a drab piece of white cloth. I put my hand to the rusted iron frame of the old bed and was stabbed to the heart by the memory of Melissa turning her candid eyes upon me in the dusky half-light of the little room. I was ashamed and surprised by my grief. And when Justine came into the room behind me I kicked the door shut and immediately began to kiss her lips and hair and forehead, squeezing her almost breathless in my arms lest she should surprise the tears in my eyes. But she knew at once, and returning my kisses with that wonderful ardour that only friendship can give to our actions, she murmured: "I know. I know."

Then softly disengaging herself she led me out of the room and closed the door behind us. "I must tell you about Nessim," she said in a low voice. "Listen to me. On Wednesday, the day before we left the Summer Palace, I went for a ride alone by the sea. There was a big flight of herring-gulls over the shoreline and all of a sudden I saw the car in the distance rolling and scrambling down the dunes towards the sea with Selim at the wheel. I couldn't make out what they were doing. Nessim was in the back. I thought she would surely get stuck, but no: they raced down to the water's edge where the sand was firm and began to speed along the shore towards me. I was not on the beach but in a hollow about fifty yards from the sea. As they came racing level with me and the gulls rose I saw that Nessim had the old repeating-gun in his hands. He raised it and fired again and again into the cloud of gulls, until the magazine was exhausted. Three or four fell fluttering into the sea, but the car did not stop. They were past me in a flash. There must have been a way back from the long beach to the sandstone and so back on to the main road because when I rode in half an hour later the car was back. Nessim was in his observatory. The door was locked and he said he was busy. I asked Selim the meaning of this scene and he simply shrugged his shoulders and pointed at Nessim's door. 'He gave me the orders,' was all he said. But, my dear, if you had seen Nessim's face as he raised the gun. . . ." And thinking of it she involuntarily raised her long fingers to her own cheeks as if to adjust the expression on her own face. "He looked mad."

In the other room they were talking politely of world politics and the situation in Germany. Nessim had perched himself gracefully on Pordre's chair. Pombal was swallowing yawns which kept returning distressingly enough in the form of belches. My mind was still full of Melissa. I had sent her some money that afternoon and the thought of her buying herself some fine clothes—or even spending it in some foolish way—warmed me. "Money," Pombal was saying playfully to an elderly woman who had the appearance of a contrite camel. "One should always make sure of a supply. For only with money can one make more money. Madame certainly knows the Arabic proverb which says: 'Riches can buy riches, but poverty will scarcely buy one a leper's kiss.' "

"We must go," said Justine, and staring into her warm

dark eyes as I said good-bye I knew that she divined how full of Melissa my mind was at the moment; it gave her handshake an added warmth and sympathy.

I suppose it was that night, while she was dressing for dinner that Nessim came into her room and addressed her reflection in the spade-shaped mirror. "Justine," he said firmly, "I must ask you not to think that I am going mad or anything like that but—has Balthazar ever been more than a friend to you?" Justine was placing a cigale made of gold on the lobe of her left ear; she looked up at him for a long second before answering in the same level, equable tone: "No, my dear."

"Thank you."

Nessim stared at his own reflection for a long time, boldly, comprehensively. Then he sighed once and took from the waistcoat-pocket of his dress-clothes a little gold key, in the form of an ankh. "I simply cannot think how this came into my possession," he said, blushing deeply and holding it up for her to see. It was the little watch-key whose loss had caused Balthazar so much concern. Justine stared at it and then at her husband with a somewhat startled air. "Where was it?" she said.

"In my stud-box."

Justine went on with her toilette at a slower pace, looking curiously at her husband who for his part went on studying his own features with the same deliberate rational scrutiny. "I must find a way of returning it to him. Perhaps he dropped it at a meeting. But the strange thing is. . . ." He sighed again. "I don't remember." It was clear to them both that he had stolen it. Nessim turned on his heel and said: "I shall wait for you downstairs." As the door closed softly behind him Justine examined the little key with curiosity.

*   *   *   *   *

At this time he had already begun to experience that

great cycle of historical dreams which now replaced the dreams of his childhood in his mind, and into which the City now threw itself—as if at last it had found a responsive subject through which to express the collective desires, the collective wishes, which informed its culture. He would wake to see the towers and minarets printed on the exhausted, dust-powdered sky, and see as if *en montage* on them the giant footprints of the historical memory which lies behind the recollections of individual personality, its mentor and guide: indeed its inventor, since man is only an extension of the spirit of place.

These disturbed him for they were not at all the dreams of the night-hours. They overlapped reality and interrupted his waking mind as if the membrane of his consciousness had been suddenly torn in places to admit them.

Side by side with these giant constructions—Palladian galleries of images drawn from his reading and meditation on his own past and the city's—there came sharper and sharper attacks on unreasoning hatred against the very Justine he had so seldom known, the comforting friend and devoted lover. They were of brief duration but of such fierceness that, rightly regarding them as the obverse of the love he felt for her, he began to fear not for her safety but for his own. He became afraid of shaving, in the sterile white bathroom every morning. Often the little barber noticed tears in the eyes of his subject as he noiselessly spread the white apron over him.

But while the gallery of historical dreams held the foreground of his mind the figures of his friends and acquaintances, palpable and real, walked backwards and forwards among them, among the ruins of classical Alexandria, inhabiting an amazing historical space-time as living personages. Laboriously, like an actuary's clerk he recorded all he saw and felt in his diaries, ordering the impassive Selim to type them out.

He saw the Mouseion, for example, with its sulky, heavily-subsidized artists working to a mental fashion-plate of its founders: and later among the solitaries and wise men the philosopher, patiently wishing the world into a special private state useless to anyone but himself—for at each stage of development each man resumes the whole universe and makes it suitable to his own inner nature: while each thinker, each thought fecundates the whole universe anew.

The inscriptions on the marbles of the Museum murmured to him as he passed like moving lips. Balthazar and Justine were there waiting for him. He had come to meet them, dazzled by the moonlight and drenching shadow of the colonnades. He could hear their voices in the darkness and he thought, as he gave the low whistle which Justine would always recognize as his: "It is mentally vulgar to spend one's time being so certain of first principles as Balthazar is." He heard the elder man saying: "And morality is nothing if it is merely a form of good behaviour."

He walked slowly down through the arches towards them. The marble stones were barred with moonlight and shadow like a zebra. They were sitting on a marble sarcophagus-lid while somewhere in the remorseless darkness of the outer court Pursewarden was walking up and down on the springy turf lazily whistling a phrase from an aria of Donizetti. The gold cigales at Justine's ears transformed her at once into a projection from one of his dreams and indeed he saw them both dressed vaguely in robes carved heavily of moonlight. Balthazar in a voice tortured by the paradox which lies at the heart of all religion was saying: "Of course in one sense even to preach the gospel is evil. This is one of the absurdities of human logic. At least it is not the gospel but the preaching which involves us with the powers of

darkness. That is why the Cabal is so good for us; it posits
nothing beyond a science of Right Attention."

They had made room for him on their marble perch
but here again, before he could reach them the fulcrum
of his vision was disturbed and other scenes gravely intervened, disregarding congruence and period, disregarding historic time and common probability.

He saw so clearly the shrine the infantry built to
Aphrodite of the Pigeons on that desolate alluvial coast.
They were hungry. The march had driven them all to
extremities, sharpening the vision of death which inhabits the soldier's soul until it shone before them with
an unbearable exactness and magnificence. Baggage-
animals dying for lack of fodder and men for lack of
water. They dared not pause at the poisoned springs and
wells. The wild asses, loitering so exasperatingly just out
of bowshot, maddened them with the promise of meat
they would never secure as the column evolved across the
sparse vegetation of that thorny coast. They were supposed to be marching upon the city despite the omens.
The infantry marched in undress though they knew it
to be madness. Their weapons followed them in carts
which were always lagging. The column left behind it
the sour smell of unwashed bodies—sweat and the stale
of oxen: Macedonian slingers-of-the-line farting like
goats.

Their enemies were of a breath-taking elegance—
cavalry in white armour which formed and dissolved
across the route of their march like clouds. At close range
one saw they were men in purple cloaks, embroidered
tunics and narrow silk trousers. They wore gold chains
round their intricate dark necks and bracelets on their
javelin-arms. They were as desirable as a flock of women.
Their voices were high and fresh. What a contrast they
offered to the slingers, case-hardened veterans of the
line, conscious only of winters which froze their sandals

to their feet or summers whose sweat dried the leather underfoot until it became as hard as dry marble. A gold bounty and not passion had entrained them in this adventure which they bore with the stoicism of all wage-earners. Life had become a sexless strap sinking deeper and ever deeper into the flesh. The sun had parched and cured them and the dust had rendered them voiceless. The brave plumed helmets which they had been issued were too hot to wear at midday. Africa, which they had somehow visualized as an extension of Europe—an extension of terms, of references to a definitive past—had already asserted itself as something different: a forbidding darkness where the croaking of ravens matched the dry exclamations of spiritless men, and rationed laughter fashioned from breath simply the chittering of baboons.

Sometimes they captured someone—a solitary frightened man out hunting hares—and were amazed to see that he was human like themselves. They stripped his rags and stared at human genitals with an elaborate uncomprehending interest. Sometimes they despoiled a township or a rich man's estate in the foothills, to dine on pickled dolphin in jars (drunken soldiers feasting in a barn among the oxen, unsteadily wearing garlands of wild nettles and drinking from captured cups of gold or horn). All this was before they even reached the desert. . . .

Where the paths had crossed they had sacrificed to Heracles (and in the same breath murdered the two guides, just to be on the safe side); but from that moment everything had begun to go wrong. Secretly they knew they would never reach the city and invest it. And God! Never let that winter bivouac in the hills be repeated. The fingers and noses lost by frostbite! The raids! In his memory's memory he could still hear the squeaking munching noise of the sentry's footsteps all winter in the snow. In this territory the enemy wore fox-

skins on their heads in a ravenous peak and long hide
tunics which covered their legs. They were silent, belonging uniquely as the vegetation did to these sharp
ravines and breath-stopping paths of the great water-
shed.

With a column on the march memory becomes an
industry, manufacturing dreams which common ills unite
in a community of ideas based on privation. He knew
that the quiet man there was thinking of the rose found
in her bed on the day of the Games. Another could not
forget the man with the torn ear. The wry scholar
pressed into service felt as dulled by battle as a chamber-
pot at a symposium. And the very fat man who retained
the curious personal odour of a baby; the joker whose
sallies kept the vanguard in a roar? He was thinking of a
new depilatory from Egypt, of a bed trade-marked
Heracles for softness, of white doves with clipped wings
fluttering round a banqueting-table. All his life he had
been greeted at the brothel door by shouts of laughter
and a hail of slippers. There were others who dreamed
of less common pleasures—hair dusty with white lead,
or else schoolboys in naked ranks marching two abreast
at dawn to the school of the Harpmaster, through falling
snow as thick as meal. At vulgar country Dionysia they
carried amid roars the giant leather phallus, but once
initiated took the proffered salt and the phallus in trembling silence. Their dreams proliferated in him, and
hearing them he opened memory to his consciousness
royally, prodigally, as one might open a major artery.

It was strange to move to Justine's side in that brindled
autumn moonlight across such an unwholesome tide of
memories: he felt his physical body displacing them by
its sheer weight and density. Balthazar had moved to
give him room and he was continuing to talk to his wife
in low tones. (They drank the wine solemnly and
sprinkled the lees on their garments. The generals had

just told them they would never get through, never find
the city.) And he remembered so vividly how Justine,
after making love, would sit cross-legged on the bed and
begin to lay out the little pack of Tarot cards which were
always kept on the shelf among the books—as if to com-
pute the degree of good fortune left them after this
latest plunge into the icy underground river of passion
which she could neither subdue nor slake. ("Minds
dismembered by their sexual part," Balthazar had said
once, "never find peace until old age and failing powers
persuade them that silence and quietness are not hos-
tile.")

Was all the discordance of their lives a measure of the
anxiety which they had inherited from the city or the
age? "O my God," he almost said, "why don't we leave
this city, Justine, and seek an atmosphere less impregnated with the sense of deracination and failure?" The
words of the old poet came into his mind, pressed down
like the pedal of a piano, to boil and reverberate around
the frail hope which the thought had raised from its dark
sleep.

> *There's no new land, my friend, no new sea,*
> *For the city will follow you: in the same*
> *Streets entangle endlessly, the same*
> *Mental suburbs slip from youth to age,*
> *In the same house go white at last—*
> *The city is a cage.*
> *No better landfall waits for you but this,*
> *No ship to take you— Ah! can you not see*
> *How just as your whole life you've spoiled*
> *In this one spot, you've ruined its worth*
> *Everywhere now over the whole earth?*

"My problem," he said to himself quietly, feeling his
forehead to see if he had a fever, "is that the woman I

loved brought me a faultless satisfaction which never
touched her own happiness;" and he thought over all
the delusions which were now confirming themselves in
physical signs. I mean: he had beaten Justine, beaten
her until his arm ached and the stick broke in his hands.
All this was a dream of course. Nevertheless on waking
he had found his whole arm aching and swollen. What
could one believe when reality mocked the imagination
by its performance?

At the same time, of course, he fully recognized that
suffering, indeed all illness, was itself an acute form of
self-importance, and all the teachings of the Cabal came
like a following wind to swell his self-contempt. He
could hear, like the distant reverberations of the city's
memory, the voice of Plotinus speaking, not of flight
away from intolerable temporal conditions but towards
a new light, a new city of Light. "This is no journey for
the feet, however. Look into yourself, withdraw into
yourself and look." But this was the one act of which he
now knew himself forever incapable.

It is astonishing for me, in recording these passages to
recall how little of all this interior change was visible on
the surface of his life—even to those who knew him in-
timately. There was little to put one's finger on—only a
sense of hollowness in the familiar—as of a well-known
air played slightly out of key. It is true that at this period
he had already begun to entertain with a prodigality
hitherto unknown to the city, even among the richest
families. The great house was never empty now. The
great kitchen-quarters where we so often boiled ourselves an egg or a glass of milk after a concert or a play
—dusty and deserted then—were now held by a permanent garrison of cooks, surgical and histrionic, capped in
floury steeples. The upper rooms, tall staircase, galleries
and salons echoing to the mournful twining of clocks
were patrolled now by black slaves who moved as regally

as swans about important tasks. Their white linen, smelling of the goose-iron, was spotless—robes divided by scarlet sashes punctuated at the waist by clasps of gold fashioned into turtles' heads: the rebus Nessim had chosen for himself. Their soft porpoise eyes were topped by the conventional scarlet flower-pots, their gorilla hands were cased in white gloves. They were as soundless as death itself.

If he had not so far outdone the great figures of Egyptian society in lavishness he might have been thought to be competing with them for advancement. The house was perpetually alive to the cool fern-like patterns of a quartet, or to the foundering plunge of saxophones crying to the night like cuckolds.

The long beautiful reception-rooms had been pierced with alcoves and unexpected corners to increase their already great seating-capacity and sometimes as many as two or three hundred guests sat down to elaborate and meaningless dinners—observing their host lost in the contemplation of a rose lying upon an empty plate before him. Yet his was not a remarkable distraction for he could offer to the nonentities of common conversation a smile—surprising as one who removes an upturned glass to show, hidden by it, some rare entomological creature whose scientific name he had not learned.

What else is there to add? The small extravagances of his dress were hardly noticeable in one whose fortune had always seemed oddly matched against a taste for old flannel trousers and tweed coats. Now in his ice-smooth sharkskin with the scarlet cummerbund he seemed only what he should always have been—the richest and most handsome of the city's bankers: those true foundlings of the gut. People felt that at last he had come into his own. This was how someone of his place and fortune should live. Only the diplomatic corps smelt in this new prodigality a run of hidden motives, a plot perhaps to capture the King, and began to haunt his drawing-room with their studied politenesses. Under the slothful or foppish faces one was conscious of curiosity stirring, a desire to study Nessim's motives and designs, for nowadays the King was a frequent visitor to the great house.

Meanwhile all this advanced the central situation not at all. It was as if the action which Nessim had been contemplating grew with such infinite slowness, like a stalactite, that there was time for all this to fill the interval—the rockets ploughing their furrows of sparks across the velvet sky, piercing deeper and ever deeper into the night where Justine and I lay, locked in each other's arms and minds. In the still water of the fountains one saw the splash of human faces, ignited by these gold and scarlet stars as they rose hissing into heaven like thirsty swans. In the darkness, her warm hand on my arm, I could watch the autumn sky thrown into convulsions of coloured light with the calm of someone for whom the whole unmerited pain of the human world had receded and diffused itself—as pain does when it goes on too long, spreading from a specific member to flood a whole area of the body or the mind. The lovely grooves of the rockets upon the dark sky filled us only with the sense of a breath-taking congruence to the whole nature of the world of love which was soon to relinquish us.

This particular night was full of a rare summer lightning; and hardly had the display ended when from the desert to the east a thin crust of thunder formed like a scab upon the melodious silence. A light rain fell, youthful and refreshing, and all at once the darkness was full of figures hurrying back into the shelter of the lamplit houses, dresses held ankle-high and voices raised in shrill pleasure. The lamps printed for a second their bare bodies against the transparent materials which sheathed them. For our part we turned wordlessly into the alcove behind the sweet-smelling box-hedges and lay down

upon the stone bench carved in the shape of a swan. The
laughing chattering crowd poured across the entrance
of the alcove towards the light; we lay in the cradle of
darkness feeling the gentle prickle of the rain upon our
faces. The last fuses were being defiantly lit by men in
dinner-jackets and through her hair I saw the last pale
comets gliding up into the darkness. I tasted, with the
glowing pleasure of the colour in my brain, the warm
guiltless pressure of her tongue upon mine, her arms
upon mine. The magnitude of this happiness—we could
not speak but gazed abundantly at each other with eyes
full of unshed tears.

From the house came the dry snap of champagne-corks
and the laughter of human beings. "Never an evening
alone now."

"What is happening to Nessim?"

"I no longer know. When there is something to hide
one becomes an actor. It forces all the people round one
to act as well."

The same man, it was true, walked about on the surface of their common life—the same considerate, gentle
punctual man: but in a horrifying sense everything had
changed, he was no longer there. "We've abandoned
each other," she said in a small expiring whisper and
drawing herself closer pressed to the very hilt of sense
and sound the kisses which were like summaries of all we
had shared, held precariously for a moment in our
hands, before they should overflow into the surrounding darkness and forsake us. And yet it was as if in every
embrace she were saying to herself: "Perhaps through
this very thing, which hurts so much and which I do not
want ever to end—maybe through this I shall find my
way back to Nessim." I was filled suddenly by an intolerable depression.

Later, walking about in the strident native quarter
with its jabbing lights and flesh-wearing smells, I won-

dered as I had always wondered, where time was leading us. And as if to test the validity of the very emotions upon which so much love and anxiety could base themselves I turned into a lighted booth decorated by a strip of cinema poster—the huge half-face of a screen-lover, meaningless as the belly of a whale turned upwards in death—and sat down upon the customer's stool, as one might in a barber's shop, to wait my turn. A dirty curtain was drawn across the inner door and from behind it came faint sounds, as of the congress of creatures unknown to science, not specially revolting—indeed interesting as the natural sciences are for those who have abandoned any claims of cultivating a sensibility. I was of course drunk by this time and exhausted—drunk as much on Justine as upon the thin-paper-bodied *Pol Roget.*

There was a tarbush lying upon the chair beside me and absently I put it on my head. It was faintly warm and sticky inside and the thick leather lining clung to my forehead. "I want to know what it really means," I told myself in a mirror whose cracks had been pasted over with the trimmings of postage stamps. I meant of course the whole portentous scrimmage of sex itself, the act of penetration which could lead a man to despair for the sake of a creature with two breasts and *le croissant* as the picturesque Levant slang has it. The sound within had increased to a sly groaning and squeaking—a combustible human voice adding itself to the jostling of an ancient wooden-slatted bed. This was presumably the identical undifferentiated act which Justine and I shared with the common world to which we belonged. How did it differ? How far had our feelings carried us from the truth of the simple, devoid beast-like act itself? To what extent was the treacherous mind—with its interminable *catalogue raisonné* of the heart—responsible? I wished to answer an unanswerable question; but I was so des-

perate for certainty that it seemed to me that if I surprised the act in its natural state, motivated by scientific
money and not love, as yet undamaged by the idea, I
might surprise the truth of my own feelings and desires.
Impatient to deliver myself from the question I lifted
the curtain and stepped softly into the cubicle which was
fitfully lighted by a buzzing staggering paraffin lamp
turned down low.

The bed was inhabited by an indistinct mass of flesh
moving in many places at once, vaguely stirring like an
ant-heap. It took me some moments to define the pale
and hairy limbs of an elderly man from those of his partner—the greenish-hued whiteness of convex woman
with a boa-constrictor's head—a head crowned with
spokes of toiling black hair which trailed over the edges
of the filthy mattress. My sudden appearance must have
suggested a police raid for it was followed by a gasp and
complete silence. It was as if the ant-hill had suddenly
become deserted. The man gave a groan and a startled
half-glance in my direction and then as if to escape de-
tection buried his head between the immense breasts of
the woman. It was impossible to explain to them that I
was investigating nothing more particular than the act
upon which they were engaged. I advanced to the bed
firmly, apologetically, and with what must have seemed
a vaguely scientific air of detachment I took the rusty
bed-rail in my hands and stared down, not upon them
for I was hardly conscious of their existence, but upon
myself and Melissa, myself and Justine. The woman
turned a pair of large gauche charcoal eyes upon me and
said something in Arabic.

They lay there like the victims of some terrible accident, clumsily engaged, as if in some incoherent experimental fashion they were the first partners in the
history of the human race to think out this peculiar
means of communication. Their posture, so ludicrous

and ill-planned, seemed the result of some early trial which might, after centuries of experiment, evolve into a disposition of bodies as breathlessly congruent as a ballet-position. But nevertheless I recognized that this had been fixed immutably, for all time—this eternally tragic and ludicrous position of engagement. From this sprang all those aspects of love which the wit of poets and madmen had used to elaborate their philosophy of polite distinctions. From this point the sick, the insane started growing; and from here too the disgusted and dispirited faces of the long-married, tied to each other back to back, so to speak, like dogs unable to disengage after coupling.

The peal of soft cracked laughter I uttered surprised me, but it reassured my specimens. The man raised his face a few inches and listened attentively as if to assure himself that no policeman could have uttered such a laugh. The woman re-explained me to herself and smiled. "Wait one moment," she cried, waving a white blotched hand in the direction of the curtain. "I will not be long." And the man, as if reprimanded by her tone, made a few convulsive movements, like a paralytic attempting to walk—impelled not by the demands of pleasure but by the purest courtesy. His expression betrayed an access of politeness—as of someone rising in a crowded tram to surrender his place to a *mutilé de la guerre*. The woman grunted and her fingers curled up at the edges.

Leaving them there, fitted so clumsily together, I stepped laughing out into the street once more to make a circuit of the quarter which still hummed with the derisive, concrete life of men and women. The rain had stopped and the damp ground exhaled the tormentingly lovely scent of clay, bodies and stale jasmine. I began to walk slowly, deeply bemused, and to describe to myself in words this whole quarter of Alexandria for I knew

that soon it would be forgotten and revisited only by
those whose memories had been appropriated by the
fevered city, clinging to the minds of old men like traces
of perfume upon a sleeve: Alexandria, the capital of
Memory.

The narrow street was of baked and scented terra
cotta, soft now from rain but not wet. Its whole length
was lined with the coloured booths of prostitutes whose
thrilling marble bodies were posed modestly each before her doll's house, as before a shrine. They sat on
three-legged stools like oracles wearing coloured slippers,
out in the open street. The originality of the lighting
gave the whole scene the colours of deathless romance,
for instead of being lit from above by electric light the
whole street was lit by a series of stabbing carbide-lamps
standing upon the ground: throwing thirsty, ravishing
violet shadows upwards into the nooks and gables of
the dolls' houses, into the nostrils and eyes of its inhabitants, into the unresisting softness of that furry darkness. I walked slowly among these extraordinary human
blooms, reflecting that a city like a human being collects
its predispositions, appetites and fears. It grows to maturity, utters its prophets, and declines into hebetude, old
age or the loneliness which is worse than either. Unaware that their mother city was dying, the living still
sat there in the open street, like caryatids supporting
the darkness, the pains of futurity upon their very eye-
lids; sleeplessly watching, the immortality-hunters,
throughout the whole fatidic length of time.

Here was a painted booth entirely decorated by
fleur-de-lis carefully and correctly drawn upon a peach-
coloured ground in royal blue. At its door sat a giant
bluish child of a Negress, perhaps eighteen years of
age, clad in a red flannel nightgown of a vaguely mis-
sion-house *allure*. She wore a crown of dazzling narcissus
on her black woollen head. Her hands were gathered

humbly in her lap—an apron full of chopped fingers. She resembled a heavenly black bunny sitting at the entrance of a burrow. Next door a woman fragile as a leaf, and next her one like a chemical formula rinsed out by anaemia and cigarette smoke. Everywhere on these brown flapping walls I saw the basic talisman of the country—imprint of a palm with outspread fingers, seeking to ward off the terrors which thronged the darkness outside the lighted town. As I walked past them now they uttered, not human monetary cries, but the soft cooing propositions of doves, their quiet voices filling the street with a cloistral calm. It was not sex they offered in their monotonous seclusion among the yellow flares, but like the true inhabitants of Alexandria, the deep forgetfulness of parturition, compounded of physical pleasures taken without aversion.

The dolls' houses shivered and reeled for a second as the wind of the sea intruded, pressing upon loose fragments of cloth, unfastened partitions. One house lacked any backcloth whatever and staring through the door one caught a glimpse of a courtyard with a stunted palm-tree. By the light thrown out from a bucket of burning shavings three girls sat on stools, dressed in torn kimonos, talking in low tones and extending the tips of their fingers to the elf-light. They seemed as rapt, as remote as if they had been sitting around a camp fire on the steppes.

(In the back of my mind I could see the great banks of ice—snowdrifts in which Nessim's champagne-bottles lay, gleaming bluish-green like aged carp in a familiar pond. And as if to restore my memory I smelt my sleeves for traces of Justine's perfume.)

I turned at last into an empty café where I drank coffee served by a Saidi whose grotesque squint seemed to double every object he gazed upon. In the far corner, curled up on a trunk and so still that she was invisible at

first sat a very old lady smoking a *narguileh* which from
time to time uttered a soft air-bubble of sound like the
voice of a dove. Here I thought the whole story through
from beginning to end, starting in the days before I
ever knew Melissa and ending somewhere soon in an idle
pragmatic death in a city to which I did not belong; I say
that I thought it through, but strangely enough I
thought of it not as a personal history with an individual
accent so much as part of the historical fabric of
the place. I described it to myself as part and parcel of
the city's behaviour, completely in keeping with everything that had gone before, and everything that would
follow it. It was as if my imagination had become subtly
drugged by the ambience of the place and could not respond to personal, individual assessments. I had lost the
capacity to feel even the thrill of danger. My sharpest regret, characteristically enough, was for the jumble of
manuscript notes which might be left behind. I had always hated the incomplete, the fragmentary. I decided
that they at least must be destroyed before I went a step
further. I rose to my feet—only to be struck by a sudden
realization that the man I had seen in the little booth
had been Mnemjian. How was it possible to mistake that
misformed back? This thought occupied me as I re-
crossed the quarter, moving towards the larger thorough-
fares in the direction of the sea. I walked across this mi-
rage of narrow intersecting alleys as one might walk
across a battlefield which had swallowed up all the
friends of one's youth; yet I could not help in delighting
at every scent and sound—a survivor's delight. Here at
one corner stood a flame-swallower with his face turned
up to the sky, spouting a column of flames from his
mouth which turned black with flapping fumes at the
edges and bit a hole in the sky. From time to time he
took a swig at a bottle of petrol before throwing back his
head once more and gushing flames six feet high. At ev-

ery corner the violet shadows fell and foundered, striped
with human experience—at once savage and tenderly
lyrical. I took it as a measure of my maturity that I was
filled no longer with despairing self-pity but with a desire to be claimed by the city, enrolled among its trivial
or tragic memories—if it so wished.

It was equally characteristic that by the time I reached
the little flat and disinterred the grey exercise books in
which my notes had been scribbled I thought no longer
of destroying them. Indeed I sat there in the lamp-light
and added to them while Pombal discoursed on life from
the other easy chair.

"Returning to my room I sit silent, listening to the
heavy tone of her scent: a smell perhaps composed of
flesh, faeces and herbs, all worked into the dense brocade
of her being. This is a peculiar type of love for I do not
feel that I possess her—nor indeed would wish to do so.
It is as if we joined each other only in self-possession,
became partners in a common stage of growth. In fact we
outrage love, for we have proved the bonds of friendship
stronger. These notes, however they may be read, are intended only as a painstaking affectionate commentary on
a world into which I have been born to share my most
solitary moments—those of coitus—with Justine. I can
get no nearer to the truth.

"Recently, when it had been difficult to see her for one
reason or another, I found myself longing so much for
her that I went all the way down to Pietrantoni to try
and buy a bottle of her perfume. In vain. The good-tem-
pered girl-assistant dabbed my hands with every make
she had in stock and once or twice I thought that I had
discovered it. But no. Something was always missing—I
suppose the flesh which the perfume merely costumed.
The undertow of the body itself was the missing factor.
It was only when in desperation I mentioned Justine's

name that the girl turned immediately to the first perfume we had tried. 'Why did you not say so at first?' she
asked with an air of professional hurt; everyone, her
tone implied, knew the perfume Justine used except
myself. It was unrecognizable. Nevertheless I was surprised to discover that *Jamais de la vie* was not among
the most expensive or exotic of perfumes.

"(When I took home the little bottle they found in
Cohen's waistcoat-pocket the wraith of Melissa was still
there, imprisoned. She could still be detected.)"

Pombal was reading aloud the long terrible passage
from *Moeurs* which is called "The Dummy Speaks." In
all these fortuitous collisions with the male animal I had
never known release, no matter what experiences I had
submitted my body to. I always see in the mirror the
image of an ageing fury crying: *"J'ai raté mon propre
amour—mon amour à moi. Mon amour-propre, mon
propre amour. Je l'ai raté. Je n'ai jamais souffert, jamais
eu de joie simple et candid."*

He paused only to say: "If this is true you are only
taking advantage of an illness in loving her," and the
remark struck me like the edge of an axe wielded by
someone of enormous and unconscious strength.

When the time for the great yearly shoot on Lake
Mareotis came round Nessim began to experience a
magical sense of relief. He recognized at last that what
had to be decided would be decided at this time and at
no other. He had the air of a man who has fought a long
illness successfully. Had his judgement indeed been so
faulty even though it had not been conscious? For seven
long years of marriage he had repeated on every day
the words, "I am so happy"—fatal as the striking of a
grandfather-clock upon which silence is forever encroaching. Now he could say so no longer. Their common life was like some cable buried in the sand which,
in some inexplicable way, at a point impossible to dis-

cover, had snapped, plunging them both into an un-accustomed and impenetrable darkness.

The madness itself, of course, took no account of cir-cumstances. It appeared to superimpose itself not upon personalities tortured beyond the bounds of endurance but purely upon a given situation. In a real sense we all shared it, though only Nessim acted it out, exemplified it in the flesh, as a person. The short period which preceded the great shoot on Mareotis lasted for perhaps a month—certainly for very little more. Here again to those who did not know him nothing was obvious. Yet the delusions multiplied themselves at such a rate that in his own rec-ords they give one the illusion of watching bacteria un-der a microscope—the pullulation of healthy cells, as in cancer, which have gone off their heads, renounced their power to repress themselves.

The mysterious series of code messages transmitted by the street names he encountered showed definite irref-utable signs of a supernatural agency at work full of the threat of unseen punishment—though whether for him-self or for others he could not tell. Balthazar's treatise lying withering in the window of a bookshop and the *same day* coming upon his father's grave in the Jewish cemetery—with those distinguishing names engraved upon the stone which echoed all the melancholy of Eu-ropean Jewry in exile.

Then the question of noises in the room next door: a sort of heavy breathing and the sudden simultaneous playing of three pianos. These, he knew, were not de-lusions but links in an occult chain, logical and per-suasive only to the mind which had passed beyond the frame of causality. It was becoming harder and harder to pretend to be sane by the standards of ordinary be-haviour. He was going through the *Devastatio* described by Swedenborg.

The coal fires had taken to burning into extraor-

dinary shapes. This could be proved by relighting
them over again to verify his findings—terrifying land-
scapes and faces. The birth-mark on Justine's wrist was
also troubling. At meal times he fought against his desire
to touch it so feverishly that he turned pale and almost
fainted.

One afternoon a crumpled sheet began breathing and
continued for a space of about half an hour, assuming
the shape of the body it covered. One night he woke to
the soughing of great wings and saw a bat-like creature
with the head of a violin resting upon the bedrail.

Then the counter-agency of the powers of good—a
message brought by a ladybird which settled on the note-
book in which he was writing; the music of Weber's *Pan*
played *every day* between three and four on a piano in
an adjoining house. He felt that his mind had become
a battle-ground for the forces of good and evil and that
his task was to strain every nerve to recognize them, but
it was not easy. The phenomenal world had begun to
play tricks on him so that his senses were beginning to
accuse reality itself of inconsistency. He was in peril of a
mental overthrow.

Once his waistcoat started ticking as it hung on the
back of a chair, as if inhabited by a colony of foreign
heartbeats. But when investigated it stopped and refused
to continue for the benefit of Selim whom he had called
into the room. The same day he saw his initials in gold
upon a cloud reflected in a shop-window in the Rue St.
Saba. *Everything seemed proved by this.*

That same week a stranger was seated in the corner
always reserved for Balthazar in the Café Al Aktar sipping an *arak*—the *arak* he had intended to order. The
figure bore a strong yet distorted resemblance to himself
as he turned in the mirror, unfolding his lips from white
teeth in a smile. He did not wait but hurried to the door.
As he walked the length of Rue Fuad he felt the entire

pavement turn to sponge beneath his feet; he was foundering waist-deep in it before the illusion vanished. At
two-thirty that afternoon he rose from a feverish sleep,
dressed and set off to confirm an overpowering intuition
that both Pastroudi and the Café Dordali were empty.
They were, and the fact filled him with triumphant relief; but it was short-lived, for on returning to his room
he felt all of a sudden as if his heart were being expelled
from his body by the short mechanical movements of
an air-pump. He had come to hate and fear this room of
his. He would stand for a long time listening until the
noise came again—the slither of wires being uncoiled
upon the floor and the noise of some small animal, its
shrieks being stifled, as it was bundled into a bag. Then
distinctly the noise of suitcase-hasps being fastened with
a snap and the breathing of someone who stood against
the wall next door, listening for the least sound. Nessim
removed his shoes and tip-toed to the bay-window in an
attempt to see into the room next door. His assailant, it
seemed to him, was an elderly man, gaunt and sharp-
featured, with the sunk reddish eyes of a bear. He was
unable to confirm this. Then, waking early on the very
morning upon which the invitations for the great shoot
must be issued he saw with horror from the bedroom
window two suspicious-looking men in Arab dress ty-
ing a rope to a sort of windlass on the roof. They pointed
to him and spoke together in low tones. Then they began to lower something heavy, wrapped in a fur coat,
into the open street below. His hands trembled as he
filled in the large white squares of pasteboard with that
flowing script, selecting his names from the huge type-
written list which Selim had left on his desk. Nevertheless he smiled as well when he recalled how large a
space was devoted in the local press each year to this
memorable event—the great shoot on Mareotis. With
so much to occupy him he felt that nothing should be

left to chance and though the solicitous Selim hovered near, he pursed his lips and insisted on attending to all the invitations himself. My own, charged with every presage of disaster, stared at me now from the mantelpiece. I gazed at it, my attention scattered by nicotine and wine, recognizing that here, in some indefinable way, was the solution towards which we all had moved. ("Where science leaves off nerves begin." *Moeurs.*)

"Of course you will refuse. You will not go?" Justine spoke so sharply that I understood that her gaze had followed mine. She stood over me in the misty early morning light, and between sentences cocked an ear towards the heavily-breathing wraith of Hamid behind the door. "You are not to tempt providence. Will you? Answer me." And as if to make persuasion certain she slipped off her skirt and shoes and fell softly into bed beside me— warm hair and mouth, and the treacherous nervous movements of a body which folded against one as if hurt, as if tender from unhealed wounds. It seemed to me then—and the compulsion had nothing of bravado in it—it seemed to me then that I could no longer deprive Nessim of the satisfaction he sought of me, or indeed the situation of its issue. There was, too, underneath it all a vein of relief which made me feel almost gay until I saw the grave sad expression of my companion-in-arms. She lay, staring out of those wonderfully expressive dark eyes, as if from a high window in her own memory. She was looking, I knew, into the eyes of Melissa—into the troubled candid eyes of one who, with every day of increasing danger, moved nearer and nearer to us. After all, the one most to be wounded by the issue Nessim might be contemplating was Melissa—who else? I thought back along the iron chain of kisses which Justine had forged, steadily back into memory, hand over fist, like a mariner going down an anchor-chain into the darkest depths of some great stagnant harbour memory.

From among many sorts of failure each selects the one which least compromises his self-respect: which lets him down the lightest. Mine had been in art, in religion, and in people. In art I had failed (it suddenly occurred to me at this moment) because I did not believe in the discrete human personality. ("Are people," writes Pursewarden, "continuously themselves, or simply over and over again so fast that they give the illusion of continuous features —the temporal flicker of old silent film?") I lacked a belief in the true authenticity of people in order to successfully portray them. In religion? Well, I found no religion worth while which contained the faintest grain of propitiation—and which can escape the charge? *Pace* Balthazar it seemed to me that all churches, all sects, were at the best mere academies of self-instruction against fear. But the last, the worst failure (I buried my lips in the dark living hair of Justine), the failure with people: it had been brought about by a gradually increasing detachment of spirit which, while it freed me to sympathize, forbade me possession. I was gradually, inexplicably, becoming more and more deficient in love, yet better and better at self-giving—the best part of loving. This, I realized with horror, was the hold I now had over Justine. As a woman, a natural possessive, she was doomed to try and capture the part of myself which was forever beyond reach, the last painful refuge of which was, for me, laughter, and friendship. This sort of loving had made her, in a way, desperate for I did not depend on her; and the desire to possess can, if starved, render one absolutely possessed in the spirit oneself. How difficult it is to analyse these relationships which lie under the mere skin of our actions; for loving is only a sort of skin-language, sex a terminology merely.

And further to render down this sad relationship which had caused me so much pain—I saw that pain itself was the only food of memory: for pleasure ends in itself—all they had bequeathed me was a fund of permanent health—life-giving detachment. I was like a dry-cell battery. Uncommitted, I was free to circulate in the world of men and women like a guardian of the true rights of love—which is not passion, nor habit (they only qualify it) but which is the divine trespass of an immortal among mortals—Aphrodite-in-arms. Beleaguered thus, I was nevertheless defined and realized in myself by the very quality which (of course) hurt me most: selflessness. *This* is what Justine loved in me—not my personality. Women are sexual robbers, and it was this treasure of detachment she hoped to steal from me—the jewel growing in the toad's head. It was the signature of this detachment she saw written across my life with all its haphazardness, discordance, disorderliness. My value was not in anything I achieved or anything I owned. Justine loved me because I presented to her something which was indestructible—a person already formed who could not be broken. She was haunted by the feeling that even while I was loving her I was wishing at the same time only to die! This she found unendurable.

And Melissa? She lacked of course the insight of Justine into my case. She only knew that my strength supported her where she was at her weakest—in her dealings with the world. She treasured every sign of my human weakness—disorderly habits, incapacity over money affairs, and so on. She loved my weaknesses because there she felt of use to me; Justine brushed all this aside as unworthy of her interest. She had detected another kind of strength. I interested her only in this one particular which I could not offer her as a gift nor she steal from me. This is what is meant by possession—to be passionately at war for the qualities in one another: to contend for the treasures of each other's personalities. But how can such a war be anything but destructive and hopeless?

And yet, so entangled are human motives: it would be

Melissa herself who had driven Nessim from his refuge
in the world of fantasy towards an action which he knew
we would all bitterly regret—our death. For it was she
who, overmastered by the impulse of her unhappiness
one night, approached the table at which he sat, before
an empty champagne-glass, watching the cabaret with a
pensive air: and blushing and trembling in her false eyelashes, blurted out eight words, *"Your wife is no longer
faithful to you"*—a phrase which stood quivering in his
mind from then on, like a thrown knife. It is true that
for a long time now his dossiers had been swollen with
reports of this dreaded fact but these reports were like
newspaper-accounts of a catastrophe which had occurred a long way off, in a country which one had not visited.
Now he was suddenly face to face with an eye-witness,
a victim, a survivor. . . . The resonance of this one
phrase refecundated his powers of feeling. The whole
dead tract of paper suddenly rose up and screeched
at him.

Melissa's dressing-room was an evil-smelling cubicle
full of the coiled pipes which emptied the lavatories. She
had a single poignant strip of cracked mirror and a little shelf dressed with the kind of white paper upon which
wedding-cakes are built. Here she always set out the jumble of powders and crayons which she misused so fearfully.

In this mirror the image of Selim blistered and
flickered in the dancing gas-jets like a spectre from the
underworld. He spoke with an incisive finish which was
a copy of his master's; in this copied voice she could
feel some of the anxiety the secretary felt for the only
human being he truly worshipped, and to whose anxi-
eties he reacted like a planchette.

Melissa was afraid now, for she knew that offence given
to the great could, by the terms of the city, be punished
swiftly and dreadfully. She was aghast at what she

had done and fought back a desire to cry as she picked
off her eyelashes with trembling hands. There was no
way of refusing the invitation. She dressed in her shabby
best and carrying her fatigue like a heavy pack followed
Selim to the great car which stood in deep shadow. She
was helped in beside Nessim. They moved off slowly into
the dense crepuscular evening of an Alexandria which,
in her panic, she no longer recognized. They scouted a
sea turned to sapphire and turned inland, folding up the
slums, towards Mareotis and the bituminous slag-heaps
of Mex where the pressure of the headlights now peeled
off layer after layer of the darkness, bringing up small
intimate scenes of Egyptian life—a drunkard singing, a
biblical figure on a mule with two children escaping from
Herod, a porter sorting sacks—swiftly, like someone dealing cards. She followed these familiar sights with emotion, for behind lay the desert, its emptiness echoing like
a seashell. All this time her companion had not spoken,
and she had not dared to risk so much as a glance in his
direction.

Now when the pure steely lines of the dunes came up
under the late moon Nessim drew the car to a standstill.
Groping in his pocket for his cheque-book he said in a
trembling voice, his eyes full of tears: "What is the price
of your silence?" She turned to him and, seeing for the
first time the gentleness and sorrow of that dark face,
found her fear replaced by an overwhelming shame. She
recognized in his expression the weakness for the good
which could never render him an enemy of her kind. She
put a timid hand on his arm and said: "I am so ashamed.
Please forgive me. I did not know what I was saying."
And her fatigue overcame her so that her emotion which
threatened her with tears turned to a yawn. Now they
stared at one another with a new understanding, recognizing each other as innocents. For a minute it was almost

as if they had fallen in love with each other from sheer relief.

The car gathered momentum again like their silence —and soon they were racing across the desert towards the steely glitter of stars, and a horizon stained black with the thunder of surf. Nessim, with this strange sleepy creature at his side, found himself thinking over and over again: "Thank God I am not a genius—for a genius has nobody in whom he can confide."

The glances he snatched at her enabled him to study her, and to study me in her. Her loveliness must have disarmed and disturbed him as it had me, for he afterwards described it as a beauty which filled one with the terrible premonition that it had been born to be a target for the forces of destruction. It was with a shock that he remembered an anecdote of Pursewarden's in which she figured, for the latter had found her as Nessim himself had done, in the same stale cabaret; only on this particular evening she had been sitting in a row of dance-hostesses selling dance-tickets. Pursewarden, who was gravely drunk, took her to the floor and, after a moment's silence, addressed her in his sad yet masterful way: *"Comment vous défendez-vous contre la solitude?"* he asked her. Melissa turned upon him an eye replete with all the candour of experience and replied softly: *"Monsieur, je suis devenue la solitude même."* Pursewarden was sufficiently struck to remember and repeat this passage later to his friends, adding: "I suddenly thought to myself that here was a woman one might very well love." Yet he did not take the risk of revisiting her, for the book was going well, and he recognized in the kindling of this sympathy a trick being played on him by the least intent part of his nature. He was writing about love at the time and did not wish to disturb the ideas he had formed on the subject. ("I cannot fall in love," he made a character exclaim, "for I belong to that ancient secret society—the Jokers!"; and elsewhere speaking about his marriage he wrote: "I found that as well as displeasing another I also displeased myself; now, alone, I have only myself to displease. Joy!")

Justine was still standing over me, watching my face as I composed these scorching scenes in my mind. "You will make some excuse," she repeated hoarsely. "You will not go." Selim had been particularly insistent on the point; he had left the room with a single dry sob. It seemed to me impossible to find a way out of this predicament. "How *can* I refuse?" I said. "How can you?"

They had driven across that warm, tideless desert night, Nessim and Melissa, consumed by a sudden sympathy for each other, yet speechless. On the last scrap before Bourg El Arab he switched off the engine and let the car roll off the road. "Come," he said, "I want to show you Justine's Summer Palace."

Hand in hand they took the road to the little house. The caretaker was asleep but he had the key. The rooms smelt damp and uninhabited, but were full of light reflected from the white dunes. It was not long before he had kindled a fire of thorns in the great fireplace, and taking his old *abba* from the cupboard he clothed himself in it and sat down before it saying: "Tell me now, Melissa, who sent you to persecute me?" He meant it as a joke but forgot to smile, and Melissa turned crimson with shame and bit her lip. They sat there for a long time enjoying the firelight and the sensation of sharing something—their common hopelessness.

(Justine stubbed out her cigarette and got slowly out of bed. She began to walk slowly up and down the carpet. Fear had overcome her and I could see that it was only with an effort that she overcame the need for a characteristic outburst. "I have done so many things in my

life," she said to the mirror. "Evil things, perhaps. But
never inattentively, never wastefully. I've always thought
of acts as messages, wishes from the past to the future,
which invited self-discovery. Was I wrong? Was I wrong?"
It was not to me she addressed the question now but to
Nessim. It is so much easier to address questions intended for one's husband to one's lover. "As for the
dead," she went on after a moment, "I have always
thought that the dead think of us as dead. They have re-
joined the living after this trifling excursion into quasi-
life." Hamid was stirring now and she turned to her
clothes in a panic. "So you must go," she said sadly,
"and so must I. You are right. We must go." And then
turning to the mirror to complete her toilet she added:
"Another grey hair," studying that wicked fashionable
face.

Watching her thus, trapped for a moment by a rare
sunbeam on the dirty window-pane, I could not help reflecting once more that in her there was nothing to control or modify the intuition which she had developed
out of a nature gorged upon introspection: no education,
no resources of intellection to battle against the impera-
tives of a violent heart. Her gift was the gift one finds
occasionally in ignorant fortune-tellers. Whatever passed
for thought in her was borrowed—even the remark about the dead which occurs in *Moeurs;* she had
picked out what was significant in books not by reading
them but by listening to the matchless discourses of
Balthazar, Arnauti, Pursewarden, upon them. She was
a walking abstract of the writers and thinkers whom she
had loved or admired—but what clever woman is more?)

Nessim now took Melissa's hands between his own
(they lay there effortless, cool, like wafers) and began to
question her about me with an avidity which might have
easily suggested that his passion was not Justine, but my-

self. One always falls in love with the love-choice of the
person one loves. What would I not give to learn all that
she told him, striking ever more deeply into his sym-
pathies with her candours, her unexpected reserves? All
I know is that she concluded stupidly, "Even now they
are not happy: they quarrel dreadfully: Hamid told me
so when last I met him." Surely she was experienced
enough to recognize in these reported quarrels the very
subject-matter of our love? I think she saw only the sel-
fishness of Justine—that almost deafening lack of interest in other people which characterized my tyrant. She
utterly lacked the charity of mind upon which Melissa's
good opinion alone could be grounded. She was not
really human—nobody wholly dedicated to the ego is.
What on earth could I see in her?—I asked this question
of myself for the thousandth time. Yet Nessim, in beginning to explore and love Melissa as an extension of Justine, delineated perfectly the human situation. Melissa
would hunt in him for the qualities which she imagined
I must have found in his wife. The four of us were un-
recognized complementaries of one another, inextricably
bound together. ("We who have travelled much and
loved much: we who have—I will not say suffered for
we have always recognized through suffering our own
self-sufficiency—only we appreciate the complexities of
tenderness, and understand how narrowly love and
friendship are related." *Moeurs*.)

They talked now as a doomed brother and sister
might, renewing in each other the sense of relief which
comes to those who find someone to share the burden of
unconfessed preoccupations. In all this sympathy an unexpected shadow of desire stirred within them, a wraith
merely, the stepchild of confession and release. It fore-
shadowed, in a way, their own love-making, which was
to come, and which was so much less ugly than ours—
mine and Justine's. Loving is so much truer when sym-

pathy and not desire makes the match; for it leaves no
wounds. It was already dawn when they rose from their
conversation, stiff and cramped, the fire long since out,
and marched across the damp sand to the car, scouting
the pale lavender light of dawn. Melissa had found a
friend and patron; as for Nessim, he was transfigured.
The sensation of a new sympathy had enabled him, magically, to become his own man again—that is to say, a man
who could act (could murder his wife's lover if he so
wished)!

Driving along that pure and natal coastline they
watched the first tendrils of sunlight uncoil from horizon
to horizon across the dark self-sufficient Mediterranean
sea whose edges were at one and the same moment touching lost hallowed Carthage and Salamis in Cyprus.

Presently, where the road dips down among the dunes
to the sea-shore Nessim once more slowed down and involuntarily suggested a swim. Changed as he was he felt
a sudden desire that Melissa should see him naked,
should approve the beauty which for so long had lain,
like a suit of well-cut clothes in an attic cupboard, forgotten.

Naked and laughing, they waded out hand in hand,
into the icy water feeling the tame sunlight glowing on
their backs as they did so. It was like the first morning
since the creation of the world. Melissa, too, had shed
with her clothes the last residual encumbrance of the
flesh, and had become the dancer she truly was; for
nakedness always gave her fulness and balance: the craft
she lacked in the cabaret.

They lay together for a long time in perfect silence,
seeking through the darkness of their feelings for the
way forward. He realized that he had won an instant
compliance from her—that she was now his mistress in
everything.

They set off together for the city, feeling at the same time happy and ill-at-ease—for both felt a kind of hollowness at the heart of their happiness. Yet since they were reluctant to surrender each other to the life which awaited them they lagged, the car lagged, their silence lagged between endearments.

At last Nessim remembered a tumbledown café in Mex where one could find a boiled egg and coffee. Early though it was the sleepy Greek proprietor was awake and set chairs for them under a barren fig-tree in a backyard full of hens and their meagre droppings. All around them towered corrugated iron wharves and factories. The sea was present only as a dank and resonant smell of hot iron and tar.

He set her down at last on the street-corner she named and said good-bye in a "wooden perfunctory" sort of way —afraid perhaps that some of his own office employees might oversee him. (This last is my own conjecture as the words "wooden" and "perfunctory," which occur in his diaries, seem somehow out of place.) The inhuman bustle of the city intervened once more, committing them to past feelings and preoccupations. For her part, yawning, sleepy and utterly natural as she was, she left him only to turn into the little Greek church and set a candle to the saint. She crossed herself from left to right as the orthodox custom is and brushed back a lock of hair with one hand as she stooped to the ikon, tasting in its brassy kiss all the consolation of a forgotten childhood habit. Then wearily she turned to find Nessim standing before her. He was deathly white and staring at her with a sweet burning curiosity. She at once understood everything. They embraced with a sort of anguish, not kissing, but simply pressing their bodies together, and he all at once began to tremble with fatigue. His teeth began to chatter. She drew him to a choir stall where he sat for

some abstracted moments, struggling to speak, and drawing his hand across his forehead like someone who is re-
covering from drowning. It was not that he had anything to say to her, but this speechlessness made him fear
that he was experiencing a stroke. He croaked: "It is ter-
ribly late, nearly half past six." Pressing her hand to his
stubbled cheek he rose and like a very old man groped
his way back through the great doors into the sunlight,
leaving her sitting there gazing after him.

Never had the early dawn-light seemed so good to
Nessim. The city looked to him as brilliant as a precious
stone. The shrill telephones whose voices filled the
great stone buildings in which the financiers really lived,
sounded to him like the voices of great fruitful mechanical birds. They glittered with a pharaonic youthfulness.
The trees in the park had been rinsed down by an unaccustomed dawn rain. They were covered in brilliants and
looked like great contented cats at their toilet.

Sailing upwards to the fifth floor in the lift, making
awkward attempts to appear presentable (feeling the
dark stubble on his chin, retying his tie) Nessim ques-
tioned his reflection in the cheap mirror, puzzled by the
whole new range of feelings and beliefs these brief scenes
had given him. Under everything, however, aching like a
poisoned tooth or finger, lay the quivering meaning of
those eight words which Melissa had lodged in him. In a
dazed sort of way he recognized that Justine was dead
to him—from a mental picture she had become an engraving, a locket which one might wear over one's heart
forever. It is always bitter to leave the old life for the
new—and every woman is a new life, compact and self-
contained and *sui generis*. As a person she had suddenly
faded. He did not wish to possess her any longer but to
free himself from her. From a woman she had become a
situation.

He rang for Selim and when the secretary appeared he dictated to him a few of the duller business letters with a calm so surprising that the boy's hand trembled as he took them down in his meticulous crowsfoot shorthand. Perhaps Nessim had never been more terrifying to Selim than he appeared at this moment, sitting at his great polished desk with the gleaming battery of telephones ranged before him.

Nessim did not meet Melissa for some time after this episode but he wrote her long letters, all of which he destroyed in the lavatory. It seemed necessary to him, for some fantastic reason, to explain and justify Justine to her and each of these letters began with a long painful exegesis of Justine's past and his own. Without this preamble, he felt, it would be impossible ever to speak of the way in which Melissa had moved and captivated him. He was defending his wife, of course, not against Melissa who had uttered no criticism of her (apart from the one phrase) but against all the new doubts about her which emerged precisely from his experience with Melissa. Just as my own experience of Justine had illuminated and re-evaluated Melissa for me so he looking into Melissa's grey eyes saw a new and unsuspected Justine born therein. You see, he was now alarmed at the extent to which it might become possible to hate her. He recognized now that hate is only unachieved love. He felt envious when he remembered the single-mindedness of Pursewarden who on the flyleaf of the last book he gave Balthazar had scribbled the mocking words:

> *Pursewarden on Life*
> N.B. Food is for eating
>   Art is for arting
>   Women for ———
>   Finish
>   RIP

And when next they met, under very different circumstances. . . . But I have not the courage to continue. I have explored Melissa deeply enough through my own mind and heart and cannot bear to recall what Nessim found in her—pages covered with erasures and emendations. Pages which I have torn from his diaries and destroyed. Sexual jealousy is the most curious of animals and can take up a lodgement anywhere, even in memory. I avert my face from the thought of Nessim's shy kisses, of Melissa's kisses which selected in Nessim only the nearest mouth to mine. . . .

From a crisp packet I selected a strip of pasteboard on which, after so many shame-faced importunities, I had persuaded a local jobbing printer to place my name and address, and taking up my pen wrote:

> mr ——— accepts with pleasure the
> kind invitation of mr ——— to a duck
> shoot on Lake Mareotis.

It seemed to me that now one might learn some important truths about human behaviour.

*   *   *   *   *

Autumn has settled at last into the clear winterset. High seas flogging the blank panels of stone along the Corniche. The migrants multiplying on the shallow reaches of Mareotis. Waters moving from gold to grey, the pigmentation of winter.

The parties assemble at Nessim's house towards twilight—a prodigious collection of cars and shooting-brakes. Here begins the long packing and unpacking of wicker baskets and gun-bags, conducted to the accompaniment of cocktails and sandwiches. Costumes burgeon. Comparison of guns and cartridges, conversation inseparable from a shooter's life, begin now, rambling, inconsequent, wise. The yellowish moonless dusk settles; the angle of the sunlight turns slowly upwards into the vitreous lilac of the evening sky. It is brisk weather, clear as waterglass.

Justine and I are moving through the spiderweb of our preoccupations like people already parted. She wears the familiar velveteen costume—the coat with its deeply cut and slanted pockets: and the soft *velours* hat pulled down over her brows—a schoolgirl's hat: leather jack-boots. We do not look directly at each other any more, but talk with a hollow impersonality. I have a splitting headache. She has urged upon me her own spare gun—a beautiful light twelve by Purdy, ideal for such an unpractised hand and eye as mine.

There is laughter and clapping as lots are drawn for the make-up of the various parties. We will have to take up widely dispersed positions around the lake, and those who draw the western butts will have to make a long detour by road through Mex and the desert fringes. The leaders of each party draw paper strips in turn from a hat, each with a guest's name written upon it. Nessim has already drawn Capodistria who is clad in a natty leather jerkin with velvet cuffs, khaki gaberdine plus-fours and check socks. He wears an old tweed hat with a cock-pheasant's feather in it, and is festooned with bandoliers full of cartridges. Next comes Ralli the old Greek general, with ash-coloured bags under his eyes and darned riding-breeches; Pallis the French chargé d'affaires in a sheep-skin coat; lastly myself.

Justine and Pombal are joining Lord Errol's party. It is clear now that we are to be separated. All of a sudden, for the first time, I feel real fear as I watch the expressionless glitter of Nessim's eyes. We take our various places in the shooting-brakes. Selim is doing up the straps of a heavy pigskin gun-case. His hands tremble.

With all the dispositions made the cars start up with a
roar of engines, and at this signal a flock of servants scamper out of the great house with glasses of champagne to
offer us as a stirrup-cup. This diversion enables Justine
to come across to our car and under the pretext of hand-
ing me a packet of smokeless cartridges to press my arm
once, warmly, and to fix me for a half-second with those
expressive black eyes shining now with an expression I
might almost mistake for relief. I try to form a smile with
my lips.

We move off steadily with Nessim at the wheel and
catch the last rays of the sunset as we clear the town to
run along the shallow dunelands towards Aboukir. Everyone is in excellent spirits, Ralli talking nineteen to the
dozen and Capodistria keeping us entertained with
anecdotes of his fabulous mad father. ("His first act on
going mad was to file a suit against his two sons accus-
ing them of wilful and persistent illegitimacy.") From
time to time he raises a finger to touch the cotton com-
press which is held in position over his left eye by the
black patch. How is it that I have never yet recognized
in Capodistria the author of all Justine's misfortunes—
the man with the black patch? Pallis has produced an
old deer-stalker with large ear-flaps which make him
look like a speculative Gallic rabbit. From time to time
in the driving mirror I catch Nessim's eye and he smiles.

The dusk has settled as we come to the shores of the
lake. The old hydroplane whimpers and roars as it waits
for us. It is piled high with decoys. Nessim assembles
a couple of tall duck-guns and tripods before joining us
in the shallow punt to set off across the reed-fringed
wilderness of the lake to the desolate lodge where we
are to spend the night. All horizons have been abruptly
cut off now as we skirt the darkening channels in our
noisy craft, disturbing the visitants of the lake with the

roar of our engines; the reeds tower over us, and everywhere the sedge hassocks of islands rise out of the water
with their promise of cover. Once or twice a long vista
of water opens before us and we catch sight of the flurry
of birds rising—mallard trailing their webs across the
still surface. Nearer at hand the hither-and-thithering
cormorants keep a curiosity-shop with their long slave-
to-appetite beaks choked with sedge. All round us now,
out of sight the teeming colonies of the lake are settling
down for the night. When the engines of the hydroplane
are turned off the silence is suddenly filled with groaning
and gnatting of duck.

A faint green wind springs up and ruffles the water
round the little wooden hut on the balcony of which sit
the loaders waiting for us. Darkness has suddenly fallen,
and the voices of the boatmen sound hard, sparkling,
gay. The loaders are a wild crew; they scamper from island to island with shrill cries, their *galabeahs* tucked up
round their waists, impervious to the cold. They seem
black and huge, as if carved from the darkness. They pull
us up to the balcony one by one and then set off in shallow punts to lay their armfuls of decoys while we turn
to the inner room where paraffin lamps have already
been lit. From the little kitchen comes the encouraging
smell of food which we sniff appreciatively as we divest
ourselves of our guns and bandoliers, and kick off our
boots. Now the sportsmen fall to backgammon or tric-
trac and bag-and-shot talk, the most delightful and absorbing masculine conversation in the world. Ralli is
rubbing pigsfat into his old much-darned boots. The
stew is excellent and the red wine has put everyone in a
good humour.

By nine however most of us are ready to turn in; Nessim is busy in the darkness outside giving his last instructions to the loaders and setting the rusty old alarm clock

for three. Capodistria alone shows no disposition to
sleep. He sits, as if plunged in reflection, sipping his wine
and smoking a cheroot. We speak for a while about
trivialities; and then all of a sudden he launches into a
critique of Pursewarden's third volume which has just
appeared in the bookshops. "What is astonishing," he
says, "is that he presents a series of spiritual problems as
if they were commonplaces and illustrates them with his
characters. I have been thinking over the character of
Parr the sensualist. He resembles me so closely. His
apology for a voluptuary's life is fantastically good—as
in the passage where he says that people only see in us
the contemptible skirt-fever which rules our actions but
completely miss the beauty-hunger underlying it. To be
so struck by a face sometimes that one wants to devour
it feature by feature. Even making love to the body beneath it gives no surcease, no rest. What is to be done
with people like us?" He sighs and abruptly begins to
talk about Alexandria in the old days. He speaks with a
new resignation and gentleness about those far-off days
across which he sees himself moving so serenely, so effortlessly as a youth and a young man. "I have never got
to the bottom of my father. His view of things was mor-
dant, and yet it is possible that his ironies concealed a
wounded spirit. One is not an ordinary man if one can
say things so pointed that they engage the attention
and memory of others. As once in speaking of marriage
he said: 'In marriage they legitimized despair,' and,
'Every kiss is the conquest of a repulsion.' He struck me
as having a coherent view of life but madness intervened
and all I have to go on is the memory of a few incidents
and sayings. I wish I could leave behind as much."

I lie awake in the narrow wooden bunk for a while
thinking over what he has been saying: all is darkness
now and silence save for the low rapid voice of Nessim

on the balcony outside talking to the loaders. I cannot
catch the words. Capodistria sits for a while in the darkness to finish his cheroot before climbing heavily into
the bunk under the window. The others are already
asleep to judge by the heavy snoring of Ralli. My fear
has given place to resignation once more; now at the
borders of sleep I think of Justine again for a moment
before letting the memory of her slide into the limbo
which is peopled now only with far-away sleepy voices
and the rushing sighing waters of the great lake.

It is pitch-dark when I awake at the touch of Nessim's
gentle hand shaking my shoulder. The alarm clock has
failed us. But the room is full of stretching yawning figures climbing from their bunks. The loaders have been
curled up asleep like sheep-dogs on the balcony outside.
They busy themselves in lighting the paraffin lamps
whose unearthly glare is to light our desultory breakfast
of coffee and sandwiches. I go down the landing stage
and wash my face in the icy lake-water. Utter blackness
all around. Everyone speaks in low voices, as if weighed
down by the weight of the darkness. Snatches of wind
make the little lodge tremble, built as it is on frail
wooden stilts over the water.

We are each allotted a punt and a gun-bearer. "You'll
take Faraj," says Nessim. "He's the most experienced and
reliable of them." I thank him. A black barbaric face under a soiled white turban, unsmiling, spiritless. He takes
my equipment and turns silently to the dark punt. With
a whispered farewell I climb in and seat myself. With a
lithe swing of the pole Faraj drives us out into the channel and suddenly we are scoring across the heart of a black
diamond. The water is full of stars, Orion down, Capella
tossing out its brilliant sparks. For a long while now we
crawl upon this diamond-pointed star-floor in silence
save for the suck and lisp of the pole in the mud. Then

we turn abruptly into a wider channel to hear a string of
wavelets pattering against our prow while draughts of
wind fetch up from the invisible sea-line tasting of salt.

Premonitions of the dawn are already in the air as we
cross the darkness of this lost world. Now the approaches
to the empty water ahead are shivered by the faintest
etching of islands, sprouts of beard, reeds and sedge. And
on all sides now comes the rich plural chuckle of duck
and the shrill pinched note of the gulls to the seaboard.
Faraj grunts and turns the punt towards a nearby island. Reaching out upon the darkness my hands grasp
the icy rim of the nearest barrel into which I laboriously
climb. The butts consist merely of a couple of dry wood-
slatted barrels tied together and festooned with tall reeds
to make them invisible. The loader holds the punt steady
while I disembarrass him of my gear. There is nothing to
do now but to sit and wait for the dawn which is rising
slowly somewhere, to be born from this black expressionless darkness.

It is bitterly cold now and even my heavy greatcoat
seems to offer inadequate protection. I have told Faraj
that I will do my own loading as I do not want him han-
dling my spare gun and cartridges in the next barrel. I
must confess to a feeling of shame as I do so, but it sets
my nerves at rest. He nods with an expressionless face
and stands off with the punt in the next cluster of reeds,
camouflaged like a scarecrow. We wait now with our
faces turned towards the distant reaches of the lake—it
seems for centuries.

Suddenly at the end of the great couloir my vision is
sharpened by a pale disjunctive shudder as a bar of but-
tercup-yellow thickening gradually to a ray falls slowly
through the dark masses of cloud to the east. The ripple
and hurry of the invisible colonies of birds around us in-
creases. Slowly, painfully, like a half-open door the dawn

is upon us, forcing back the darkness. A minute more
and stairway of soft kingcups slides smoothly down out
of heaven to touch in our horizons, to give eye and mind
an orientation in space which it has been lacking. Faraj
yawns heavily and scratches himself. Now rose-madder
and warm burnt gold. Clouds move to green and yellow.
The lake has begun to shake off its sleep. I see the black
silhouette of teal cross my vision eastward. "It is time,"
murmurs Faraj; but the minute hand of my wrist watch
shows that we still have five minutes to go. My bones feel
as if they have been soaked in the darkness. I feel
suspense and inertia struggling for possession of my
sleepy mind. By agreement there is to be no shooting before four-thirty. I load slowly and dispose my bandolier
across the butt next me within easy reach. "It is time,"
says Faraj more urgently. Nearby there is a plop and a
scamper of some hidden birds. Out of sight a couple of
coot squat in the middle of the lake pondering. I am
about to say something when the first chapter of guns
opens from the south—like the distant click of cricket-
balls.

Now solitaries begin to pass, one, two, three. The light
grows and waxes, turning now from red to green. The
clouds themselves are moving to reveal enormous cavi-
ties of sky. They peel the morning like a fruit. Four separate arrowheads of duck rise and form two hundred
yards away. They cross me trimly at an angle and I open
up with a tentative right barrel for distance. As usual they
are faster and higher than they seem. The minutes are
ticking away in the heart. Guns open up nearer to hand,
and by now the lake is in a general state of alert. The
duck are coming fairly frequently now in groups, three,
five, nine: very low and fast. Their wings purr, as they
feather the sky, their necks reach. Higher again in mid-
heaven there travel the clear formations of mallard,

grouped like aircraft against the light, ploughing a soft slow flight. The guns squash the air and harry them as they pass, moving with a slow curling bias towards the open sea. Even higher and quite out of reach come chains of wild geese, their plaintive honking sounding clearly across the now sunny waters of Mareotis.

There is hardly time to think now: for teal and widgeon like flung darts whistle over me and I begin to shoot slowly and methodically. Targets are so plentiful that it is often difficult to choose one in the split second during which it presents itself to the gun. Once or twice I catch myself taking a snap shot into a formation. If hit squarely a bird staggers and spins, pauses for a moment, and then sinks gracefully like a handkerchief from a lady's hand. Reeds close over the brown bodies, but now the tireless Faraj is out poling about like mad to retrieve the birds. At times he leaps into the water with his *galabeah* tucked up to his midriff. His features blaze with excitement. From time to time he gives a shrill whoop.

They are coming in from everywhere now, at every conceivable angle and every speed. The guns bark and jumble in one's ears as they drive the birds backwards and forwards across the lake. Some of the flights though nimble are obviously war-weary after heavy losses; other solitaries seem quite out of their minds with panic. One young and silly duck settles for a moment by the punt, almost within reach of Faraj's hands, before it suddenly sees danger and spurts off in a slither of foam. In a modest way I am not doing too badly though in all the excitement it is hard to control oneself and to shoot deliberately. The sun is fairly up now and the damps of the night have been dispersed. In an hour I shall be sweating again in these heavy clothes. The sun shines on the ruffled waters of Mareotis where the birds still fly. The punts by now will be full of the sodden bodies of the vic-

tims, red blood running from the shattered beaks on to
the floor-boards, marvellous feathers dulled by death.

I eke out my remaining ammunition as best I can but
already by quarter past eight I have fired the last
cartridge; Faraj is still at work painstakingly tracking
down stragglers among the reeds with the single-mindedness of a retriever. I light a cigarette, and for the first
time feel free from the shadow of omens and premonitions—free to breathe, to compose my mind once more.
It is extraordinary how the prospect of death closes down
upon the free play of the mind, like a steel shutter, cutting off the future which alone is nourished by hopes
and wishes. I feel the stubble on my unshaven chin and
think longingly of a hot bath and a warm breakfast. Faraj
is still tirelessly scouting the islands of sedge. The guns
have slackened, and in some quarters of the lake are already silent. I think with a dull ache of Justine, somewhere out there across the sunny water. I have no great
fear for her safety for she has taken as her own gun-
bearer my faithful servant Hamid.

I feel all at once gay and light-hearted as I shout to
Faraj to cease his explorations and bring back the punt.
He does so reluctantly and at last we set off across the
lake, back through the channels and corridors of reed
towards the lodge.

"Eight brace no good," says Faraj, thinking of the large
professional bags we will have to face when Ralli and
Capodistria return. "For me it is very good," I say. "I
am a rotten shot. Never done as well." We enter the
thickly sown channels of water which border the
lake like miniature canals.

At the end, against the light, I catch sight of another
punt moving towards us which gradually defines itself
into the familiar figure of Nessim. He is wearing his old
moleskin cap with the ear-flaps up and tied over the top.

I wave but he does not respond. He sits abstractedly in
the prow of the punt with his hands clasped about his
knees. "Nessim," I shout. "How did you do? I got eight
brace and one lost." The boats are nearly abreast now,
for we are heading towards the mouth of the last canal
which leads to the lodge. Nessim waits until we are
within a few yards of each other before he says with a
curious serenity, "Did you hear? There's been an accident. Capodistria . . ." and all of a sudden my heart
contracts in my body. "Capodistria?" I stammer. Nessim
still has the curious impish serenity of someone resting
after a great expenditure of energy. "He's dead," he
says, and I hear the sudden roar of the hydroplane engines starting up behind the wall of reeds. He nods towards the sound and adds in the same still voice: "They
are taking him back to Alexandria."

A thousand conventional commonplaces, a thousand
conventional questions spring to my mind, but for a long
time I can say nothing.

On the balcony the others have assembled uneasily,
almost shamefacedly; they are like a group of thought-
less schoolboys for whom some silly prank has ended in
the death of one of their fellows. The furry cone of noise
from the hydroplane still coats the air. In the middle
distance one can hear shouts and the noise of car-engines
starting up. The piled bodies of the duck, which would
normally be subject matter for gloating commentaries,
lie about the lodge with anachronistic absurdity. It appears that death is a relative question. We had only been
prepared to accept a certain share of it when we entered
the dark lake with our weapons. The death of Capodistria hangs in the still air like a bad smell, like a bad
joke.

Ralli had been sent to get him and had found the body
lying face down in the shallow waters of the lake with

the black eye-patch floating near him. It was clearly an accident. Capodistria's loader was an elderly man, thin as a cormorant, who sits now hunched over a mess of beans on the balcony. He cannot give a coherent account of the business. He is from Upper Egypt and has the weary half-crazed expression of a desert father.

Ralli is extremely nervous and is drinking copious draughts of brandy. He retells his story for the seventh time, simply because he must talk in order to quieten his nerves. The body could not have been long in the water, yet the skin was like the skin of a washerwoman's hands. When they lifted it to get it into the hydroplane the false teeth slipped out of the mouth and crashed on to the floor-boards frightening them all. This incident seems to have made a great impression on him. I suddenly feel overcome with fatigue and my knees start to tremble. I take a mug of hot coffee and, kicking off my boots, crawl into the nearest bunk with it. Ralli is still talking with deafening persistence, his free hand coaxing the air into expressive shapes. The others watch him with a vague and dispirited curiosity, each plunged in his own reflections. Capodistria's loader is still eating noisily like a famished animal, blinking in the sunlight. Presently a punt comes into view with three policemen perched precariously in it. Nessim watches their antics with an imperturbability flavoured ever so slightly with satisfaction; it is as if he were smiling to himself. The clatter of boots and musket-butts on the wooden steps, and up they come to take down our depositions in their notebooks. They bring with them a grave air of suspicion which hovers over us all. One of them carefully manacles Capodistria's loader before helping him into the punt. The servant puts out his wrists for the iron cuffs with a bland uncomprehending air such as one sees on the faces of old apes when called upon to perform a human action which they have learned but not understood.

It is nearly one o'clock before the police have finished
their business. The parties will all have ebbed back from
the lake by now to the city where the news of Capodistria's death will be waiting for them. But this is not to
be all.

One by one we straggle ashore with our gear. The cars
are waiting for us, and now begins a long chaffering ses-
sion with the loaders and boatmen who must be paid off;
guns are broken up and the bag distributed; in all this
incoherence I see my servant Hamid advancing timidly
through the crowd with his good eye screwed up against
the sunlight. I think he must be looking for me but
no: he goes up to Nessim and hands him a small blue
envelope. I want to describe this exactly. Nessim takes it
absently with his left hand while his right is reaching
into the car to place a box of cartridges in the glove-box.
He examines the superscription once thoughtlessly and
then once more with marked attention. Then keeping
his eyes on Hamid's face he takes a deep breath and
opens the envelope to read whatever is written on the
half sheet of notepaper. For a minute he studies it and
then replaces the letter in the envelope. He looks about
him with a sudden change of expression, as if he suddenly felt sick and was looking about for a place where
he might be so. He makes his way through the crowd and
putting his head against a corner of mud wall utters a
short panting sob, as of a runner out of breath. Then he
turns back to the car, completely controlled and dry-
eyed, to complete his packing. This brief incident goes
completely unremarked by the rest of his guests.

Clouds of dust rise now as the cars begin to draw away
towards the city; the wild gang of boatmen shout and
wave and treat us to carved water-melon smiles studded
with gold and ivory. Hamid opens the car door and
climbs in like a monkey. "What is it?" I say, and folding
his small hands apologetically towards me in an attitude

of supplication which means "Blame not the bearer of
ill tidings," he says in a small conciliatory voice: "Master, the lady has gone. There is a letter for you in the
house."

It is as if the whole city had crashed about my ears: I
walk slowly to the flat, aimlessly as survivors must walk
about the streets of their native city after an earthquake,
surprised to find how much that had been familiar has
changed. Rue Piroua, Rue de France, the Terbana
Mosque (cupboard smelling of apples), Rue Sidi Abou
El Abbas (water-ices and coffee), Anfouchi, Ras El Tin
(Cape of Figs), Ikingi Mariut (gathering wild flowers
together, convinced she cannot love me), equestrian
statue of Mohammed Ali in the square. . . . General
Earle's comical little bust, killed Sudan 1885. . . . An
evening multitudinous with swallows . . . the tombs at
Kom El Shugaffa, darkness and damp soil, both terrified
by the darkness. . . . Rue Fuad as the old Canopic Way,
once Rue Rosette. . . . Hutchinson disturbed the whole
water-disposition of the city by cutting the dykes. . . .
The scene in *Moeurs* where he tries to read her the book
he is writing about her. "She sits in the wicker chair with
her hands in her lap, as if posing for a portrait, but with
a look of ever-growing horror on her face. At last I can
stand it no longer, and I throw down the manuscript in
the fireplace, crying out: 'What are they worth, since you
understand nothing, these pages written from a heart
pierced to the quick?'" In my mind's eye I can see Nessim racing up the great staircase to her room to find a
distraught Selim contemplating the empty cupboards
and a dressing table swept clean as if by a blow from a
leopard's paw.

In the harbour of Alexandria the sirens whoop and
wail. The screws of ships crush and crunch the green oil-
coated waters of the inner bar. Idly bending and inclining, effortlessly breathing as if in the rhythm of the

earth's own systole and diastole, the yachts turn their spars against the sky. Somewhere in the heart of experience there is an order and a coherence which we might surprise if we were attentive enough, loving enough, or patient enough. Will there be time?

THE DISAPPEARANCE of Justine was something new to be borne. It changed the whole pattern of our relationship. It was as if she had removed the keystone to an arch: Nessim and I, left among the ruins, so to speak were faced with the task of repairing a relationship which she herself had invented and which her absence now rendered hollow, echoing with a guilt which would, I thought, henceforward always overshadow affection.

His suffering was apparent to everyone. That expressive face took on a flayed unhealthy look—the pallor of a church martyr. In seeing him thus I was vividly reminded of my own feelings during the last meeting with Melissa before she left for the clinic in Jerusalem where she had now been for almost a whole year. The candour and gentleness with which she said: "The whole thing is gone. . . . It may never come back. . . . At least this separation." Her voice grew furry and moist, blurring the edges of the words. At this time she was quite ill. The lesions had opened again. "Time to reconsider ourselves. . . . If only I were Justine. . . . I know you think of her when you make love to me. . . . Don't deny it. . . . I know my darling. . . . I'm even jealous of your imagination. . . . Horrible to have self-reproach heaped on top of the other miseries. . . . Never mind." She blew her nose shakily and managed a smile. "I need rest so badly. . . . And now Nessim has fallen in love with me." I put my hand over her sad mouth. The taxi throbbed on remorselessly, like someone living on his nerves. All round us walked the wives of the Alexandrians, smartly turned out, with the air of well-lubricated phantoms. The driver watched us in the mirror like a

spy. The emotions of white people, he perhaps was thinking, are odd and excite prurience. He watched as one
might watch cats making love.

"I shall never forget you."

"Nor I. Write to me."

"I shall always come back if you want."

"Never doubt it. Get well, Melissa, you must get
well. I'll wait for you. A new cycle will begin. It is all
there inside me, intact. I feel it."

The words that lovers use at such times are charged
with distorting emotions. Only their silences have the
cruel precision which aligns them to truth. We were silent, holding hands. She embraced me and signalled to
the driver to set off.

"With her going the city took on an unnerving
strangeness for him," writes Arnauti. "Wherever his
memory of her turned a familiar corner she re-created
herself swiftly, vividly, and superimposed those haunted
eyes and hands on the streets and squares. Old conversations leaped up and hit him among the polished table-
tops of cafés where once they had sat, gazing like leopards
into each other's eyes. Sometimes she appeared walking
a few paces ahead of him in the dark street. She would
stop to adjust the strap of a sandal and he would over-
take her with beating heart—only to find it was someone else. Particular doors seemed just about to admit
her. He would sit and watch them doggedly. At other
times he was suddenly seized by the irresistible convic-
tion that she was about to arrive on a particular train,
and he hurried to the station and breasted the crowd of
passengers like a man fording a river. Or he might sit
in the stuffy waiting-room of the airport after midnight
watching the departures and arrivals, in case she were
coming back to surprise him. In this way she controlled
his imagination and taught him how feeble reason was;
and he carried the consciousness of her going heavily

about with him—like a dead baby from which one could
not bring oneself to part."

The night after Justine went away there was a freak
thunder-storm of tremendous intensity. I had been wan-
dering about in the rain for hours, a prey not only to
feelings which I could not control but also to remorse
for what I imagined Nessim must be feeling. Frankly, I
hardly dared to go back to the empty flat, lest I should be
tempted along the path Pursewarden had already taken
so easily, with so little premeditation. Passing Rue Fuad
for the seventh time, coatless and hatless in that blinding
downpour, I happened to catch sight of the light in Clea's
high window and on an impulse rang the bell. The front
door opened with a whine and I stepped into the silence
of the building from the dark street with its booming
of rain in gutters and the splash of overflowing man-
holes.

She opened the door to me and at a glance took in
my condition. I was made to enter, peel off my sodden
clothes and put on the blue dressing-gown. The little
electric fire was a blessing, and Clea set about making me
hot coffee.

She was already in pyjamas, her gold hair combed out
for the night. A copy of *A Rebours* lay face down on the
floor beside the ash-tray with the smouldering cigarette
in it. Lightning kept flashing fitfully at the window, lighting up her grave face with its magnesium
flashes. Thunder rolled and writhed in the dark heavens
outside the window. In this calm it was possible partly
to exorcise my terrors by speaking of Justine. It appeared
she knew all—nothing can be hidden from the curiosity
of the Alexandrians. She knew all about Justine, that is
to say.

"You will have guessed," said Clea in the middle of
all this, "that Justine was the woman I told you once I
loved so much."

This cost her a good deal to say. She was standing with a coffee cup in one hand, clad in her blue-striped pyjamas by the door. She closed her eyes as she spoke, as if she were expecting a blow to fall upon the crown of her head. Out of the closed eyes came two tears which ran slowly down on each side of her nose. She looked like a young stag with a broken ankle. "Ah! let us not speak of her any more," she said at last in a whisper. "She will never come back."

Later I made some attempt to leave but the storm was still at its height and my clothes still impossibly sodden. "You can stay here," said Clea, "with me;" and she added with a gentleness which brought a lump into my throat, "But please—I don't know how to say this—please don't make love to me."

We lay together in that narrow bed talking of Justine while the storm blew itself out, scourging the window-panes of the flat with driven rain from the seafront. She was calm now with a sort of resignation which had a moving eloquence about it. She told me many things about Justine's past which only she knew: and she spoke of her with a wonder and tenderness such as people might use in talking of a beloved yet infuriating queen. Speaking of Arnauti's ventures into psycho-analysis she said with amusement: "She was not really clever, you know, but she had the cunning of a wild animal at bay. I'm not sure she really understood the object of these investigations. Yet though she was evasive with the doctors she was perfectly frank with her friends. All that correspondence about the words 'Washington D.C.,' for example, which they worked so hard on—remember? One night while we were lying here together I asked her to give me her free associations from the phrase. Of course she trusted my discretion absolutely. She replied unerringly (it was clear she had already worked it out though she would not tell Arnauti): 'There is a town near Washing-

ton called Alexandria. My father always talked of going
to visit some distant relations there. They had a daughter called Justine who was exactly my age. She went mad
and was put away. She had been raped by a man.' I then
asked her about D.C. and she said, 'Da Capo. Capodistria.' "

I do not know how long this conversation lasted or
how soon it melted into sleep, but we awoke next morning in each other's arms to find that the storm had ceased.
The city had been sponged clean. We took a hasty breakfast and I made my way towards Mnemjian's shop for a
shave through streets whose native colours had been
washed clean by the rain so that they glowed with
warmth and beauty in that soft air. I still had Justine's
letter in my pocket but I did not dare to read it again
lest I destroy the peace of mind which Clea had given me.
Only the opening phrase continued to echo in my mind
with an obstinate throbbing persistence: "If you should
come back alive from the lake you will find this letter
waiting for you."

On the mantelpiece in the drawing-room of the flat
there is another letter offering me a two-year contract as
a teacher in a Catholic school in Upper Egypt. I sit down
at once without thinking and draft my acceptance. This
will change everything once more and free me from the
streets of the city which have begun to haunt me of late
so that I dream that I am walking endlessly up
and down, hunting for Melissa among the dying flares of
the Arab quarter.

With the posting of this letter of acceptance a new
period will be initiated, for it marks my separation from
the city in which so much has happened to me, so much
of momentous importance: so much that has aged me.
For a little while, however, life will carry its momentum
forwards by hours and days. The same streets and squares
will burn in my imagination as the Pharos burns in his-

tory. Particular rooms in which I have made love, particular café tables where the pressure of fingers upon a
wrist held me spellbound, feeling through the hot pavements the rhythms of Alexandria transmitted upwards
into bodies which could only interpret them as famished
kisses, or endearments uttered in voices hoarse with wonder. To the student of love these separations are a school,
bitter yet necessary to one's growth. They help one to
strip oneself mentally of everything save the hunger for
more life.

Now, too, the actual framework of things is undergoing a subtle transformation, for other partings are also
beginning. Nessim is going to Kenya for a holiday. Pombal has achieved crucifixion and a posting to the Chan-
cery in Rome where I have no doubt he will be happier.
A series of leisurely farewell parties have begun to serve
the purposes of all of us; but they are heavy with the
absence of the one person whom nobody ever mentions
any more—Justine. It is clear too that a world war is
slowly creeping upon us across the couloirs of history—
doubling our claims upon each other and upon life. The
sweet sickly smell of blood hangs in the darkening air
and contributes a sense of excitement, of fondness and
frivolity. This note has been absent until now.

The chandeliers in the great house whose ugliness
I have come to hate, blaze over the gatherings which
have been convened to say farewell to my friend. They
are all there, the faces and histories I have come to know
so well, Sveva in black, Clea in gold, Gaston, Claire,
Gaby. Nessim's hair I notice has during the last few
weeks begun to be faintly touched with grey. Ptolemeo
and Fuad are quarrelling with all the animation of old
lovers. All around me the typical Alexandrian animation swells and subsides in conversations as brittle and
frivolous as spun glass. The women of Alexandria in all
their stylish wickedness are here to say good-bye to some-

one who has captivated them by allowing them to be-
friend him. As for Pombal himself, he has grown fatter,
more assured since his elevation in rank. His profile
now has a certain Neronian cast. He is professing himself worried about me in *sotto voce;* for some weeks we
have not met properly, and he has only heard about my
schoolmastering project tonight. "You should get out,"
he repeats, "back to Europe. This city will undermine
your will. And what has Upper Egypt to offer? Blazing
heat, dust, flies, a menial occupation. . . . After all you
are not Rimbaud."

The faces surging round us sipping toasts prevent my
answering him, and I am glad of it for I have nothing
to say. I gaze at him with a portentous numbness, nod-
ding my head. Clea catches my wrist and draws me aside
to whisper: "A card from Justine. She is working in a
Jewish *kibbutz* in Palestine. Shall I tell Nessim?"

"Yes. No. I don't know."

"She asks me not to."

"Then don't."

I am too proud to ask if there is any message for me.
The company has started to sing the old song "For He's
a Jolly Good Fellow" in a variety of times and accents.
Pombal has turned pink with pleasure. I gently shake off
Clea's hand in order to join in the singing. The little
Consul-General is fawning and gesticulating over Pombal; his relief at my friend's departure is so great that he
has worked himself up into a paroxysm of friendship and
regret. The English consular group has the disconsolate
air of a family of moulting turkeys. Madame de Venuta
is beating time with an elegant gloved hand. The black
servants in their long white gloves move swiftly from
group to group of the guests like eclipses of the moon. If
one were to go away, I catch myself thinking, to Italy
perhaps or to France: to start a new sort of life: not a city
life this time, perhaps an island in the Bay of Naples.

. . . But I realize that what remains unresolved in my life is not the problem of Justine but the problem of Melissa. In some curious way the future, if there is one, has always been vested in her. Yet I feel powerless to influence it by decisions or even hopes. I feel that I must wait patiently until the shallow sequences of our history match again, until we can fall into step once more. This may take years—perhaps we will both be grey when the tide suddenly turns. Or perhaps the hope will die stillborn, broken up like wreckage by the tides of events. I have so little faith in myself. The money Pursewarden left is still in the bank—I have not touched a penny of it. For such a sum we might live for two years in some cheap spot in the sun.

Melissa still writes the spirited nonchalant letters which I have such difficulty in answering save by whining retorts about my circumstances or my improvidence. Once I leave the city it will be easier. A new road will open. I will write to her with absolute frankness, telling her all I feel—even those things which I believe her forever incapable of understanding properly. "I shall return in the spring," Nessim is saying to the Baron Thibault, "and take up my summer quarters at Abu Sir. I am determined to slack off for about two years. I've been working too hard at business and it isn't worth it." Despite the haunted pallor of his face one cannot help seeing in him a new repose, a relaxation of the will; the heart may be distracted, but the nerves are at last at rest. He is weak, as a convalescent is weak; but he is no longer ill. We talk and joke quietly for a while; it is clear that our friendship will repair itself sooner or later—for we now have a common fund of unhappiness upon which to draw. "Justine," I say, and he draws in his breath slightly, as if one had run a small thorn under his fingernail, "writes from Palestine." He nods quickly and motions me with a small gesture. "I know. We have traced her. There is no need to . . . I'm writing to her. She can stay away as long as she wishes. Come back in her own good time." It would be foolish to deprive him of the hope and the consolation it must give him, but I know now that she will never return on the old terms. Every phrase of her letter to me made this clear. It is not us she had abandoned so much but a way of life which threatened her reason—the city, love, the sum of all that we had shared. What had she written to him, I wondered, as I recalled the short sobbing breath he had drawn as he leaned against the whitewashed wall?

*   *   *   *   *

On these spring mornings while the island slowly un-curls from the sea in the light of an early sun I walk about on the deserted beaches, trying to recover my memories of the two years spent in Upper Egypt. It is strange when everything about Alexandria is so vivid that I can recover so little of that lost period. Or perhaps it is not so strange—for compared to the city life I had lived my new life was dull and uneventful. I remember the back-breaking sweat of school work: walks in the flat rich fields with their bumper crops feeding upon dead men's bones: the black silt-fed Nile moving corpulently through the Delta to the sea: the bilharzia-ridden peas-antry whose patience and nobility shone through their rags like patents of dispossessed royalty: village patriarchs intoning: the blind cattle turning the slow globe of their waterwheels, blindfolded against monotony—how small can a world become? Throughout this period I read nothing, thought nothing, was nothing. The fathers of the school were kindly and left me alone in my spare time, sensing perhaps my distaste for the cloth, for the apparatus of the Holy Office. The children of course were a torment—but then what teacher of sensibility does not echo in his heart the terrible words of Tolstoy: "Whenever I enter a school and see a multitude of children, ragged thin and dirty but with their clear eyes and sometimes angelic expressions, I am seized with restlessness and terror, as though I saw people drowning?"

Unreal as all correspondence seemed, I kept up a desultory contact with Melissa whose letters arrived punctually. Clea wrote once or twice, and surprisingly enough old Scobie who appeared to be rather annoyed that he should miss me as much as he obviously did. His letters were full of fantastic animadversion against Jews (who were always referred to jeeringly as "snipcocks") and, surprisingly enough, to passive pederasts (whom he labelled "Herms," i.e. Hermaphrodites). I was not surprised to learn that the Secret Service had gravelled him, and he was now able to spend most of the day in bed with what he called a "bottle of wallop" at his elbow. But he was lonely, hence his correspondence.

These letters were useful to me. My feeling of unreality had grown to such a pitch that at times I distrusted my own memory, finding it hard to believe that there had ever been such a town as Alexandria. Letters were a lifeline attaching me to an existence in which the greater part of myself was no longer engaged.

As soon as my work was finished I locked myself in my room and crawled into bed; beside it lay the green jade box full of hashish-loaded cigarettes. If my way of life was noticed or commented upon at least I left no loophole for criticism in my work. It could be hard to grudge me simply an inordinate taste for solitude. Father Racine, it is true, made one or two attempts to rouse me. He was the most sensitive and intelligent of them all and perhaps felt that my friendship might temper his own intellectual loneliness. I was sorry for him and regretted in a way not being able to respond to these overtures. But I was afflicted by a gradually increasing numbness, a mental apathy which made me shrink from contact.

Once or twice I accompanied him for a walk along the
river (he was a botanist) and heard him talk lightly and
brilliantly on his own subject. But my taste for the landscape, its flatness, its unresponsiveness to the seasons had
gone stale. The sun seemed to have scorched up my ap-
petite for everything—food, company and even speech.
I preferred to lie in bed staring at the ceiling and listening to the noises around me in the teachers' block: Father Gaudier sneezing, opening and shutting drawers;
Father Racine playing a few phrases over and over
again on his flute; the ruminations of the organ moulder-
ing away among its harmonies in the dark chapel. The
heavy cigarettes soothed the mind, emptying it of every
preoccupation.

One day Gaudier called to me as I was crossing the
close and said that someone wished to speak to me on the
telephone. I could hardly comprehend, hardly believe
my ears. After so long a silence who would telephone?
Nessim perhaps?

The telephone was in the Head's study, a forbidding
room full of elephantine furniture and fine bindings.
The receiver, crepitating slightly, lay on the blotter before him. He squinted slightly and said with distaste: "It
is a woman from Alexandria." I thought it must be Melissa but to my surprise Clea's voice suddenly swam up
out of the incoherence of memory: "I am speaking
from the Greek Hospital. Melissa is here, very ill indeed.
Perhaps even dying."

Undeniably my surprise and confusion emerged as
a ▓▓▓. "But she would not let me tell you before. She
did▓▓ want you to see her ill—so thin. But I simply must
now. Can you come quickly? She will see you now."

In my mind's eye I could see the jogging night train
with its interminable stoppings and startings in dust-
blown towns and villages—the dirt and the heat. It
would take all night. I turned to Gaudier and asked his

permission to absent myself for the whole week-end. "In exceptional cases we do grant permission," he said thoughtfully. "If you were going to be married, for example, or if someone was seriously ill." I swear that the idea of marrying Melissa had not entered my head until he spoke the words.

There was another memory, too, which visited me now as I packed my cheap suitcase. The rings, Cohen's rings, were still in my stud-box wrapped in brown paper. I stood for a while looking at them and wondering if inanimate objects also had a destiny as human beings have. These wretched rings, I thought—why, it was as if they had been anxiously waiting here all the time like human beings; waiting for some shabby fulfilment on the finger of someone trapped into a *mariage de convenance*. I put the poor things in my pocket.

Far off events, transformed by memory, acquire a burnished brilliance because they are seen in isolation, divorced from the details of before and after, the fibres and wrappings of time. The actors, too, suffer a transformation; they sink slowly deeper and deeper into the ocean of memory like weighted bodies, finding at every level a new assessment, a new evaluation in the human heart.

It was not anguish I felt so much at Melissa's defection, it was rage, a purposeless fury based, I imagine, in contrition. The enormous vistas of the future which in all my vagueness I had nevertheless peopled with images of her had gone by default now; and it was only now that I realized to what an extent I had been nourishing myself on them. It had all been there like a huge trust, an account upon which I would one day draw. Now I was suddenly bankrupt.

Balthazar was waiting for me at the station in his little car. He pressed my hand with rough and ready sympathy as he said, in a matter of fact voice: "She died last

night poor girl. I gave her morphia to help her away.
Well." He sighed and glanced sideways at me. "A pity
you are not in the habit of shedding tears. *Ça aurait
été un soulagement."*

"*Soulagement grotesque.*"

"*Approfondir les émotions . . . les purger.*"

"*Tais-toi,* Balthazar, shut up."

"She loved you I suppose."

"*Je le sais.*"

"*Elle parlait de vous sans cesse. Cléa a été avec elle
toute la semaine.*"

"*Assez.*"

Never had the city looked so entrancing in that soft
morning air. I took the light wind from the harbour on
my stubbled cheek like the kiss of an old friend. Mareotis
glinted here and there between the palm-tops, between
the mud huts and the factories. The shops along Rue
Fuad seemed to have all the glitter and novelty of Paris.
I had, I realized, become a complete provincial in Upper
Egypt. Alexandria seemed a capital city. In the trim garden nurses were rolling their prams and children their
hoops. The trams squashed and clicked and rattled.
"There is something else," Balthazar was saying as we
raced along. "Melissa's child, Nessim's child. But I suppose you know all about it. It is out at the summer villa.
A little girl."

I could not take all this in, so drunk was I on
the beauty of the city which I had almost forgotten.
Outside the Municipality the professional scribes sat at
their stools, inkhorns, pens and stamped paper beside
them. They scratched themselves, chattering amiably.
We climbed the low bluff on which the hospital stood
after threading the long bony spine of the Canopic Way.
Balthazar was still talking as we left the lift and started
to negotiate the long white corridors of the second floor.
"A coolness has sprung up between Nessim and my-

self. When Melissa came back he refused to see her out
of a sort of disgust which I found inhuman, hard to comprehend. I don't know. . . . As for the child he is trying
to get it adopted. He has come almost to hate it, I suppose. He thinks Justine will never come back to him so
long as he has Melissa's child. For my part," he added
more slowly, "I look at it this way: by one of those fearful displacements of which only love seems capable the
child Justine lost was given back by Nessim not to her
but to Melissa. Do you see?"

The sense of ghostly familiarity which was growing
upon me now was due to the fact that we were approaching the little room in which I had visited Cohen when
he was dying. Of course Melissa must be lying in the same
narrow iron bed in the corner by the wall. It would be
just like real life to imitate art at this point.

There were some nurses in the room busy whispering
round the bed, arranging screens; but at a word from
Balthazar they scattered and disappeared. We stood
arm in arm in the doorway for a moment looking in.
Melissa looked pale and somehow wizened. They had
bound up her jaw with tape and closed the eyes so that
she looked as if she had fallen asleep during a beauty
treatment. I was glad her eyes were closed; I had been
dreading their glance.

I was left alone with her for a while in the huge silence
of that whitewashed ward and all of a sudden I found
myself suffering from acute embarrassment. It is hard to
know how to behave with the dead; their enormous
deafness and rigidity is so studied. One becomes awkward as if in the presence of royalty. I coughed behind
my hand and walked up and down the ward stealing little glances at her out of the corner of my eye, remembering the confusion which had once beset me when she
called upon me with a gift of flowers. I would have liked
to slip Cohen's rings on her fingers but they had already

swathed her body in bandages and her arms were bound stiffly to her sides. In this climate bodies decompose so quickly that they have to be almost unceremoniously rushed to the grave. I said "Melissa" twice in an uncertain whisper bending my lips to her ear. Then I lit a cigarette and sat down beside her on a chair to make a long study of her face, comparing it to all the other faces of Melissa which thronged my memory and had established their identity there. She bore no resemblance to any of them—and yet she set them off, concluded them. This white little face was the last term of a series. Beyond this point there was a locked door.

At such times one gropes about for a gesture which will match the terrible marble repose of the will which one reads on the faces of the dead. There is nothing in the whole ragbag of human emotions. "Terrible are the four faces of love," wrote Arnauti in another context. I mentally told the figure on the bed that I would take the child if Nessim would part with her, and this silent agreement made I kissed the high pale forehead once and left her to the ministrations of those who would parcel her up for the grave. I was glad to leave the room, to leave a silence so elaborate and forbidding. I suppose we writers are cruel people. The dead do not care. It is the living who might be spared if we could quarry the message which lies buried in the heart of all human experience.

("In the old days the sailing ships in need of ballast would collect tortoises from the mainland and fill great barrels with them, alive. Those that survived the terrible journey might be sold as pets for children. The putrefying bodies of the rest were emptied into the East India Docks. There were plenty more where they came from.")

I walked lightly effortlessly about the town like an escaped prisoner. Mnemjian had violet tears in his violet eyes as he embraced me warmly. He settled down to

shave me himself, his every gesture expressing an emol-
lient sympathy and tenderness. Outside on the pavements drenched with sunlight walked the citizens of
Alexandria each locked into a world of personal relationships and fears, yet each seeming to my eyes infinitely remote from those upon which my own thoughts and feelings were busy. The city was smiling with a heartbreaking indifference, a *cocotte* refreshed by the darkness.

There remained only one thing to do now, to see Nessim. I was relieved to learn that he was due to come into
town that evening. Here again time had another surprise in store for me for the Nessim who lived in my
memories of two years before had changed.

He had aged like a woman—his hips and face had
both broadened. He walked now with his weight distributed comfortably on the flats of his feet as if his body
had already submitted to a dozen pregnancies. The queer
litheness of his step had gone. Moreover he radiated now
a flabby charm mixed with concern which made him at
first all but unrecognizable. A foolish authoritativeness
had replaced the delightful old diffidence.

I had hardly time to capture and examine these new
impressions when he suggested that we should visit the
Etoile together—the night-club where Melissa used to
dance. It had changed hands, he added, as if this somehow excused our visiting it on the very evening when her
funeral was due to take place. Shocked and surprised as
I was I agreed without hesitation, prompted both by
curiosity as to his own feelings and a desire to discuss the
transaction which concerned the child.

When we walked down the narrow airless stairway
into the white light of the place a cry went up and the
girls came running to him from every corner like cock-
roaches. It appeared that he was well known now as an
habitué. He opened his arms to them with a shout of
laughter, turning to me for approval as he did so. Then

taking their hands one after another he pressed them
voluptuously to the breast pocket of his coat so that they
might feel the outlines of the thick wallet he now carried,
stuffed with banknotes. This gesture at once reminded
me of how, when I was accosted one night in the dark
streets of the city by a pregnant woman and trying to
make my escape, she took my hand, as if to give me an
idea of the pleasure she was offering (or perhaps to em-
phasize her need) and pressed it upon her swollen abdomen. Now, watching Nessim, I suddenly recalled the
tremulous beat of the foetal heart in the eighth month.

It is difficult to describe how unspeakably strange I
found it to sit beside this vulgar double of the Nessim I
had once known. I studied him keenly but he avoided
my eye and confined his conversation to laboured commonplaces which he punctuated by yawns that were one
by one tapped away behind ringed fingers. Here and
there, however, behind this new façade stirred a hint of
the old diffidence but buried—as a fine physique may
get buried in a mountain of fat. In the washroom Zoltan
the waiter confided in me: "He has become truly himself
since his wife went away. All Alexandria says so." The
truth was that he had become like all Alexandria.

Late that night the whim seized him to drive me to
Montaza in the late moonlight; we sat in the car for a
long time in silence, smoking, gazing out at the moonlit
waves hobbling across the sand bar. It was during this
silence that I apprehended the truth about him. He had
not really changed inside. He had merely adopted a new
mask.

* * * * *

In the early summer I received a long letter from Clea
with which this brief introductory memorial to Alexandria may well be brought to a close.

"You may perhaps be interested in my account of a

brief meeting with Justine a few weeks ago. We had, as
you know, been exchanging occasional cards from our
respective countries for some time past, and hearing that
I was due to pass through Palestine into Syria she herself suggested a brief meeting. She would come, she said,
to the border station where the Haifa train waits for half
an hour. The settlement in which she works is somewhere
near at hand, she could get a lift. We might talk for a
while on the platform. To this I agreed.

"At first I had some difficulty in recognizing her. She
has gone a good deal fatter in the face and has chopped
off her hair carelessly at the back so that it sticks out in
rats' tails. I gather that for the most part she wears it
done up in a cloth. No trace remains of the old elegance
or *chic*. Her features seem to have broadened, become
more classically Jewish, lip and nose inclining more towards each other. I was shocked at first by the glittering
eyes and the quick incisive way of breathing and talking
—as if she were feverish. As you can imagine we were
both mortally shy of each other.

"We walked out of the station along the road and
sat down on the edge of a dry ravine, a wadi, with a few
terrified-looking spring flowers about our feet. She gave
the impression of already having chosen this place for
our interview: perhaps as suitably austere. I don't know.
She did not mention Nessim or you at first but spoke only
about her new life. She had achieved, she claimed, a new
and perfect happiness through 'community-service'; the
air with which she said this suggested some sort of religious conversion. Do not smile. It is hard, I know, to be
patient with the weak. In all the back-breaking sweat of
the Communist settlement she claimed to have achieved
a 'new humility.' (Humility! The *last trap* that awaits the
ego in search of absolute truth. I felt disgusted but said
nothing.) She described the work of the settlement
coarsely, unimaginatively, as a peasant might. I noticed

that those once finely-tended hands were callused and
rough. I suppose people have a right to dispose of their
bodies as they think fit, I said to myself, feeling ashamed
because I must be radiating cleanliness and leisure, good
food and baths. By the way, she is not a Marxist as yet—
simply a work-mystic after the manner of Panayotis at
Abu Sir. Watching her now and remembering the touching and tormenting person she had once been for us
all I found it hard to comprehend the change into this
tubby little peasant with the hard paws.

"I suppose events are simply a sort of annotation of
our feelings—the one might be deduced from the other.
Time carries us (boldly imagining that we are discrete
egos modelling our own personal futures)—time carries
us forward by the momentum of those feelings inside us
of which we ourselves are least conscious. Too abstract
for you? Then I have expressed the idea badly. I mean,
in Justine's case, having become cured of the mental aberrations brought about by her dreams, her fears, she has
been deflated like a bag. For so long the fantasy occupied
the foreground of her life that now she is dispossessed of
her entire stock-in-trade. It is not only that the death of
Capodistria has removed the chief actor in this shadow-
play, her chief gaoler. The illness itself had kept her on
the move, and when it died it left in its place total exhaustion. She has, so to speak, extinguished with her
sexuality her very claims on life, almost her reason. People driven like this to the very boundaries of freewill
are forced to turn somewhere for help, to make absolute
decisions. If she had not been an Alexandrian (i.e.
sceptic) this would have taken the form of religious conversion. How is one to say these things? It is not a question of growing to be happy or unhappy. A whole block
of one's life suddenly falls into the sea, as perhaps yours
did with Melissa. But (this is how it works in life, the
retributive law which brings good for evil and evil for

good) her own release also released Nessim from the inhibitions governing his passional life. I think he always
felt that so long as Justine lived he would never be able
to endure the slightest human relationship with anyone
else. Melissa proved him wrong, or at least so he thought;
but with Justine's departure the old heartsickness
cropped up and he was filled with overwhelming disgust
for what he had done to her—to Melissa.

"Lovers are never equally matched—do you think?
One always overshadows the other and stunts his or her
growth so that the overshadowed one must always be
tormented by a desire to escape, to be free to grow.
Surely this is the only tragic thing about love?

"So that if from another point of view Nessim did
plan Capodistria's death (as has been widely rumoured
and believed) he could not have chosen a more calamitous path. It would indeed have been wiser to kill you.
Perhaps he hoped in releasing Justine from the succubus
(as Arnauti before him) he would free her for himself.
(He said so once—you told me.) But quite the opposite
has happened. He has granted her a sort of absolution, or
poor Capodistria unwittingly did—with the result that
she thinks of him now not as a lover but as a sort of arch-
priest. She speaks of him with a *reverence* which would
horrify him to hear. She will never go back, how could
she? And if she did he would know at once that he had
lost her forever—for those who stand in a confessional
relationship to ourselves can never love us, never truly
love us.

" (Of you Justine said simply, with a slight shrug: 'I
had to put him out of my mind.')

"Well, these are some of the thoughts that passed
through my mind as the train carried me down through
the orange groves to the coast; they were thrown into
sharp relief by the book I had chosen to read on the
journey, the last volume of *God Is a Humorist*. How

greatly Pursewarden has gained in stature since his death! It was before as if he stood between his own books and our understanding of them. I see now that what we found enigmatic about the man was due to a fault in ourselves. An artist does not live a personal life as we do, he hides it, forcing us to go to his books if we wish to touch the true source of his feelings. Underneath all his preoccupations with sex, society, religion, etc. (all the staple abstractions which allow the forebrain to chatter) there is, quite simply, a man *tortured beyond endurance by the lack of tenderness in the world.*

"And all this brings me back to myself, for I too have been changing in some curious way. The old self-sufficient life has transformed itself into something a little hollow, a little empty. It no longer answers my deepest needs. Somewhere deep inside a tide seems to have turned in my nature. I do not know why but it is towards you, my dear friend, that my thoughts have turned more and more of late. Can one be frank? Is there a friendship possible this side of love which could be sought and found? I speak no more of love—the word and its conventions have become odious to me. But is there a friendship possible to attain which is deeper even, limitlessly deep, and yet wordless, idealess? It seems somehow necessary to find a human being to whom one can be faithful, not in the body (I leave that to the priests) but in the culprit mind? But perhaps this is not the sort of problem which will interest you much these days. Once or twice I have felt the absurd desire to come to you and offer my services in looking after the child perhaps. But it seems clear now that you do not really need anybody any more, and that you value your solitude above all things. . . ."

There are a few more lines and then the affectionate superscription.

*   *   *   *   *   *

The cicadas are throbbing in the great plains, and the summer Mediterranean lies before me in all its magnetic blueness. Somewhere out there, beyond the mauve throbbing line of the horizon lies Africa, lies Alexandria, maintaining its tenuous grasp on one's affections through memories which are already refunding themselves slowly into forgetfulness; memory of friends, of incidents long past. The slow unreality of time begins to grip them, blurring the outlines—so that sometimes I wonder whether these pages record the actions of real human beings; or whether this is not simply the story of a few inanimate objects which precipitated drama around them—I mean a black patch, a green fingerstall, a watch-key and a couple of dispossessed wedding-rings. . . .

Soon it will be evening and the clear night sky will be dusted thickly with summer stars. I shall be here, as always, smoking by the water. I have decided to leave Clea's last letter unanswered. I no longer wish to coerce anyone, to make promises, to think of life in terms of compacts, resolutions, covenants. It will be up to Clea to interpret my silence according to her own needs and desires, to come to me if she has need or not, as the case may be. Does not everything depend on our interpretation of the silence around us?

CONSEQUENTIAL DATA

* * *

Landscape-tones: steep skylines, low cloud, pearl ground with shadows in oyster and violet. Accidie. On the lake gunmetal and lemon. Summer: sand lilac sky. Autumn: swollen bruise greys. Winter: freezing white sand, clear skies, magnificent starscapes.

* * *

CHARACTER-SQUEEZES

Sveva Magnani: pertness, malcontent.
Georges Pombal: honey-bear, fleshly opiates.
Teresa di Petromonti: farded Berenice.
Ptolomeo Dandolo: astronomer, astrologer, Zen.
Fuad El Said: black moon-pearl.
Josh Scobie: piracy.
Justine Hosnani: arrow in darkness.
Clea Montis: still waters of pain.
Gaston Phipps: nose like a sock, black hat.
Ahmed Zananiri: pole-star criminal.
Nessim Hosnani: smooth gloves, face frosted glass.
Melissa Artemis: patron of sorrow.
S. Balthazar: fables, work, unknowing.

* * *

Pombal asleep in full evening dress. Beside him on the bed a chamber-pot full of banknotes he had won at the Casino.

* * *

Da Capo: "To bake in sensuality like an apple in its jacket."

* * *

Spoken impromptu by Gaston Phipps:
*   "The lover like a cat with fish*
*   Longs to be off and will not share his dish."*

Accident or attempted murder? Justine racing along the desert road to Cairo in the Rolls when suddenly the lights give out. Sightless, the great car swarms off the road and whistling like an arrow buries itself in a sand-dune. It looked as if the wires had been filed down to a thread. Nessim reached her within half an hour. They embrace in tears. (From her diary.)

*   *   *

Balthazar on Justine: "You will find that her formidable manner is constructed on a shaky edifice of childish timidities."

*   *   *

Clea always has a horoscope cast before any decision reached.

*   *   *

Clea's account of the horrible party; driving with Justine they had seen a brown cardboard box by the road. They were late so they put it in the back and did not open it until they reached the garage. Inside was dead baby wrapped in newspaper. What to do with this wizened homunculus? Perfectly formed organs. Guests were due to arrive, they had to rush. Justine slipped it into drawer of the hall desk. Party a great success.

*   *   *

Pursewarden on the "n-dimensional novel" trilogy: "The narrative momentum forward is counter-sprung by references backwards in time, giving the impression of a book which is not travelling from a to b but standing above time and turning slowly on its own axis to comprehend the whole pattern. Things do not all lead forward to other things: some lead backwards to things which have passed. A marriage of past and present with the flying multiplicity of the future racing towards one. Anyway, that was my idea. . . ."

*   *   *

"Then how long will it last, this love?" (in jest).
"I don't know."
"Three weeks, three years, three decades . . . ?"

"You are like all the others . . . trying to shorten eternity with numbers," spoken quietly, but with intense feeling.

* * *

Conundrum: a peacock's eye. Kisses so amateurish they resembled an early form of printing.

* * *

Of poems: "I like the soft thudding of Alexandrines" (Nessim).

* * *

Clea and her old father whom she worships. White haired, erect, with a sort of haunted pity in his eyes for the young unmarried goddess he has fathered. Once a year on New Year's Eve they dance at the Cecil, stately, urbanely. He waltzes like a clockwork man.

* * *

Pombal's love for Sveva: based on one gay message which took his fancy. When he awoke she'd gone, but she had neatly tied his dress tie to his John Thomas, a perfect bow. This message so captivated him that he at once dressed and went round to propose marriage to her because of her sense of humour.

* * *

Pombal was at his most touching with his little car which he loved devotedly. I remember him washing it by moonlight very patiently.

* * *

Justine: "Always astonished by the force of my own emotions—tearing the heart out of a book with my fingers like a fresh leaf."

* * *

Places: street with arcade: awnings: silverware and doves for sale. Pursewarden fell over a basket and filled the street with apples.

* * *

Message on the corner of a newspaper. Afterwards the closed
cab, warm bodies, night, volume of jasmine.

* * *

A basket of quail burst open in the bazaar. They did not try to
escape but spread out slowly like spilt honey. Easily recaptured.

* * *

Postcard from Balthazar: "Scobie's death was the greatest fun.
How he must have enjoyed it. His pockets were full of love-
letters to his aide Hassan, and the whole vice squad turned out
to sob at his grave. All these black gorillas crying like babies.
A very Alexandrian demonstration of affection. Of course the
grave was too small for the coffin. The grave-diggers had
knocked off for lunch, so a scratch team of policemen was
brought into action. Usual muddle. The coffin fell over on its
side and the old man nearly rolled out. Shrieks. The padre was
furious. The British Consul nearly died of shame. But all Alex-
andria was there and a good time was had by all."

* * *

Pombal walking in stately fashion down Rue Fuad, dead drunk
at ten in the morning, clad in full evening dress, cloak and
opera hat—but bearing on his shirt-front, written in lipstick,
the words: "Torche-cul des républicains."

* * *

(Museum)
Alexander wearing the horns of Ammon (Nessim's madness).
He identified himself with A. because of the horns?

* * *

Justine reflecting sadly on the statue of Berenice mourning her
little daughter whom the Priests deified: "Did that assuage her
grief I wonder? Or did it make it more permanent?"

* * *

Tombstone of Apollodorus giving his child a toy. "Could bring tears to one's eyes." (Pursewarden) "They are all dead. Nothing to show for it."

* * *

Aurelia beseeching Petesouchos the crocodile god. . . .

* * *

Lioness Holding a Golden flower. . . .

* * *

Ushabti . . . little serving figures which are supposed to work for the mummy in the underworld.

* * *

Somehow even Scobie's death did not disturb our picture of him. I had already seen him long before in Paradise—the soft conklin-coloured yams like the haunches of newly cooked babies: the night falling with its deep-breathing blue slur over Tobago, softer than parrot-plumage. Paper flamingoes touched with gold-leaf, rising and falling on the sky, touched by the keening of the bruise-dark water-bamboos. His little hut of reeds with the cane bed, beside which still stands the honoured cake-stand of his earthly life. Clea once asked him: "Do you not miss the sea, Scobie?" and the old man replied simply, without hesitation, "Every night I put to sea in my dreams."

I copied out and gave her the two translations from Cavafy which had pleased her though they were by no means literal. By now the Cavafy canon has been established by the fine thoughtful translations of Mavrogordato and in a sense the poet has been freed for other poets to experiment with; I have tried to transplant rather than translate—with what success I cannot say.

THE CITY

You tell yourself: I'll be gone
To some other land, some other sea,
To a city lovelier far than this

Could ever have been or hoped to be—
Where every step now tightens the noose:
A heart in a body buried and out of use:
How long, how long must I be here
Confined among these dreary purlieus
Of the common mind? Wherever now I look
Black ruins of my life rise into view.
So many years have I been here
Spending and squandering, and nothing gained.
There's no new land, my friend, no
New sea; for the city will follow you,
In the same streets you'll wander endlessly,
The same mental suburbs slip from youth to age,
In the same house go white at last—
The city is a cage.
No other places, always this
Your earthly landfall, and no ship exists
To take you from yourself. Ah! don't you see
Just as you've ruined your life in this
One plot of ground you've ruined its worth
Everywhere now—over the whole earth?

THE GOD ABANDONS ANTONY

When suddenly at darkest midnight heard,
The invisible company passing, the clear voices,
Ravishing music of invisible choirs—
Your fortunes having failed you now,
Hopes gone aground, a lifetime of desires
Turned into smoke. Ah! do not agonize
At what is past deceiving
But like a man long since prepared
With courage say your last good-byes
To Alexandria as she is leaving.
Do not be tricked and never say
It was a dream or that your ears misled,
Leave cowards their entreaties and complaints,
Let all such useless hopes as these be shed,
And like a man long since prepared,

Deliberately, with pride, with resignation
Befitting you and worthy of such a city
Turn to the open window and look down
To drink past all deceiving
Your last black rapture from the mystical throng,
And say farewell, farewell to Alexandria leaving.

NOTES IN THE TEXT

Page 5. "The Poet of the city." C. P. Cavafy.

Page 5. "The old man." C. P. Cavafy.

Page 32. Caballi. The astral bodies of men who died a premature death. "They imagine to perform bodily actions while in fact they have no physical bodies but act in their thoughts." *Paracelsus.*

Page 32. "Held the Gnostic doctrine that creation is a mistake. . . . He imagines a primal God, the centre of a divine harmony, who sent out manifestations of himself in pairs of male and female. Each pair was inferior to its predecessor and Sophia ('wisdom') the female of the thirtieth pair, least perfect of all. She showed her imperfection not, like Lucifer, by rebelling from God, but by desiring too ardently to be united to him. She fell through love."

E. M. Forster, *Alexandria.*

Page 34. Quotation from Paracelsus.

Page 48. Taphia, or Egyptian "Red Biddy."

Page 51. Greek text. Ὅταν θά βγῶ, ἄν δέν ἔχης φιλενάδα, φώναξέ με.

Page 70. Fosca died in childbirth. Ashes scattered in the desert.

Page 83. Amr, Conqueror of Alexandria, was a poet and soldier. Of the Arab invasion E. M. Forster writes: "Though they had no intention of destroying her, they destroyed her, as a child might a watch. She never functioned again properly for over 1,000 years."

Page 182. Among the Consequential Data the reader will find the full translation.

CURRENT BEST SELLERS

A MATTER OF CONVICTION
by Evan Hunter (50¢)

Author of *The Blackboard Jungle, Strangers When We Meet,* etc. The story of good people caught up in a sensational murder. The book from which the movie was made. Order GC-94.

AN ESSAY ON MORALS
by Philip Wylie (50¢)

Author of *Generation of Vipers,* etc. A bold and provocative statement of the author's beliefs about God, about men as animals and about modern man's need to seek integrity within himself. Order GC-93.

THE LOTUS EATERS
by Gerald Green (75¢)

Author of *The Last Angry Man.* "It portrays corruption, vulgarity and sensuality, but it contains anger and judgment."—*The Chicago Tribune.* Order GC-761.

THE DARKNESS AND THE DAWN
by Thomas B. Costain (50¢)

A superlative novel about Attila the Hun. "An excellent book, a stirring book and one of Costain's best..."—*The New York Times.* Order M-5029.

THIS HALLOWED GROUND
by Bruce Catton (50¢)

Author of *A Stillness at Appomattox,* etc. "A classic work—certainly the best single-volume treatment of the Civil War..."—*Chicago Sun-Times.* Order GC-95.

[MORE→]

COMMAND THE MORNING
by Pearl S. Buck　　　　　　　　　　　(35¢)

A novel about the terrible consequences of man's conquest of the atom. Order C-410.

THE YOUNG TITAN
by F. van Wyck Mason　　　　　　　　(75¢)

"If you have been waiting for a really great historical novel dealing with the young America, then your search is over."—*Boston Herald.* Order GC-762.

RANDOM HARVEST
by James Hilton　　　　　　　　　　(35¢)

The world-famous novel of a man who found perfect love—then lost it when he regained his memory. Order C-418.

THE FIERY FLOWER
by Paul I. Wellman　　　　　　　　　(35¢)

A strange and compelling story of pagan passion on an exotic South Sea island. Order M-4192.

DEAR FOLKS
by Juliet Lowell　　　　　　　　　　(35¢)

An unexpurgated, illustrated collection of screwball letters to, from and about the youngest generation. Order M-4195.

THESE SYMBOLS GUARANTEE
THE BEST IN READING

POCKET BOOKS, INC., is the largest publisher of books in the world today in terms of the number of copies it has sold and is currently selling. Nearly 800,000,000 copies have carried the symbol of "Gertrude," the little kangaroo, or the perky cardinal, or the stylized anchor and dolphin—all trademarks guaranteeing you books of exceptional merit and value.

Only genuine POCKET BOOK, CARDINAL and PERMABOOK editions carry these symbols. The titles are carefully chosen from the lists of all leading publishers and present the most distinguished and most widely diversified group offered today by any publisher of paper-bound books. Watch for these symbols. They are your guarantee of the best in reading at the lowest possible price.